BIRTHDAY

C.H.B. (Clifford Henry Benn) Kitchin was born in Yorkshire in 1895. He attended Exeter College, Oxford, and published his first book, a collection of poems, in 1919. His first novel, *Streamers Waving*, appeared in 1925, and he scored his first success with the crime novel *Death of My Aunt* (1929), which has been frequently reprinted and translated into a number of foreign languages.

Kitchin was a man of many interests and talents, being called to the bar in 1924 and later amassing a small fortune in the stock market. He was also, at various times, a farmer and a schoolmaster, and his many talents included playing the piano, chess, and bridge. He was also an avid collector of antiques and *objets d'art*.

Kitchin was a lifelong friend of L.P. Hartley, with whose works Kitchin's were often compared, and was also a friend and mentor to Francis King, who later acted as Kitchin's literary executor. Some of Kitchin's finest works appeared towards the end of his life, including *Ten Pollitt Place* (1957) and *The Book of Life* (1960), but though they earned critical acclaim, Kitchin was bitterly disappointed at their lack of success with the reading public. Kitchin, who was gay, lived with his partner Clive Preen, an accountant, from 1930 until Preen's death in 1944. C.H.B. Kitchin died in 1967.

Adrian Wright is an actor and writer. His works include *Foreign Country: The Life of L. P. Hartley*; *John Lehmann: A Pagan Adventure*; *The Innumerable Dance: The Life and Work of William Alwyn*; *A Tanner's Worth of Tune: Rediscovering the Post-War British Musical*; *West End Broadway: The Golden Age of the American Musical in London*; the novel *Maroon* and *The Boy Detective Stories*. For more information, visit www.mustclosesaturday.co.uk.

By C.H.B. Kitchin

Curtains (1919) (poetry)

Winged Victory (1921) (poetry)

Streamers Waving (1925)

Mr. Balcony (1927)

Death of My Aunt (1929)

The Sensitive One (1931)*

Crime at Christmas (1934)

Olive E. (1937)

Birthday Party (1938)*

Death of His Uncle (1939)

The Cornish Fox: A Detective Story (1949)

The Auction Sale (1949)

Jumping Joan, and Other Stories (1954)

The Secret River (1956)

Ten Pollitt Place (1957)*

The Book of Life (1960)*

A Short Walk in Williams Park (1971)*

* Available or forthcoming from Valancourt Books

BIRTHDAY PARTY

by

C.H.B. KITCHIN

With a new introduction by

ADRIAN WRIGHT

VALANCOURT BOOKS

Birthday Party by C.H.B. Kitchin
First published London: Constable, 1938
First Valancourt Books edition 2014

Published by Valancourt Books, Richmond, Virginia
Publisher & Editor: James D. Jenkins
20th Century Series Editor: Simon Stern, University of Toronto
http://www.valancourtbooks.com

All Valancourt Books publications are printed on acid free paper that meets all ANSI standards for archival quality paper.

ISBN 978-1-941147-19-1 (trade paperback)
Also available as an electronic book.

Set in Dante MT 11/13.2

INTRODUCTION

Clifford Henry Benn Kitchin is the only writer I have ever stalked. When other teenagers were in thrall to Batman and James Bond, my nose was buried in the novels of the much less glamorous Kitchin and L. P. Hartley. By an extraordinary chain of circumstance, I went on to write Hartley's biography, but I knew that publishers would never consider a life of Clifford Kitchin. Determined to get my man into the spotlight, I anyway managed to sneak him prominently into the Hartley biography.

Years later, when I wrote the novel *Maroon*, my principal player, the ageing novelist Jocelyn Hawk, was based on Kitchin, and I had the temerity to borrow Kitchin's description of the central character in his last book, *A Short Walk in Williams Park*: "There goes an old man, to whom nothing has ever happened." This has always seemed to me to be a chastening reminder of the writer's place in the world. Visits to Brighton also revive the links with Kitchin, when I make a pilgrimage to the block of flats where he once lived, imagining him counting the crowds on Bank Holiday days teeming onto the West Pier, in which he held shares. Somehow, this does not seem at odds with the generosity toward humankind and constant sense of ecstasy that pours through Kitchin's work, or through the lines of a letter in which he recalls his delight at riding the rollercoaster at a pleasure beach. Hartley and Kitchin were both observers of life, but only Kitchin collaborated with it, and beneath the reticent note of his novels, passions run deep.

Kitchin perhaps muddied his literary waters by winning a reputation as the author of detective stories, beginning in 1929 with *Death of My Aunt* and winding up with *The Cornish Fox* twenty years later. Even Agatha Christie had difficulty establishing her non-detective Mary Westmacott novels; similarly, admirers of Kitchin's detective fiction may have looked to his "straight" novels with puzzlement, and the balancing act possibly detracted from Kitchin's more serious intent.

Birthday Party, Kitchin's seventh novel, published in 1938, marks the beginning of a sea-change in his novels proper, which resumed ten years later with *The Auction Sale*. Between those years, much happened to the man to whom nothing had ever happened, not least the death of his partner, Clive Preen. "I feel as if my real life began in 1930 and ended in 1944," Kitchin wrote. "The steady purpose, which during the last thirteen and a half years had given everything, even in my nerviest moods, a reality and a justification, has gone, except for such faint gleams as an uncertain faith occasionally gives me."

It is from this time of "steady purpose" that *Birthday Party* springs, perhaps a cousin to the novel that preceded it, *Olive E.*, the story of Olive Everett, a not out of the ordinary young woman. Women are at the heart of Kitchin's fiction: the kindly Miss Elton is the driving force of *The Auction Sale*; *The Secret River* (1956) is wholly concerned with the life of Harriet Ashworth and her domineering mother; *Ten Pollitt Place* (1957) is presided over by the watchful Miss Tredennick; *The Book of Life* (1960) is overlooked by a gallery of aunts. Kitchin's empathy with the opposite sex is just as obvious in *Birthday Party*, in which half of the book is taken up by first person accounts from Isabel Carlice and Dora Carlice, with the males represented by first person accounts from Dora's hapless brother Stephen Payne and Dora's stepson Ronald Carlice, who warns us about first person narratives: "Art, especially modern art, is always in the first person. *I, me, my.* It emphasises our differences rather than our homogeneity. It panders to the cell, rather than the whole body of the state. It differentiates and divides, harps on personal interests, personal importance, even personal property— everything we're out to smash." It is a brave thing to attempt first person accounts from a quartet of voices, at the same time as Kitchin is pulling another trick, for *Birthday Party* is as much an experiment in detective story writing as a novel proper, framed at top and tail by two deaths in the gun-room at Carlice Abbey. Kitchin brings it off with some deft touches that might have impressed Christie, but it is the human dilemma that dominates.

No matter how effective each of the four characterisations is in *Birthday Party*, Kitchin cannot resist using at least one of them as his representative, and it may be that he identifies most closely with Isabel. She has learned Kitchin's manifesto of life, and is fed lines that suggest the sermonizing passages that often creep into his books, as in Mrs. Rivett's speech at the close of *The Auction Sale* and in the final pages of *A Short Walk in Williams Park*. So it is that Isabel, as Britain awaits the announcement of a great war (the inevitable consequences of which haunt the novel), defines a society that is about to recede: ". . . if I believe anything, I believe that life must have a drawing-room if it's to be civilised. We've built up the drawing-room by centuries of struggle, and to destroy it, just because it doesn't hold everybody, is to my mind a reversion to savagery. I admit, we may have underrated the bathroom." Thirteen years later, Kitchin still believed as much. He wrote to a friend, "I have never had any instinctive veneration for the moral law as such, and have regarded its existence—if it exists— as a necessary evil—no more an end in itself than lavatories or bathrooms which make one fitter to enjoy gold music-boxes in the boudoir."

The now and again tendency to preach on the meaning of life (and very wisely he does it too) cannot account for Kitchin's tussle with popularity. As early as 1921 he wrote to Hartley, "I feel convinced that nothing I write can ever appeal either to the gross but lucrative public, or to the select and jealous circle of literary critics. I shall always be a little out of touch . . . out of tune. When I pipe, they dance not. When I weep, they laugh." There is a revealing exchange in *Birthday Party*, when Stephen admits to Ronald that he is not a proletarian novelist. Ronald replies that "I suppose you write for a few dyspeptic escapists who feel as you feel, and then you're surprised at not being a best-seller . . . You write for people you think count."

The celebration towards which *Birthday Party* inexorably travels, is not a jolly affair of ice-cream and jellies; how could it be, when it is the continuance of tradition, intellectual comfort and financial contentment that drives the novel along. The great prize is Carlice Abbey, the family pile in Wiltshire. Isabel speaks of "the essential earth of Carlice", which may be "quite worth a murder". Will it, after all, be saved from the hands of the Communists? Three years after writing *Birthday Party*, Kitchin believed that it "is strange how to be a member of a privileged class—at one time thought worthy of so much admiration—is now regarded as a criminal offence".

That remark suggests that Kitchin was removed from the everyday world that most of us are condemned to occupy, but that is far from the truth. For me, Kitchin's voice rings true in all his books, the author interested in each passing shadow of man or woman or flower. He wrote of critics that they "lap up proletarian studies of delinquency and they tolerate a plunge into high life, but they can't abide the stratum between these extremes, though to me it seems the basis of our civilisation". An admiring visitor to Carlice tells Isabel, "The world will be much poorer when these standards disappear." In Kitchin's hands, much that has been lost comes back with a radiance that is distinctive and compelling.

ADRIAN WRIGHT
Poringland, Norfolk

May 8, 2014

BIRTHDAY PARTY

To
DARCY BUTTERWORTH KITCHIN

CONTENTS

This story is told by four of the characters.
The name at the head of each chapter is that of the narrator.

Chapter I: ISABEL CARLICE

I

THIS afternoon we had tea without artificial light for the first time since October. My visitor, the female novelist, who has just left me, must have noticed a wistfulness in my voice when I told Simmonds not to draw the curtains; for she said, with that quiet sophistication which some of these London women still affect, "Dusk has already become a feature you would like to enjoy?"

I looked at her. She was vivacious and wore gay colours. There was something of the parrot about her. I felt her to be young—compared with me.

Then she began to "draw me out."

"I like to think of you, in these days, just sitting here," she said, "enjoying a later sunset every day, and filling this lovely room with spring flowers. You're one of those people who make us feel that life hasn't yet gone to pieces."

I demurred.

"Oh no," she replied. "I don't mean that you're bucolic or self-satisfied. But you do lead the right kind of life—the elegant life. It sets a standard for those who can't or won't. The world will be much poorer when these standards disappear."

"Will they?"

She gave me a look of pity.

"But of course! You're not really a Londoner, are you?"

"No. I was brought up in the country, and lived there again when my brother's first wife died."

"Oh yes, at Carlice Abbey. I should have remembered. Do tell me about it. Is the Abbey really very old?"

"It was one of the first religious establishments to be dissolved

5

by Henry VIII, when it was given to someone who took the name Carlice, or *Cœur de Lys*, which was its earlier form. We trace ourselves to him very deviously."

I told the well-worn story. Someone said once that I have the knack of making my listener feel as if I were divulging a secret. I hope I have.

"And is it really very beautiful?"

"It is, or was, hideous. My grandfather, who married a rich wife, enriched the building in a mid-Victorian way, adding a billiard-room and a conservatory. At that time they thought the Georgian house, which had been superimposed on the remains of the Abbey, too plain for words."

"But the remains of the Abbey——?"

"The original Abbey was largely destroyed in the Civil War. It was rebuilt, on a smaller scale, after the Restoration, and burnt down a hundred years later."

She looked at me with penetration.

"You know the exact date, of course?"

"Yes, as a matter of fact."

"But you were afraid of sounding too pedantic?"

"Perhaps."

She smiled at the point she had made—a little touch, perhaps, for her next novel.

"And now, do tell me what it's like to-day."

"My father——"

"The Ambassador?"

"He was never actually even a Minister."

"He disagreed, I suppose, with your grandfather's taste?"

"Yes, and as he didn't marry money, like my grandfather, the house was far too big. He pulled down the billiard-room and the conservatory, and other additions too. The house became smaller, though it was (and is) still too big."

"But it regained its beauty?"

"It's now not much more than a Georgian house gone a little wrong."

"Oh, I'm sure it's lovely, and that you adored living there."

I said nothing, and feeling perhaps that she had touched a sore place (though she was soon to touch a sorer), she hurried on:

"I want to know much more. I suppose you have a huge hall, a vast drawing-room and dining-room, a morning-room, a smoking-room, a boudoir and a dozen spare bedrooms?"

"No, it's not so big as that. But we have three bathrooms."

"You disappoint me. I had hoped for one only—a big room in a high tower, draughty but panoramic."

"There are no towers. It's too Georgian."

"No, it was a silly joke. And outside? Stabling, I suppose, and a coach-house?"

"Yes."

"And marvellous shooting for miles?"

"A little bad shooting. Mostly rabbits."

She clapped her hands with sudden delight.

"Oh, and of course, you have a *gunroom*?"

2

It was with the gunroom that I had intended to begin the auto-biography which I shall not write. Why go too far back? It is the *me* of to-day which I must give other people—if they want me at all. It's no use my showing them someone who has ceased to exist, someone I should be guessing at. Memories? Of course. But they will be the past possessed by the *me* of the present. They must emerge as I recall them, not be set forth in any historical sequence.

I was asked once, almost seriously, by a publisher whom I met at a dinner party, to write my memoirs.

"You must have seen so much. Your father——"

"No one under sixty will remember him."

"Oh, come——"

"And he never had any great position, you know. He was not even a Minister."

"But as *chargé d'affaires* in the —— incident. Weren't you there too, acting as his hostess?"

"Yes, but that wouldn't make a book."

"You met Lubinsky, Prince Osric and the Duchess of Malfi. And I'm forgetting. It was your father who replied to the Emperor's telegram. They say he saved us a war. Weren't you there then?"

"Yes."

"Then do think it over, dear Miss Carlice. And of course you must describe your lovely home. Make a start to-morrow and send me the first chapter or two."

I began in bed the same night, with these sentences:

One very lovely afternoon in August, when I was six years old, I noticed a tall trumpet-shaped flower, in colour a velvety crimson streaked with bronze, growing in a border at the foot of our oldest wall. The gardener told me later that its name was salpiglossis. It stood quite still, for there was no breeze at all, and I stood still, too, for five minutes, which is a long time at that age, and watched it and enjoyed it. It gave me a feeling I hadn't felt before, and made me love the wall that was its background, and the other walls, and the house and garden and the fields beyond. . . .

This might do, I thought. Only there mustn't be too much of that kind of thing. It's not really what people will want. They'll be waiting for Lubinsky, Prince Osric and the Duchess of Malfi—for the important things. But my first conscious sight of a salpiglossis was far more important for me than any of my diplomatic encounters. The more I realised this divergence of values, the more convinced I was that I should never produce publishable memoirs. I began to argue mentally and somewhat cantankerously with my unknown readers.

"What you treasure most," I imagined them saying, "is not necessarily what we want. You put sensation before action, but why should we care a hoot for your sensations—the sensations of one person?"

"Because," I replied, "they may be your sensations, too, and enrich your lives."

"Oh, we haven't time for that. Give us the big things that affect the lives of millions."

"You mean the temporary things, that make a good headline. My salpiglossis mood goes far deeper than any Emperor's telegram. After all, the final object of all action is only to provide a background or means to sensation. . . ."

This seemed so clinching an argument—and still does to me—that here I would rest upon my laurels. My readers became speechless, if alienated. Nothing remained except not to bother with them—perhaps not to write at all.

But, for a time, I toyed with the idea. And the gunroom episode, the memory of which I could not lose, was my beginning.

It was in November, about nine and a half years ago. My nephew Ronnie was eleven years and two months old. His birthday is on the eighth of September. Dora, his stepmother, his sister Joan and I, who was hostess to the party, had gone to see him for half-term at his preparatory school. It was near Leamington and we were staying at an hotel there—an old-fashioned place, furnished as provincial hotels, till just recently perhaps, have always been furnished. Happily, it was almost empty. I remember my bedroom, with the wash-stand and its massive floral toilet-ware in front of the window. In the middle of the lounge there was a palm in a huge china pot. The chairs were fantastic and contorted—caricatures of these which my grandfather in his last phase had bought for home. I mean, for Carlice Abbey. It had already ceased to be my home four years before.

On the Saturday we went to see a football match at Ronnie's school. He wasn't in the eleven. None of us have ever excelled at games, except my brother at lawn tennis and his successes didn't go very far. Ronnie's school won, amid tremendous cheers. Ronnie cheered too, loudly, with an enthusiasm I was sure he did not feel. Boys' schools are monstrously like totalitarian states. I felt thankful to have been a Victorian girl; for I believe even girls nowadays are made to cheer in chorus. He was self-conscious with us, and feared probably that Dora would kiss him in public. But I had warned her against that. He may have hoped that one of the older boys would be dazzled by Joan—"I say, Carlice, you've got a stunningly pretty sister"—though Joan was never dazzling. He was, I knew, longing for us to go, and we went early, soon after the misty dusk had fallen. Living in London as I did—and do—I relished the crackling of dead leaves in the drive.

The next day, Sunday, Ronnie came to tea with us in our

hotel. The headmaster was one of those who resent the visits of
parents in term-time and would not allow him to come over for
luncheon—a relief to Dora, perhaps, who even then liked a nap in
the afternoon. Four years at Carlice had made her lazy and relaxed
the tension of her earlier suburban brightness. Joan complained a
little that Ronnie didn't spend the whole day with us. "No, dear," I
explained, "it isn't because he would miss any lessons, but because
Mr. Peters doesn't like to see home-influences at work in term-
time. He thinks it's bad for a boy's character to be too much in
touch with his relations. It was the same in your father's time.
They were even stricter then." "Then," she said, "it was hardly
worth coming here." "I think," I told her, "Auntie Dora"—(that
was what we called Dora to the children)—"enjoys the change
from home." "Then you could have left me at home with Daddy."
"Nonsense, my dear, some day you'll only be too eager to have
these little holidays." Joan was at school too, a school much nearer
home, but it had been closed three weeks before by an epidemic,
and she was to stay at home another fortnight before she returned.
I had to caution both her and Dora not to mention the epidemic to
Mr. Peters, or Ronnie might not have been allowed even to come
to us for tea.

He arrived about four o'clock in a four-wheeler, bringing his
friend Bunny Andrews, a bright boy more talkative than Ronnie,
and, I thought, with better manners. A drizzle was falling, and it
had become damply cold outside. Dora, who was a conscientious
stepmother, made both the boys take off their shoes and dry them,
though they could hardly have got wet. Her solicitude reminded
me of a summer's day, two years before, when we had been staying
together at Tunbridge Wells and she saw Ronnie making a boat
out of a piece of newspaper he had picked up on the common.
"Put that down at once, dear," she had said. "You don't know who
touched it before you. It may be covered with germs for all you
know." It was the doctor's daughter speaking. She may have been
quite right, but I could not help feeling that such an attitude must
make life seem very formidable to a child of eight. There has been
a good deal of "You don't know who touched it before you" in
Ronnie's life since then. It explains, up to a point, what he is now.

So the two boys sat with their stockinged feet near the hearth, while the panting waiter brought in tea. We had the drawing-room to ourselves. A tall woman looked in once, but the children's voices drove her away. One by one the Venetian blinds were lowered. Dora made up the fire, and a smell of hot buttered teacake filled the big room. A grandfather clock struck half-past four.

"You'll remind Mrs. Carlice," Bunny said to Ronnie, "that Mr. Peters said we must be back by six."

Was he bored already, I wondered? But Ronnie supported him so strongly that I felt that it was probably fear of Mr. Peters and not boredom. "Oh yes, dear, you shall be back," Dora said. "Now put on your shoes and come to this nice big table." Ronnie was used to such adjectives, but I think they lowered Dora a little in Bunny's eyes.

The boys ate largely. One would have been alarmed if they had not. Then, when the remains of the meal had been cleared away, they sprang a surprise on us—some parlour fireworks which they had made themselves. Apparently the school had a firework display on the fifth of November, and one or two of the bigger fireworks had failed to go off properly. A search next day had disclosed a wealth of "stars" and unexploded powder lying about the games field. One of the bolder spirits had put some of these ingredients in a burnt-out Roman Candle, and let it off, with great success. It was not long before most of the boys had imitated him.

Ronnie and Bunny produced their creations with great pride and caressed them with their fingers.

"It gives me a lovely taste in the mouth," Ronnie said, "whenever I touch fireworks." I remembered the taste too and the strange exultation which it engendered. Dora did not, but she hadn't the strength of mind to ban the display.

"You must promise only to let them off in the hearth and stand well away," she said, despite all their assurances that there would be no explosion and no danger. Indeed, the fireworks were harmless enough, though they made ugly marks on the dark green tiles of the hearth. When it was too late, Dora noticed them. "Oh dear," she said, "look what you've done. They may make us pay for a new hearth." "How much would that cost?" Bunny asked. "Far more than all the pocket-money you have in a year," she replied. "Well, if any harm's been done, we've done it now," said Bunny.

"And there's only one more. This one should have coloured stars."
I ought, I suppose, to have helped Dora, but I was very conscious
in those days of only being the children's aunt.

The last firework was let off, but the anticlimax was not yet.
Both the boys and even Joan had become filled with an excitement
which they could no longer contain. They began to chase one
another round the room, to jump from the sofa to an armchair, to
fight with cushions. Dora watched them with helpless dismay, and
I watched Dora, wondering what her own children would have
been like if she had been able to have any. We had forgotten the
time till the hall-porter came in to tell us that the cab was waiting
for Master Carlice.

Then Dora asserted herself. "Please tell him to wait another ten
minutes," she said. "Master Carlice and his friend will not be ready
till then."

"But, Auntie Dora, we must go. We shall be late."

"You must sit down and get cool first, dear. I can't let you go
while you're so hot. You would both catch your deaths of cold.
Now sit down quietly for a few minutes."

"But we must go. Mr. Peters said——"

"Tell Mr. Peters I said you were not to go."

I feared that Ronnie might be going to appeal to me, and looked
away from him, at an oil painting of a bearded old man who was
carrying a young girl on his shoulder through a flood. In the background stood the deserted cottage, already lapped by the rising
waters. Then Joan whispered loudly to me, "They'll get into a row,
Auntie Isabel." Dora overheard and looked at me nervously, as if
fearing that her one firm stand of the afternoon would be broken
down. "After all, we pay Mr. Peters," she murmured. Bunny blushed,
while Ronnie gazed resentfully at the hot fire, and the hearth
strewn with traces of the firework display. It was a contest of wills,
though we all agreed, except Joan, that Dora must win.

When the good-nights were said, I noticed that she gave each
of the boys five shillings. Joan stood waving after the cab for a long
time, by the swing door in the hall, and Dora and I went back to
the drawing-room, to open the windows and tidy the fireplace.

"I think Joan rather liked Bunny," Dora said. "You do agree,
Isabel, don't you, that I was right to make them stay and cool

down? You know what awful colds Ronnie catches. They had him in bed for a fortnight in the school sanatorium this time last year."

"Yes," I said, "but we should have thought of it before."

"Oh, ten minutes can't matter. Besides, you can walk to the school in half an hour. I did with Claude when we came down in the summer last year. It was Ronnie's first summer term."

She knelt by the hearth, like a housemaid, her blonde little head nodding as she tried to polish up the tiles. I wondered how long she would continue to wear black which, oddly enough, didn't suit her. Her father, Dr. Payne of South Mersley, London very much S.W., had died less than a month before. She had spent several weeks in the summer hovering round his death-bed. A dutiful daughter. But when Claude asked her to marry him, four years before, she had seemed enchanted to leave home. Or had I assumed that she must be?

Once more she said, "I think Joan rather liked Bunny."

"But not so much as she likes the under-porter," I said. "You may be sure she's talking to him now, hoping to see him swing the revolving door."

She looked up at me with the fear of my disapproval in her face—an expression which made me want to bully her whenever I saw it.

"Do you think I ought to fetch her away?"

"Oh no! She'll be all right. The porter won't . . ."

I was going to use what Claude called one of my mannish phrases, when there was a sound of steps coming to the door.

"Here is Joan," Dora said, continuing to burnish the hearth. But it was the young page-boy. "Trunk call for Mrs. Carlice, please."

She got up hurriedly, rubbed her hands, smoothed her dress and hair, and looked at herself in the mirror over the fireplace, all very quickly.

"Oh dear, I hope nobody will see me in the lounge. What *can* it be, Isabel?"

"The 'phone box is behind the reception office in the hall," the page-boy said shrilly.

"Well, you must show me the way," she said. Then turning round to me, as she was just going through the door, she added: "I expect it's you they want, not me."

The page-boy slammed the door behind her, leaving me alone, while I tried to think of any reason why anyone who knew we were in Leamington should wish to ring us up. Despite the opening of the windows, there was still a smell of fireworks in the room, and as I noticed it, the old exciting taste, which Ronnie had mentioned, came suddenly into my mouth and reminded me of those Novembers when I had to let off fireworks for Claude, though he loved them more than I did. But when it came to letting them off . . . "How the devil will the boy ever learn to use a gun?" my father used to say. But, somehow, he had learnt. . . .

Then Joan came bundling in.

"Auntie Isabel, will you go at once to Auntie Dora? She's at the telephone-box. She opened the door and said I was to fetch you. I was watching her through the glass. Something's upset her. What do you think it can be? . . ."

I shook her off at the door and told her to stay in the drawing-room.

I don't think Dora was crying, but she was white enough to faint.

"Oh, Isabel . . . you speak! It's about Claude."

I shut myself in the box and took up the receiver.

"Eames, this is Miss Carlice speaking. What is it?"

"It's the master. There's been an accident. He's been shot. In the gunroom."

"*Been* shot? Is he dead?"

"Yes, miss, I'm afraid so. The gun was between his knees."

"Was it you who found him?"

"Yes, miss. Not a quarter of an hour ago."

"Have you sent for Dr. Machin?"

"Yes, miss."

"And the police?"

"Not yet, miss."

"Then you'd better. We shall come home at once—to-night if we can. I'll send a message when I know the train. And, Eames . . ."

"Yes, miss?"

"Caution everyone to say nothing, or as little as possible, to Miss Joan when we arrive. You understand? I, or Mrs. Carlice, will tell her what we think she should be told."

As I opened the door of the telephone-box, Dora fell against me heavily.

3

I have had, sometimes, to tell this story, and when I do, I feel I have made myself out as too heroic or too heartless. And each time afterwards, when I have imagined my listener going away with a disapprovingly murmured "Remarkable woman that!" I have asked myself whether I really ever did love Claude—despite our girlhood and boyhood spent together, and the three years I kept house for him after his first wife died. I make no secret that those three years were happy—till I saw he was set on marrying again.

He picked Dora up—I have allowed my friends to put it like that sometimes—at the Grangeleigh tennis tournament. Poor Claude! Having been such a duffer at all school games, it was an unexpected joy to find himself up to small tournament tennis form. At thirty-nine too and even over forty. It gave a new zest to those three summers for him. I enjoyed watching, too, and would often drive over with him on those long bright days, and hobnob with people whom otherwise perhaps one wouldn't have known very well—a cheery set, tending a little to drink, and flitting from town to town along the coast, housed in the attics of friends or on special terms in second-rate hotels. Even I, a non-player, thought it was all great fun, like a cruise or prolonged picnic, something outside the ordinary scheme of one's life and incapable—as I wrongly thought then—of interfering with it.

Needless to say, we did it all from home. We didn't bother our friends or stay in those hotels, except once in Eastbourne. But Claude was outclassed there too hopelessly to make the visit worth while. He kept to the smaller gatherings after that—Mickleton, Swan Sands, Ivemoor and Grangeleigh—where, in 1922, Maud McEwen, who was to have been his partner in the doubles, sprained her ankle in the station yard as she arrived, and Dorothea Payne, flushed with a triumph in the mixed doubles at South Mersley and, like Claude, let down by her proposed partner, was given Claude instead and led him to victory.

Seeing her now, with her would-be matronly air, those dimples and fourteen years on her age, one hardly believes it possible. But it was.

"I've never won the mixed anywhere before," Claude said, as we got into the car after the prize-giving.

"She seemed quite a nice girl," I told him. "You must play with her again."

"Yes, it's still early in the season."

He played with her twice more, though they didn't win, and then, when the week came for our local tournament, he suggested having a little party for it. I said it was an excellent idea, and the house was filled with people who did not ordinarily visit us.

"It isn't a *social* occasion," Claude explained. "You don't mind, do you?"

"Good heavens, of course I don't. Do you think Dr. Payne will let his daughter come?"

"Oh, I should think he would only be too glad to get rid of her for a time."

I watched, I remember, for a blush as he said this. He blushed again a few days later when he said, "The children seem to get on very well with Dora."

Then the tournament was over, and she went home to keep house for her father, though, as I gathered from a remark I wasn't meant to hear, her father had an efficient cook-housekeeper, who was by no means too old to be something more than that. Apparently the Paynes lived rather well. The doctor had a big practice and was clever with his investments. But—as another remark I overheard put it—"he wasn't quite everybody's cup of tea in South Mersley."

In early September, Claude said to me, "Do you know, I haven't ever played in a hard-courts tournament?"

"Would you like to?"

"I rather think I should."

"Well, where is one going to be held?"

"There's one at South Mersley the week after next."

"But it's much too far to motor there for the day."

"Oh, I shouldn't try to."

"You'd stay with——?"

"I should stay in London for the week. It's less than three-quarters of an hour by train, you know."

"Of course."

"Wouldn't you care for a few days in London too?"

"In mid-September, in weather like this?"

"I suppose not."

The early autumn was very lovely that year—as it is every year whatever the weather is like.

"I can't leave the rose garden now," I said. (I was replanning it.) "And I want to plant the daffodils myself. Jackson puts them in as if they were soldiers. There are three thousand of them."

"Three thousand! Where on earth are they all going?"

"In father's cherry tree plantation."

"But there are some there already."

"None."

"Oh, I'm thinking of the orchard."

"Yes, you are. But, Claude, you haven't to plant them. They needn't keep you here."

"I don't like gadding about while you're so busy at home."

"I do it because I like it. Besides, I needn't be lonely. I can have Gwen Rashdall here for the week. I ought to ask her down, and I know you don't care for her much."

"Well, if it all fits in——"

It all fitted in.

So Claude played in the South Mersley Hard-Courts Championship and got as far as the semifinal in the mixed doubles—an achievement, as the tournament attracted some almost good players. The following week there was another hard-courts tournament also near London. He mentioned it at some length in a letter, and I urged him to play in it. "It's as if you were the man and he were the woman," Gwen Rashdall said, when I read her parts of his letter. "You ought obviously to be owning this place, not Claude." Her habit of saying things like that was one of the reasons why Claude disliked her. I said little or nothing to her about Dora Payne, of whom (not being in our new tennis world) she had hardly heard.

On the second Saturday afternoon of Claude's absence, a telegram arrived for me. But it only stated, "We have won the mixed."
He was to come back on the next day, Sunday. Gwen had gone
two days before. I remember Sunday was a specially lovely day,
so warm in the sunshine that instead of planting my bulbs, I sat
for a long time on a seat by the orchard, while the apples seemed
to swell and ripen before my eyes. The salpiglossis—which for
the sake of preserving a childhood's memory I have kept as my
"favourite annual"—were very fine that year, and four of our
Victorian beds near the house were filled with them. Wherever
I turned, there was something to notice and be fond of. The cobs
were almost ready to pick. The autumn crocuses were spattering
the grass round the mulberry tree. The Michaelmas daisies were
beginning to turn colour and gave the long wall, which was their
background, a blue and purple tinge, broken here and there by the
tawny flash of a late-blooming red-hot poker, or a straggly shoot
of pink hollyhocks which should have been cut down three weeks
before.

I had expected Claude for luncheon, but he sent a telephone
message in the morning to say he wouldn't be home till after
dinner. In a way I was not sorry to be able to enjoy the garden by
myself, without the busy distraction of his news.

After that blaze of light and warmth it seemed absurd for the
sun to set at seven. I watched it from my window, striking through
the curved line of beeches that was one of our boundaries, over a
couple of fields and a space of lawn and lower trees, till it caught
the things on my dressing-table, each minute at a different angle,
and filled the room with changing reflexions of itself. Then the last
ray vanished.

After dinner I sat in the morning-room where, thinking it might
be chilly, Eames had lit the fire. Neither Claude nor I were fond of
the drawing-room. But it was still warm, and I drew the curtains
back and opened a window to let in the fresh air, before settling
down by a shaded lamp to read.

I hardly heard Claude coming into the room, and before I had
put my book down I felt his hand on my hair and his face touching
mine as he kissed me. It was a more affectionate greeting than
we generally gave one another. Then he sat down in an armchair

opposite mine and lit a cigarette. A moonbeam struck the carving of the gunroom door, which was between our chairs.

"Well," I said, "so you won. I'm delighted."

"Yes. It's been a marvellous fortnight."

He began to tell me about it, little things which I could have guessed, and were clearly leading up to something bigger which, though I might guess it too, would have to be expressed in difficult words.

"What did you do to-day?" I asked, thinking I had better help him.

"To-day? Oh, I met Arthur and Lilian last night, and they made me promise to spend the day with them. You know how often I've promised to go and see them. They've got a very pretty little place, but of course that part of Hertfordshire's getting very towny. It's only about fifteen miles from London."

For a short time we talked about Arthur and Lilian.

"I suppose you had a celebration dinner last night?"

"No. These tournaments break up very quickly, you know. Dora had to get back home, and I thought I'd just dine somewhere quietly and go to a show when, as I told you, I met Arthur in the bar and . . ."

"Dora must have been very pleased with herself."

"She ought to be. She won the second set entirely on her own. I played like a rabbit. . . . I suppose the children are well?"

"Oh, perfectly."

He lit another cigarette, and I prepared myself for his voice to change when he next spoke. It did.

"Isabel, I've had a letter I think I ought to show you. I found it at the hotel when I got back last night. From Dr. Payne."

"Oh!"

While I read it, he fetched himself a whisky-and-soda. I can still remember some of the pompous phrases.

"As a father and a medical man I can assert . . . This hesitation to disclose your intentions . . . In point of time a short period, but in point of the closeness of your association, a long one . . . Her acquaintance with you has already caused her to reject a very suitable offer for her hand . . . Failing an explanation, I must for her sake forbid my daughter to speak to you again . . ."

My first thought was, "The man has written too soon. He's done for himself by this."

But I was wrong.

"You see?"

"Yes, Claude. It's a most—unfortunate letter. Why rush things so?"

"You mean me?"

"No, no. Dr. Payne, of course. He ought to give you time to know your own mind, however well he thinks he knows Dora's."

"Isabel dear, I think I do know my own mind. I have enjoyed this summer so enormously. You don't suppose it was just the tennis, do you?"

"Oh, there was never any need to think that."

He looked puzzled by my remark, which indeed began to puzzle me. I think I meant two or three different things by it.

He answered it by saying, "The point is, this letter brings things to a crisis."

"In a sense, yes. But not really, if you know your own mind."

"I know my own mind so far as I'm concerned. But there are other people to think of."

"You mean——?"

"You and the children, of course."

"As for the children——" I began. I wanted to gain a little time before we discussed my position, and it was no effort to convince him that the children would not suffer if he married Dora. She had already shown that she liked them, and, more important, they seemed to like her. When their mother died Joan was seven and Ronnie only four. Now Joan was ten and Ronnie seven. They wouldn't resent a new mother.

"My only fear is she may spoil them."

This seemed greatly to reassure him. After all, who could blame him for giving them an over-indulgent stepmother?

"Well, if that's out of the way, I've only to ask you how you'd feel about having her here," he said. "Not even she would ever expect you to go. She knows how you've helped me here since Mary died."

"My dear Claude, we had all this out when you married Mary. It would be ridiculous of me to think of staying. I went away before. I only came back as a stop-gap."

"Don't speak of it like that. And Dora's not quite like Mary, you know. Dora will need your help—for a long time. She'll rely on it."

"I don't think she'll want any help from me at all. Of course, I'll do what I can. I'll pay you long visits, and——"

"Oh, Isabel, you make me feel I'm driving you away."

"Nonsense! If I don't convince you you're not, I shall feel I've never had any right to be here at all."

I took his part and he mine. We did it well. He said things on my behalf which I should hardly have liked to plead even to myself. "Your interest in this place, your devotion to the garden . . ." He was almost eloquent. So was I.

"Don't you see, Claude, this is rescuing me from a rut? Here I am, at forty-three, settling down as if I were fifty-three, or even sixty. Life still should have a few surprises for me."

I spoke almost as if I might get married. He believed it or, at least, thought it possible. So, I suppose, it was.

"I can afford," I said, "a flat in London—during the interregnum, if there is to be one. Before, I mean, something happens to show me the way. Or a cottage in the country, if the mood takes me. But I think a contrast would be—more useful to me, before I quite lose touch with all the interesting people we used to know. Why, after Christmas, I might go for a cruise."

No, I can't have said a cruise, because cruises were hardly commonplaces in 1922. How easy these anachronisms are! I suppose I actually said "travel abroad." But whatever it was, he jumped at it. The strain of holding out against me was too much—as it had always been. He gave in.

4

Claude married Dora Payne in December, 1922. I spent Christmas with them, and took a flat in London. Then, when I was preparing thoroughly to detest the year, my Aunt Eleanor died and left me some of the money her rich husband had left her. I can't pretend it made no difference to me. I got rid of the flat, which I hated already, and moved into a house—this house, this L-shaped drawing-room, where the female novelist has just had tea with me and asked me about the gunroom—this drawing-room where the first pale sunset of yet another year has struck the silver tray and sugar basin.

I have wondered, sometimes, how much Claude resented Aunt Eleanor's will. The money should have been left not to him, perhaps, but to the house in which he lived. It gave me a false importance—the power, for instance, to restore the hall when it needed doing up. I insisted on being "generous" over this. Oh, those arrivals with *my* architect, *my* builder! Even at the time I felt guilty, though no one welcomed me with anything but thanks and praise. But it was too early in my exile to be detached, to smile when I heard of the dinners Dora couldn't give, servants she couldn't manage, the long painstaking adjustment of herself that she was making. Yet the one sign I was waiting for from Claude— the sign that he had ceased to be in love with her—never came.

He hadn't "only married a tennis-racket," as Gwen Rashdall so wittily asserted. They did play tennis the summer after the wedding, but without much success. Indeed, Dora played when she ought to have given it up. Perhaps it was only fair that the game which gave Joan and Ronnie a stepmother should have prevented them from having stepbrothers and stepsisters. The following summer, after her long convalescence, Dora played again. But she had lost her skill and soon ceased to try. Claude was now definitely too old. I have no reason to think that those years were anything but happy for him.

Then suddenly came his death. Despite all our efforts at the inquest, a verdict of suicide was returned. No worry about health? None, so far as we and his doctor knew. Money? He had enough to keep things going, with a little care. His "affairs were all in order." His domestic life? Perfectly happy. Then, *why* . . . ?

We made the most of an attack of influenza, which he had caught towards the end of October. It was not a severe attack. He was not more than three whole days in bed. But might it not have produced a depression—yes, he had been rather depressed, but not to that point—or a brain-storm, sufficient to account for what he did? Sufficient, that is to say, to spare us and his children the words "while of unsound mind." The jury were not convinced, and gave the verdict we dreaded.

Joan somehow heard.

"Does it mean," she asked me, "that we've got insanity in the family?"

We were in the morning-room, while Dora, upstairs, was going through Claude's things.

"It means nothing at all," I told her. "They're old-fashioned words which the law still uses. There's been no sign of insanity ever in our family. Look at me. I come from the same stock. Do you think there's any insanity here?"

I tapped my forehead in melodramatic fashion, trying to frighten her into common sense. She said "No," doubtfully, as if making a reservation about me.

"You're quite right, dear," I went on, "to have asked me about this. And you must promise to talk to me if ever it worries you again. But it needn't. Your grandfather was perfectly lucid till an hour before he died. And his father—that's to say, my grand-father—did his accounts on his deathbed, when he was eighty-eight. Your mother, too, was a most clear-headed woman. I think you take after her."

Her thoughts had wandered a little.

"Then I can tell Ronnie——" she began.

"You must tell Ronnie nothing—because there's nothing to tell him."

"Then why didn't you let him come back for the funeral?"

I explained to her that Ronnie was three years younger than she was, which meant that, being a boy, he was really a child in comparison with her. An imaginative highly strung child, too. For her, there was no shock, because there was nothing to be shocked about, except for our natural grief at losing Daddy. But for Ronnie there would have been a shock—beyond his natural grief. It was our duty, and Joan's duty too, to see that he never heard exactly what happened—or didn't hear it for a very long time. We had written, I told her, to Ronnie's headmaster, who promised to see that Ronnie shouldn't get hold of a newspaper. He had even told Ronnie a long story about the accident, saying that Eames was in the room when it happened. Eames was prepared to support the

story if Ronnie should question him, and it was for Joan, if necessary, to support the story as well.

"Even if I have to tell an untruth?" she asked.

"Yes, even if you have to tell an untruth. Now, listen, Joan—this
is what Ronnie has been told."

I gave her the account we had sent to Mr. Peters. She listened,
as if to an interesting story, and I knew I had made her an ally over
it. If it worried her—well, she had the strength to bear it. Ronnie, I
didn't think, had. At least, I didn't care to put him to the test.

"And shall we go on living here?" she asked, when I had finished.

"Of course. You and Auntie Dora and Ronnie will go on living
here, and when Ronnie's twenty-one the place will belong to him.
But you'll be married yourself before that happens and have a
home of your own."

"But you never married, Auntie Isabel."

"You shouldn't ask older people why they never married. They
may have some intimate or sad reason which they don't want
to tell you. Mind, I don't say that I have. But if you like, you can
think that I was too busy looking after your grandfather to think
of marrying. *You* won't have anyone to look after, except Ronnie,
and I expect he'll soon get a wife to do that for him. Now, have we
talked it all over?"

"I think so. Except one thing. Why Daddy did it. . . ."

But that was a question to which I could give no answer.

5

My grandfather, who married the coal on which we have been
living ever since, disliked entails. I am not sure really that he didn't
dislike Carlice Abbey; for, with the taste of his age, he coveted a
house in the style of the Crystal Palace, and not all his additions
and enrichments could turn the Abbey into one. It may be that the
entail prevented him from leaving, or made it more difficult. At all
events, it was broken at some time or other, and my father had the
place in his own right, to bequeath as he chose. When it came to
Claude the position was the same.

Claude's will was dated the September before his death. He left
the Abbey outright to Ronnie on reaching twenty-one. If he died

before, it was to go to Joan on reaching twenty-five or marrying under that age with the consent of her guardians. If both children died before attaining vested interests it was to go to me. The bulk of the revenue from coal (which had sadly dwindled) was to pass with the estate, Dora and Joan each being given five hundred a year for life. While Ronnie was under twenty-one Dora, who was his guardian jointly with me, was to have the right to live at Carlice Abbey and to control the main funds subject to my consent. If we disagreed, the dispute was to be settled by Sir Thomas Hill, a legal friend of Claude's. I was left a few things of sentimental value.

Gwen Rashdall was full of comments, when she heard the arrangements—or, rather, she tried to make me say the things she wanted to say. Her first impression was that Claude had treated Dora with unexpected shabbiness.

"Dora's turned adrift with only £500 a year in ten years' time," she said. "Don't you think she'd be wiser to go now? After all, she might marry fairly well now, but in ten years' time—well, her face will hardly be a fortune then."

I agreed that if I were Dora I should go at once.

"Do you think," Gwen asked me, "that you ought to tell her, or let her know somehow, that you'd be ready to live here and look after the children? She may have a sense of duty in her odd way and feel she ought to stay."

I said that that was the last thing I should like to let Dora know. It would be too like telling her that she ought to make way for me.

"Besides," I asked, "what makes you think I should like to live at Carlice and look after the children?"

She laughed.

"Of course, the children might bore you. You don't like the young."

"No, I don't."

"Joan is sure to grow up into a Communist, and Ronnie will be an æsthete."

(Here Gwen was wrong, but I couldn't contradict her.)

"Still," she went on, "living at Carlice would be a compensation for you."

"To be turned away the moment Ronnie's twenty-one, like Dora?"

"Except that you'd have more than five hundred a year—thanks to your Aunt Eleanor. You know, Isabel, you seem destined to live in a detective story—I mean, to have a perpetual incentive to murder people!"

"Explain yourself, Gwen."

"Well, there was Honorine, your Aunt Eleanor's daughter. Suppose she'd lived another three years, where would you have been? Nowhere. You'd have been like me, a sponger, trading on a kind of common sense of amiability—a superior lady-companion. You were with Honorine in Paris when she caught diphtheria, weren't you?"

"You know I was."

"Did you make her drink her bath-water?"

"As usual, Gwen, you're verging on bad taste."

"Anyway, I thought that with the serum diphtheria could always be cured nowadays."

"Honorine had the serum. She had everything."

"Have you been thankful enough, though, for the difference it made to you?"

"Whom should I thank? Aunt Eleanor?"

"No, God. Or something inside you. That power to get, somehow, what you want. Well, you've a chance now to use it again. Ronnie must go. Joan must go. Then—step on Dora."

"Is this an argument to persuade me to look after my nephew and niece?"

"Oh, they mean less than nothing to me—less even than they do to you. You can't convince me, though, that your one ambition is to see Carlice descending through the male line for ever and for ever. Besides, it won't descend."

"Why?"

"Because the world is misguidedly breeding something which will stop all that kind of thing. Another death, and after paying death duties, how could the family keep up Carlice—unless Aunt Eleanor's money came to the rescue?"

"Ronnie might marry oil."

"I bet he doesn't."

"Why are you so pessimistic about him?"

"I just have a feeling he's going to be awkward for you all. But that's nothing. It isn't only death duties. It's a world movement. Things as we know them may just last our time—if we don't over-stay our welcome. Having Carlice would only put Ronnie on the wrong lines. Claude would have been kinder if he'd left it to you."

"Who am on the wrong lines already, you mean?"

I daresay she was right. There was a gay gloominess about Gwen which endeared her to people—enabled her to "sponge her way," as she would have put it, from South Kensington to Cannes and back to Scotland. She read everything—all those disconcerting books and weeklies which I prefer to avoid. She was full of the 1926 General Strike months before the papers mentioned it. (Yet we had the General Strike and nothing so very terrible happened. As it turned out, it was waste of time to worry about it before-hand.) Now, in this month of February, 1936, she is full of the next war. Or rather, she's got beyond the mere war, to a period of drab, intensive and compulsory industrialism which she says will succeed it—a period which she says will not only destroy our present values, but make even the memory of them illegal. In a crisis, of course, Gwen would be admirable. She would parry the bomb with one hand and shake a cocktail with the other. I think I have liked her, partly, because she has always been so unsuitable a friend for me. She goes with nothing that we stand for—or *stood* for—since now that my father, Aunt Eleanor and Claude are gone, there's no *we* to stand for anything. Any standing has to be done by me alone.

But she was wrong about Joan. Joan is not a Communist. She's a quite nice unattractive girl. I should like to have her as my maid. And she was wrong about Dora, who never showed any sign of wanting to leave Carlice—never even gave me a loophole for telling her that I could and would look after the children, if she preferred to start life afresh. This I found difficult to understand in her. It was almost as if something outside her had made up her mind to stay and "do her duty"—if anyone, knowing the facts, could use that phrase. And now she has about seven months to go, from this February till September the eighth, when Ronnie comes of age. And I suppose she'll stay on after that, until he marries, managing the staff with a mixture of timidity and petulance, and leaving the coast clear for Ronnie's friends, those not-very-nice young men with whom he surrounds himself. Bunny Andrews, whom Ronnie brought to tea with us at Leamington, was the best of them. But Bunny has suddenly come into a lot of money and has the wrong ideology, as Ronnie puts it now. Bunny ranges himself with the comfortable classes, about whom we are now not even supposed to read, as a reviewer told me only the other day. O Lord, preserve my egoism! If pressed, I will even say selfishness; for selfishness, in its broadest and fullest sense, seems to me to have been the main-spring of everything worth while. At least, it can hardly claim so many miseries and murders as mass-made fanaticisms.

It is Ronnie who goads me to such dicta, and makes me wish that I had beaten him well when he was a child.

6

Last time I was at Carlice—for ten days round Christmas—I was walking down the lane to the pillar-box past the curved line of beeches which I have always loved so much, when I saw a tramp sitting on the grass verge and looking up at the smooth trunks and branches which still retained some of their coppery leaves. There was a little sunlight, a reminder that the sun did really exist some-where, and I suppose it was just warm enough for a tramp to sit in the open without getting a chill. It was one of those encounters, like my more recent encounter with the fat woman who would be back in her flat at five, which meant a great deal to me. He didn't look at me for a long time, which allowed me to look at him. There was nothing very remarkable in his expression—no ecstasy, no indignation, no distress even or resignation. He was just living at that moment like a vegetable, enjoying the vegetable world—that world which I secretly value so much more than the world of human beings. I felt and still feel, when I picture him sitting there, an intimate kinship with him, as if he were ultimately "on my side" in the modern battle of values. I hoped that it was not misfortune, but laziness or self-indulgence which had made him what he was. I hoped, too, that he would never regain his "self-respect," but would struggle along, as he was, for many years, without too much external wretchedness. I say *external*, because

I had no doubt that internally he was all right. The Kingdom of Heaven was within him—as it is in me, at bedrock, whatever I say and do, however absorbed I may seem with trivial and silly things, however fearful I may be of the future, or distressed with past and present. We have learnt the great secret. We have found Grace. I use the word with the intensity, though without the orthodoxy, of a theologian. In some moods I might maintain that I mean an intimation of immortality, which has nothing to do with morality, or merit, but proceeds from an apprehension of the inner essence of material things. Wordsworth, I suppose, in part, or that modern man, J. C. Powys, whom I ought to read. Gwen has this "Grace," but with too much conscious artistry for me, and Joan may be going to develop it. Sometimes I think that even Dora has glimmerings of it, while her ne'er-do-well half-brother, the dipsomaniac, has more than his fair share, from what I've gathered. Claude had none, my father had none, Ronnie has none, or like a fool has killed it. It is this, really, which makes the essential cleavage in the world. At present our side seems to be losing. Science, organisation, short-sighted experimentalism in search of efficiency carry the day. But we have cunning forces on our side. Though we batten on the past, our powers of adaptation to a changing environment are more durable than those engendered painfully in laboratories. We slink comparatively scatheless through the crash of scientific scheming and the breakdown of an over-elaborate order. For it is in disorder that we find our secret nourishment—in the waywardness of the first fiery particle that broke the law of perpetual monotony—and will from time to time break all the other laws to give us that calm anarchy which is our hidden joy.

This is a passage from my real autobiography—which I shall write still less than the one which I began with salpiglossis—a periodical iteration of my creed which may well mark the first February evening when I have had tea without electric light.

But it is now quite dark, and ever since the female novelist was shown out, full of the Abbey architecture and our gunroom, I have been sitting here telling snippets of my story to myself. Yet I could go back to the gunroom all over again, and tell the story again from there, with other touches and other colouring. The hope for the future is that it will one day be the past and part of the same story. Even this cramp of mine which I've got through sitting here so long, and this darkness which might be midnight though it's only——

Come in.

Yes, Simmonds, you can draw the curtains now.

Chapter II: RONALD CARLICE

THE clocks of Oxford striking eleven, overlapping, jangling up the hour, on the last Sunday morning of my last term but one. A grey day, though warm. My books and papers scattered all over my big fake sofa-table. (Real sofa-tables were never made of walnut.) My gown, substitute for a pair of tongs, on the floor beside the ugly coal-scuttle. There is a clock still striking. Or is it a belated church bell? A memory to carry away—these clocks and bells of Oxford—and use when I'm being drilled for the next war, or putting on my gas-mask, or burnishing my spade in the labour corps. Dreaming spires. Compton Mackenzie. My little taste of the otiose elegances which even the last war didn't quite kill.

I must clear those club fixture-cards from the mantelpiece. There is no reason why I should have their dust next term—if there is a next term. Philosophical Society. Musical Club. Liars' Club. Prophets' Club. All except this one—St. Peter's College Labour Club (affiliated to the University Labour Club). Trinity Term, 1936. *Proof. Please correct and return by Tuesday. 14th May: Mr. R. Carlise will read a paper on "Labour and Art." Host: Mr. D. L. Cruttley.*

I might as well correct that now. Cross out the "s" and turn it into a "c," so that my father could recognise it. This was his chief small vanity. "Two 'c's' were good enough for Henry VIII," he said when he took me to school for the first time. "Don't let them spell your name with an 's,' even though it is pronounced Carliss." Poor father! In his time, of course, people didn't have cars. The boys didn't bother to spell my name with an "s." I wished they had, because they might have been less quick to call me Car-*louse.* "You're singular, not plural. Your parents are car-lice. You're a Car-louse. Aren't you?" And so on, with physical proof of it. Nasty days.

I hated them—and Peters, the headmaster. (Odd that I find myself at St. Peter's College now.) I was frightened of him, and he was unjust—especially on the night my father died. Isabel, Dora and Joan had come to Leamington to see me at midterm. God knows why. I loathed them coming to see me at school, and I didn't want to go and see them in their hotel on Sunday. I suppose I was afraid of being unsettled by the taste of two hours' civilisation. It was good of Bunny to go with me. "May Ronnie bring a friend, Mr. Peters?" It was Dora doing her stuff, while Isabel listened critically. "Oh, certainly, my dear Mrs. Carlice." Had Peters an eye for a pretty woman? I imagine she was rather pretty then. Meanwhile, I fidgeted and blushed and looked sideways, and wondered if we could show off with those damned fireworks we had made. It was the fireworks really which made us late in getting back. And Peters would choose that Sunday evening to read to the juniors. Had it been Meldrum's turn, I shouldn't have minded. I should have said, "I'm sorry I'm late, sir, but I couldn't get away from my family earlier." He'd have left it at that. But with Peters in charge, everything went wrong. We slunk in, or rather I slunk. Bunny probably was smiling very quietly to himself, with his blue eyes looking at nothing, knowing he wasn't in any way responsible. I slunk in, followed by Bunny, and *Treasure Island* suddenly ceased to boom.

"Carlice?"

"Sir."

"What is the time?"

"Ten minutes past six, sir."

"Did I remind you to be back by six o'clock?"

"Yes, sir. I'm very sorry."

"Why are you late?"

"We were playing about, sir, and got very hot and my stepmother said we must cool down before we went out."

"Why must you be so mamby-pamby, Carlice? Sit down, both of you."

And *Treasure Island* began to boom again.

The words stuck. *Why must you be so mamby-pamby, Carlice?* Even as I sat down, I felt that I was done for. *Why must you be so mamby-pamby, Car-louse?* What a slogan for my enemies, among whom I included the many who regarded me with indifference, or even liked me a little, but wouldn't want to miss a bit of fun. As it happened, I needn't have worried. I went to bed that night with the words still crawling over the raw stuff in my mind, but nobody used them at supper or in my dormitory. Perhaps the collective judgment was that Peters had been unfair. As Bunny put it, the man was a bit of a cad. He ought to have known what parents were by that time. Bunny could say amazingly adult things like that, and no one kicked him. And the next day, I gave them all something else to think about. My father had had his accident and died—probably just in those ten minutes by which I overstayed my leave. It was a very different Peters who saw me in his study the next morning and gave me the news—or, rather, the first instalment.

It was Peters, too, who gave me the second instalment a week later, after my father was buried. It was a long, painstaking account, almost illustrated with diagrams. "We must picture your dear father as standing *there*, my boy, while your butler, Eames, was *here*. Your father was about to hand the gun to Eames, when . . ."

I can't remember now what was supposed to have happened next. The details embarrassed me, and meant nothing. It seemed ghoulish to insist on them. I'm sure that, as my eyes wandered to the huge globe on its stand near the window, Peters longed to shout "Attend!" I was attending, but not to the details. What did it matter exactly how my father held the gun, or how the safety-catch failed to work? It was a relief when we came to generalities again—to the exhortation with which the interview was rounded off. "Unhappily, my dear boy, you are now an orphan. This places peculiar and difficult responsibilities upon you—responsibilities towards yourself and your own moral and physical development." And so on.

Was Peters right? Should I have grown up to be very different, if I had had a mother and father living? I remember, even while the news was fresh to me, thinking secretly: "Now I shall be able to do more as I like at home. There won't be any more talk of getting a tennis or cricket Professional over to coach me in the holidays." My father had been bad at school games, and wanted me to escape the humiliation his own failures had brought him. He had been good at tennis, and wanted me to be good too. I hated all games then, as much as I do now. I remember my first term being bullied for not knowing what a Test Match was, and thinking how unjust it was that I wasn't bullying my tormentors, who didn't even know the plots of Æschylus' plays, while I had read them all twice in a translation in Everyman's Library. But with all the tennis and cricket coaching in the world, I should never have excelled. I can't put down my athletic feebleness to lack of a father. I don't pretend the news of his death wasn't a shock. I cried a good deal, and for a few days my grief brought me prestige.

Christmas came—a quiet Christmas with Aunt Isabel as our only visitor. I went home feeling I should be made a fuss of, and I was. Even Joan embarrassed me by being strangely considerate, asking me what I should like to do, seeing that I wore my thick coat, and hardly ever contradicting me. It was as if I had had a narrow escape myself—— They were pleasant holidays—but all holidays were pleasant.

Then, less than a week before I was due to go back to school, the real news came to me, in an issue of our local paper published ten days after my father's death. It arrived by the afternoon post. I saw the postman coming up the drive and went to meet him. It was dusk, and I didn't realise that the paper was for me, till I had turned the light on in the hall and read the address:

> *Master Ronald Carlice,*
> *Carlice Abbey.*
> *Local.*

The paper was done up clumsily with string.

Auntie Dora had taken Joan to her dancing-class, and I had the house to myself. Even so, I didn't open the paper till I had gone to my bedroom and locked the door; for I recognised the illiterate writing of the address at once. It was Solly who had sent it—a groom who was dismissed at the end of the summer holidays, for (as I now see it) having a bad influence on me. It was my own fault really; for I used to ask him awkward questions about the horses and encourage him to teach me things I ought not to have known. Still, he was a bad hat. Stephens our bailiff got wind of it, and reported Solly to my father. It was typical of my father that so far from giving me a lecture, he merely said, when I asked nervously why Solly had gone, that he was an unsatisfactory character and neglected his work.

On the front page Solly had scrawled:

See page 12.

It didn't occur to me that the paper was an old one, till I obeyed the instructions and read the heading:

Inquest on owner of Carlice Abbey.
Verdict of Suicide.

The whole thing was set out in detail, the expostulations of our lawyer, Auntie Dora's "ordeal in box," the medical evidence, both as to the "accident" and the depressing effects of influenza. So that was it. Suicide. I knew the secret now.

When Auntie Dora and Joan came back, I said nothing to them about my discovery, and the next day I found it still more difficult to speak. What most deterred me was the thought of their finding out that Solly had been communicating with me again. There seemed to be something guilty in this last communication of his, just as there had been in those other communications which had corrupted my good manners. Yet this very feeling of guilt had with it, like my previous feelings of guilt, the spice of exhilaration. I remember many a night, after I had gone back to school again, lying awake and listening to the dark blue blind flapping against the dormitory window and thinking to myself, "I am the son of a man who committed suicide." And in the mornings, I used to awake very early, while all the other boys were still sleeping, and think the same thought as I watched a lozenge-shaped piece of light, let in by a rent in the same blind, move slowly along the wall opposite my bed.

I told Bunny and for once he didn't know what to say. At first he pretended to think I had invented the story. I couldn't show him the paper, as I had locked it up in my treasure-box at home. Then I guessed that he had really known the truth for some time. Probably his parents had talked in the Christmas holidays. After all, the local paper wasn't the only one to report our trouble. I found out later that there had been a paragraph in *The Times*.

"Well," he said, "even if it is true, I should say nothing." And he added characteristically, "You'd only upset other people by telling them."

This justification for saying nothing at home pleased me very much. In the Easter holidays I felt a secret amusement whenever I imagined Auntie Dora was steering clear of the forbidden subject. Once I even asked her the meaning of the words *felo de se*. The phrase had come out in a history lesson towards the end of term. She blushed, and dropped some flowers she was arranging, and said, with what indifference she could, "I haven't the least idea." I was a little ashamed of having embarrassed her by disregarding Bunny's words of wisdom. But I should never have dared to put my question to Aunt Isabel. She would very quickly have forced everything out of me and perhaps even (so I then thought) had Solly punished. Oddly enough, my chief feeling towards Solly was one of gratitude for enlightening me. It did not occur to me for a long time that his motive had been mere spite at losing a good situation. He was still in the district, and no doubt had heard of the precautions which our staff used to keep the truth from me.

It did not occur to me, either, at that age, to wonder why my father had committed suicide. Later, when halfway up my next school, I began to puzzle over it a good deal. I had started to read rather highly coloured novels, in which suicides were not infrequent, and my psychological curiosity had developed. People killed themselves for love, or to avoid indelible disgrace. Very rarely they did so because they were suffering from incurable disease. Sometimes the wrong man would do it, to leave the right girl with the right man. Mere melancholia (unaided by remorse) was not sufficient. I applied these motives to my father, one by one, but none of them seemed to meet the case. The doctor at the inquest had made no mention of disease, except for influenza, and that was not incurable. My father was not heavily in debt. He hadn't committed forgery, embezzlement or bigamy or brought any other irretrievable disgrace upon his family. He was happily married, and therefore (I assumed from my reading) not in love. Could it have been boredom—boredom with Auntie Dora? I divined that one could be happily married and yet a little bored with one's spouse. Suicide from boredom with Auntie Dora, aided perhaps by a secret unrequited passion for another woman, seemed the most likely line, though I could find no convincing precedent for it. Again, I consulted Bunny, who had moved on to the same Public School as I had. And again Bunny was indefinite, and unhelpful. I concluded that he thought it morbid of me to give my mind to the subject, and he fell a little in my esteem for being so conventional. This secret of mine gave me a silly importance to myself. I had the feeling that I was different from other people, and enjoyed it. Perhaps Bunny was jealous because there was no veiled tragedy in his own family.

I had two other close friends at that time, mentally less mature than Bunny, and as a supreme pledge of friendship confided my secret to them. They were thrilled and made suggestions so fantastic that I recoiled. My father was being blackmailed. What for? Rape, murder, anything. Then why hadn't we heard any more of it? Why should you, they asked. A blackmailer would have no object in making trouble if he couldn't get money for it. And after my father's death they would have lost their victim. Or again, had my father been in the secret service? Was he a victim of the Ogpu's vengeance? He lived at home and did nothing special? That was a blind. Assuredly he was a government agent—or agent of a foreign power. Had I seen any suspicious-looking characters in the neighbourhood? Only, of course, they wouldn't look suspicious. There were moments when our discussions became farcical. I told Bunny what they said, and he scolded me for having "given myself away." Perhaps he was jealous that I had taken the other two into my confidence.

At home, I still pretended—as I pretend now—to suspect nothing. Joan knows, I am almost sure, though I don't know when she was told. Aunt Isabel probably assumes that I have learnt by this time, though she would prefer not to know how I learnt it, and thinks that, in any event, the subject should not be mentioned. Auntie Dora no doubt thinks that I cannot possibly know, and never will know. At times I almost think she doesn't know anything herself. Since my question to her about the meaning of *felo de se* I have been careful never to put her to the test. And I still have a shrinking from saying anything to Joan—a kind of prudishness.

Besides, there is the possibility that she knows nothing, after all. Despite what one might imagine, there is little strain, after a while, in treating a subject as forbidden.

2

Now I have altered Carlise into Carlice and my father could survey our name with satisfaction. But would he? *St. Peter's College Labour Club, affiliated to the Oxford University Labour Club. 14th May: Mr. R. Carlice will read a paper on "Labour and Art." Host: Mr. D. L. Cruttley.*

"I'm rather surprised you've joined that," he would say. "Or are you a visitor?"

"No. I'm a member. In fact, I'm the secretary. Read the small print on the back page."

He would bring out his spectacles and change the subject.

I must get busy with this paper of mine. I shan't have time to do any work on it while I'm with the reading-party in the Cotswolds. (Ough! The cold of those draughty rectories and their tin baths at the end of March. I was rather a fool to say I'd go.) Then Easter at Carlice. Too many visitors, Aunt Isabel and probably her friend Gwen Rashdall, that nosey bore Sir Thomas Hill, Lady Calliton and her slick son, who might "do for Joan." Then Dora will have some of *her* friends, that Maud Criswell, I suppose, and Maud's sister and brother-in-law. Perhaps even Dora's ne'er-do-well half-brother will turn up again like a bad penny. (Could he have had anything to do with my father's death? Rubbish!)

I needn't be with that crowd much really, though I probably shall. After all, Dora hasn't much longer to go as she is. Exactly six months yesterday. I can't let her think that she bores me with her friends—or without them, for that matter. Besides, I like Dora—as one says one likes the bus better than the underground.

Then *my* friends, to finish the vac. Cruttley, Brench and Gievely. I could write then, but I shan't. We shall talk all day, and all night, till Brench finishes the whisky decanter. It was silly to have asked him, and I don't think Cruttley's right in thinking that he's got a great future before him, even though his father was in the Cabinet. It's odd how the sons of Tory Cabinet Ministers go Labour, and the sons of Labour ministers give up politics. Mem.: don't give Aunt Isabel this handle.

Labour and Art.

A bad title, because there's so much to say. Too many methods of approach. Too many possible theses.

But, obviously, a paper of this kind at Oxford should have a tilt at the æsthetes—those dreary devotees of art for art's sake. I must destroy their little hobbyhorse, even if I haven't time to build up my own. *If art is to survive it must be functional.* And its function, as the social consciousness develops, is not to show the individual to himself, or set him a pretty pattern on which to develop his personal whimsies, but to display the force and omnipresence of creative evolution and the collective will.

Now I might consider art that is manifestly wrong, the art that we must do down. A few tags from modern French poetry will come in here. I can start with Bunny's favourite poem. (A pity he won't be there to hear me.)

> Je suis comme le roi d'un pays pluvieux,
> Riche mais impuissant, jeune pourtant très vieux . . .

You could hardly have a better example of overindividualisation.

Or, even more striking, this:

> Mon âme est une infante en robe de parade . . .

I imagine that in the proletarian mouth! It's certainly much easier to find examples of what must go than what might stay.

> Dans le vieux parc, solitaire et glacé,
> Deux formes sont tout à l'heure passées . . .

Perhaps that's relatively harmless. But the nonsense I could extract from Mallarmé . . .

> Le blond torrent de mes cheveux immaculés,
> Quand il baigne mon corps solitaire, le glace
> D'horreur, et mes cheveux que la lumière enlace,
> Sont immortels . . .

Surely that's worthy of the Index, or a pathological museum? And I needn't only keep to French poetry. There's a good deal in English verse, even in classical stuff. Let's open the Golden Treasury at random.

> Not greatly moved with awe am I
> To learn that we may spy
> Five thousand firmaments beyond our own . . .

That's retrograde. He ought to have been moved by awe. At least, it would be better than the egotistical little cult of beauty he cherishes. Let's try another.

> Deep on the convent-roof, the snows
> Are sparkling to the moon:
> My breath to heaven like vapour goes:
> May my soul follow soon!

Apart from the inadmissible word *soul*, it's the first personal pronoun that damns the poet. That's a point. Art, especially modern art, is always in the first person. *I, me, my.* It emphasises our differences rather than our homogeneity. It panders to the cell, rather than the whole body of the state. It differentiates and divides, harps on personal interests, personal importance, even personal property —everything we're out to smash.

"Come in!"

Cruttley is tall, thin and dark,

> The lean and swarthy poet of despair,

and he looks a bit unhealthy.

"Hello!" He wants to borrow a book.

"Yes, I think I can. Hobbes' *Leviathan*. It should be by the Rousseau and the Locke and the Spinoza in this shelf. Here you are, Dan. I'm struggling with my paper on *Labour and Art*. It's going to make the æsthetes wriggle."

"It's a big subject," he says judicially, taking the book, "and not too easy."

"Well, you must agree with this, Dan. Labour hasn't any use for art that isn't *social* in its purpose. And nearly all modern art is chock-full of personalities."

"I suppose you're taking that line to torment yourself."

"Of course not. But even if I am . . ."

"Well, I only said it wasn't too easy."

"It's a problem we've got to deal with."

"I suspect you're a Communist, Carlice, and don't really belong to the Labour Party at all. We ought to expel you."

"We all must be Communists in theory. I happen to believe in gradualness, that's all. Labour paves the way."

"Why do you believe in gradualness?"

"Partly because I'm frightened of an upheaval, and partly because I think Communism has more chance if we go slow. If we had a real upheaval, I'm not at all sure Communism would come out on top. But I'm forgetting you're a Tory."

"Thank you! Well, I suppose there's no enthusiasm like the convert's. You've only been a member of the Labour Club a year."

"A year's a long time, at our age."

"I suppose so. Like ten when you're over forty."

"God! Shall we ever be that?"

"Probably not. Well, I must stick a bit of Hobbes into my essay. What are you doing this afternoon?"

"Taking Dicky Brench for a walk to Boar's Hill. It'll do him good. Why don't you come?"

"I'm having tea with the Ryders. Don't let me forget your book. Come and collect it any time. What marvellous flowers! Where did they come from? South of France?"

"No. From home. They're forced, of course. My stepmother sent them. I wish she wouldn't."

"Why?"

"Because it puts me under an obligation to her. Besides, I don't want them."

"Tell her to send them to me next time."

"You can ask her yourself when you come and stay at the end of the vac."

"I shall, if I dare. Well . . ."

"Well . . ."

And he's left the door open. Why can't one work with the door open? Perhaps it's that gentle, irritating swing. I'm crotchety for my age. What shall I be at forty? Damn those flowers! Why didn't I give them to Cruttley? They're all wrong. Forced hyacinths and daffodils in an undergraduate's room. It's out of date. Goes back to the 'nineties almost. Bunny would have them. But he's left us for a handful of silver—a pretty big handful, by the way—or was never with us.

How he let himself go as the typical undergraduate, bursting out into every expensive caprice—jumping over walls to escape the progs, breaking rules for fun and yet getting a first in Mods, getting drunk and paying for that insane magazine over there to be printed! *Europe in tears*. What a cover! Purple, green and yellow stripes, and that absurd hermaphrodite under an umbrella.

THE STERILISATION FRONT

Our second machine began its pacific operations on February 1st. It is still too early to produce any statistics as to the decline of fecundity induced by its beneficent rays, but we can assure our readers that our first machine (to which full reference was made in our previous number) has already aroused consternation among the heads of the governments affected. Already they envisage their enormous military roads deserted except for dotards too weak even to salute, the rusty cannon hungering in vain for fodder. Despite the most rigorous searches by the secret police, no trace of the machine has been found. Sobbing women crowd the doctors' consulting-rooms, complaining that their husbands . . .

Is it true, I wonder, that two or three embassies sent in a protest? At any rate, it's not surprising he was almost sent down. Just, I suppose, when he felt he'd had enough and thought it would be nicer to go right away and spend his money in earnest. March in the West Indies, then Bermuda till it bores him. Very nice. I hardly feel we should have anything to say to one another now. He's a different person from the Bunny who ran right through my schooldays like a chink of light coming through a door that one was glad to have open. He's changed, and I feel I'm exactly the same, except that I like fewer things. Well, I've got Dan Cruttley and Dicky Brench in exchange. Not that they mean so much to me as Bunny meant—but, after all, when one grows up, things are bound to mean less to one. A box of toy soldiers, when you're ten, gives you a much keener pleasure than a Rolls-Royce when you're twenty. Or it ought to. As we grow older we lose that pernicious egoism which makes childhood and second childhood ages of irresponsibility. We realise, if we realise anything at all, that the purpose of our existence lies outside us.

Labour and Art.

3

The clocks of Oxford striking twelve, overlapping, jangling up the noon of the last Sunday morning of my last term but one. A memory to carry away—these noisy clocks of Oxford—and use when—when . . .

Why carry away any memory at all? Live in the present. Make yourself each moment do the serviceable thing. I must bully myself out of these habits of retrospection, even at the risk of being thought a prig, or too zealous a convert to the new religion. Otherwise, I shall flop. I shall suddenly see myself sitting in the library at Carlice, looking at that very lovely view, and listening to a Sibelius symphony on the gramophone, and I shall think—or rather *feel*, since the image will be so intense—"this house is mine, this view is mine, this kind of life is mine—anyway till the catastrophe." And I shall give way, and acquiesce and just live there like a cultivated dilettante, doing little charities to ease my conscience, and being, oh, so considerate to Dora and more creditable than Aunt Isabel would have thought possible. That's my danger. I've got to bring myself up in a harder school. Evidently the two schools I went to weren't hard enough.

I've got to think this out, carefully and decisively. I've only one more vac., already accounted for, before schools and my second in Greats, and I go down and such fun as there is is over. What then? A small but natty flat in town where I can go to so-and-so's chambers and read law, rather lazily, and long week-ends at Carlice, with Dora still keeping house for me? A bit hard-up perhaps, but only because one has "got to keep up appearances." Why should

I keep up appearances? Why should I bother with any convention that doesn't tally with the future development of society? Why shouldn't I show them?

Then give up Carlice in September as soon as you're twenty-one.

Give it to whom? To Aunt Isabel? No, thank you. I don't see why she should come and sit there on a feudal throne. I know, of course, that if I stepped out, she'd very soon step in. (And yet, what is Carlice, after all? Beyond being marked in Gothic letters on the ordnance map, it's a very ordinary little country house. It takes a real antiquarian or a snob to be excited by our meagre ruins.) No. I'll not have Carlice turned into the niche in which she can nourish her egotism. I used to think she had no sense of duty, but she's full of it—duty towards herself. She regards it as not only agreeable, but as morally right that people in uniform should hand her things on silver trays. She puts luxury before comfort—for moral reasons. No one is more able than she to sit bolt upright for hours in a hard-bottomed chair. She faces draughts that would give other people neuralgia for a month. She can live, if necessary, on a starvation diet. She can work in the garden like a factory-hand, keeping an infinity of sweated hours. She goes to inordinate lengths to help the local poor—a blanket here, here a jelly or a nutritious soup—provided there's that hint of a curtsey when she's finished her errand—provided that the essential demarcations are preserved. No sybarite, Aunt Isabel. And for that very reason, how much more dangerous and damnable. I feel, oddly enough, that since I have learnt her great secret, I have her in my power. *She regards people she doesn't know, not as people, but as things.*

The personal point of view—which will only be destroyed when we destroy personality. But we shall destroy it.

No. I shall not step out and let Aunt Isabel step in. Rather leave Dora there as caretaker—Dora, who could be "liquidated" with a word or two. If our behaviour towards human individuals is of any importance—I mean as regards particular acts of kindness and forbearance without any general social purpose—I have acquired a good deal of merit in my behaviour to Dora. I realised a long time ago that she was in a difficult position. One might almost say, a false position. I don't think I have ever presumed on it. I never took the liberties with her which one would have taken with a real mother. I've observed all her little domestic taboos. I've made a great show of never questioning her authority. When that aged bore Sir Thomas Hill took me aside one day and asked me whether I approved of certain items in the Carlice budget, I answered that I wanted Auntie Dora to use her absolute discretion about such things till I was twenty-one. And when, perhaps trying to make mischief, he suggested that Aunt Isabel didn't see eye to eye with Dora over this and that, I went the whole hog for Dora. "Aunt Isabel doesn't live here," I said. "She didn't marry my father. I could never see why she was left as one of my guardians by my father's will." He hummed and hawed and tried to indicate that doubtlessly my father had seen that Dora had hardly the experience to run a place "of this kind." (Always this harping on Carlice being a *place*!) I said that at all events she'd had plenty of time to gain the necessary experience since my father's death. He pretended to agree and we changed the subject.

No. Dora has nothing to reproach me with. She knows that. In her way, I think she's rather fond of me. If I were ill, she'd do everything that she ought to do—less efficiently than Aunt Isabel, but with much more genuine feeling. It's pathetic to see how she tries to reserve the first-fruits of the *place* for me—how she keeps back the hothouse strawberries and the early asparagus till I am there to eat them, and how, since I've been living out of College, she sends me these forced narcissi and special little hampers during term-time, new-laid eggs, mushrooms in season, new peas, globe artichokes, home-grown celery—all the tit-bits of the estate. When I'm at home, she surrounds me with a multitude of *petits soins*. It was she who had central heating carried up to that lovely big room on the first floor, now called my library, where I can play Sibelius privately on the gramophone and look out of the big Georgian windows at my own delightful view—that library where I am spoilt and tempted to become something which I know categorically I ought not to become. The library at Carlice which shall not seduce me, any more than the gunroom at Carlice shall lead me to commit suicide like my father.

When I'm twenty-one, if I'm not married—and at present I see no likelihood of that—I shall keep Auntie Dora on as caretaker of Carlice, if she likes to stay. But I shall keep her there with the clear understanding that, probably sooner than later, she'll have to go away and live on her five hundred a year from my father, and the two or three hundred she has of her own. It's no pittance after all. And she might easily marry again—some slightly seedy professional man whom she'd meet at a superior boarding-house. I can't let her—or even my library—stand in the way of what's got to be done, when I see it more clearly. If they want Carlice for a Labour Summer School, they can have it. If Carlice should be sold and the proceeds given to Abyssinia, it shall be sold. (By the way, the news from Abyssinia isn't so rosy now.) I feel myself already pointed out as a "young man with great possessions." This I do vow—by all the clocks of Oxford now chiming a quarter past twelve—my great possessions shall never get me down.

Even this is put too personally. What does it matter whether *I* fail morally or not? My own private moral perfection isn't an end in itself. It's a means merely to a wider purpose. It's failure in action, not in morals that I must worry about. What a good thing I'm going that walk with Dicky Brench this afternoon. I need a dose of his scientific materialism, to keep me straight, and counteract my hereditary virus. Dan Cruttley's no use. He's only a Liberal in new clothes.

(Suppose I offered Carlice Abbey to Bunny? His people had no *place*. Plenty of money to keep it up with, a historical background and Gothic lettering on the map. In exchange, a bit of the sweated Andrews millions going back to the workers who made them. It's not a bad idea.)

If only there were a living authority to tell one what to do—a Socialist Pope in whom would be incarnated the Collective Will, with a voice like Jehovah's and a finger that would write flaming letters in the sky! Conscience? What's that but the secretion of a few sluggish glands?

4

As usual, I have forgotten Joan. Twenty-four and still no sign of a marriage in the offing, despite her season in London. Well, poor girl, she isn't pretty and she hasn't got a fortune. What has

she to offer beyond a pleasant disposition and the fact that she was
brought up in a *place*? Not enough, in these days—at least for the
kind of man they would like her to marry. And she's so fastid-
ious about men. She notices their voices, their fingernails, bits
of scurf in their hair, the smell of their clothes, and disapproves.
She was happiest when she went off with Doris Hawkes and did
her chicken-farming. "It won't last," said Auntie Dora. It lasted
nearly three years, and they didn't lose as much as one would have
thought probable. It might still be lasting if Doris hadn't leapt into
matrimony with bounder Benson. No doubt Joan went through
more than we realised, turning up again at Carlice with a wry
smile and some very dowdy clothes. "Now," she said, "I suppose
I've got to marry too."

I remember her sitting, the evening of her return, in the
morning-room and tapping her big feet on the stone fender. Dora
looked up from the blue jumper she was knitting and said, "Why,
dear? You feel at home here, don't you?" And Joan gave a mannish
kind of gulp and said, "Frankly, I don't know that I do." Then Dora
said at great length how glad she would be to have Joan's help
and company, and how she hoped that, until my marriage—this
with a quick arch look—Joan would feel herself full mistress of the
house, as she would have been if my father hadn't married again.
And Joan, as soon as she could, got up and went to her bedroom.
And Dora turned confidingly to me and said, "We must do something to help her, Ronnie. She seems to be missing her farm and
Doris terribly. Don't *you* know any young men, Ronnie, whom she
might like?"

"Do I know any young men who might like her?" I answered,
a little too brutally perhaps. "My friends are about my own age. I
don't think I know anyone who isn't two years younger than Joan."

"Well, two years isn't much."

"Did you ever think men marriageable who were two years
younger than you, Auntie Dora? I mean, when you were in the
early twenties."

She blushed, and said with a toss of the head, "It didn't occur
to me to think of men as marriageable or not. It was enough for
them to think me marriageable. What a horrid word, anyway."

"There you had the advantage of Joan," I replied, rather precociously for a boy of nineteen. (I see it now. How I have grown up during the last eighteen months!)

"Well, she's a pretty attractive girl, and after all . . ."

"She isn't pretty, Auntie Dora. You know that. And what does 'after all' mean?"

"Oh, I don't know. Perhaps I was thinking of your family. And she'll have some money of her own. She would make a very good wife, if she found the right man."

I couldn't help feeling that Dora would have liked to say, "If Mr. Right came along." But it isn't often, nowadays, that she lets the idiom of South Mersley come out.

"That's the point," I said, being suddenly bored with the conversation, "she's got to find the right man. Meanwhile, she'll probably find it isn't too bad living here. And Aunt Isabel may have something to suggest."

In due course, Aunt Isabel suggested giving Joan a season in London. Joan had her season, and nothing came of it that we could see. And since then, since we were all plotting like a *petit bourgeois* French family about their daughter's future, I've changed my views a good deal, and really can't bother myself as to whether Joan makes a dynastic marriage or not. Incidentally, Doris' experiment with bounder Benson doesn't seem to have been much of a success. Perhaps that example is keeping Joan back. Well, if she marries, she marries, and if she doesn't, she can stay on at Carlice with Dora as long as it's kept going. I want her to be happy—probably, inside me, I want her to have more than her *fair share* of happiness—but I can't let these so-called family ties interfere with the essential things of life. She'll have her five hundred a year—till the big crash comes. She's healthy and not unintelligent. She's as capable as most people of making a living. I don't see that I'm called to make my arrangements fit hers.

Good Lord! Is that Dan, coming to return the *Leviathan* already? No, it isn't his step. It must be Browne going up to his attic. Coming back from Chapel, I suppose. Well, a fine morning I've spent. Almost as uselessly as if I'd been to Chapel too. There's still another half-hour before lunch.

Labour and Art.

Chapter III: DORA CARLICE

OH, these sheets of rain—they are like sheets, dirty damp sheets on a clothes-line—flapping one after the other over the garden, breaking down the daffodils and ruining them for the house. I'm sure it's wetter here than it is anywhere else. And windier, too. What was the name of that old man who wrote in some famous book, "The most remarkable feature of Carlice Abbey is that it was built not on low ground beside a stream, but on something of a hill"? Claude told me that the first time I came here. I wish it wasn't built on something of a hill. It makes everything so draughty. There's that window open again in this storm, and the curtain waving about outside. Drenched. It's absolutely drenched, and the dye *is* running. It just shows you can't believe a word they say. I really ought to stop it out of Flora's wages. If I've told her once, I've told her a hundred times that as soon as there's any sign of rain she must go round the windows and close them— particularly on this side of the house, which catches it so.

"No, Flora. You're late again. I've just come in and closed that window. As it is, I'm afraid that curtain's spoilt. Yes, I think you'd better take it down. You see, it's wringing wet . . ."

A new curtain last Christmas. It is a shame. Another chance for Isabel to talk about shoddy modern fabrics. She's never liked this room since I did it up. Perhaps that's a good thing, because it makes it really *my* room. I think I shall call it "the boudoir" instead of "the drawing-room." After all, we use the morning-room as our living-room. Ronnie has his big library upstairs. And Joan has her nice bed-sitting-room. The arrangement has worked out very well. What a fool I was not to make myself thoroughly at home years ago, instead of living here like a visitor or a poor relation. Well, old girl, you know why that was, don't you? Now that something's going to happen soon, the whole business seems so stale and silly that I can't really bother myself about it. I shall simply say,

"Here you are, Ronnie. I don't care twopence what's inside this old box, or what you think." No, I shan't, though. I shall go trembly at the knees again, and nearly faint as I nearly fainted during that talk with Thomas Hill on Ronnie's last birthday—his twentieth. And when his twenty-first comes round, perhaps I shall quite faint. But it'll be for the last time. As things you dread come nearer, you dread them less. But I wish Thomas Hill wasn't coming for Easter. He looks at you like a doctor who suspects you of concealing a bad habit. I've always been afraid of doctors, starting with Daddy. Perhaps that explains why I fell so hopelessly for Don.

What a day! Sheets of rain still flapping over the lawns and beating down the daffodils. Not quite as many as last year, though I did pick off the seed-pods. The year before, when I told Isabel I thought the daffs were getting a little thinner, she said it was because I hadn't picked the seed-pods. It's one of the many things gardeners never do, according to her. Well, it wasn't as bad as when I told Jackson to mow them off before the leaves began to wither. That, I found, was a terrible mistake. It kills them. But they were so straggly, and how was I to know? At Elmcroft we had new daffodils every year. Only a few dozen, of course. Isabel says that while she was here she planted eighteen thousand herself. I wonder if she did.

It's so chilly, I ought to have a fire. April's always a cold month. I wish we had gas, or the main electricity supply, so that I could just turn on the stove. It seems rather a waste having a fire here before lunch when there's one in the morning-room. But I can't write in the morning-room. Who could at a silly secretaire desk, even if it is Sheraton? And the Dutch marquetry desk is far too high for me. Besides, I can think better in my own room.

I ought to have written all these letters yesterday. I did mean to, but—of course I found I only had one envelope and two or three dirty sheets of paper. Then something happened to put me off. I'd better ring now. I *must* get these done to-day.

"Oh, Eames—I've run out of stationery. Could you bring me some? Yes, notepaper, envelopes and cards."

Why don't I order my own notepaper, something a bit brighter than this plain cream with the black address? It's too silly leaving it to the butler. I would order my own if I were beginning here all over again. I intended to, I remember, but Joan put me off by saying, "Why do you want a change? Don't you think ours very nice?" And I had to say, "Yes, dear, of course I like your notepaper very much."

"Thank you, Eames. Yes, it's wonderful how one uses it up, isn't it?"

If he'd suggested lighting the fire I'd have let him. I suppose he thinks the central heating ought to be enough in April. Besides, Isabel never feels the cold. Or pretends she doesn't. She doesn't understand comfort. None of these people do. She'd rather spend her money on lime for the irises, or soup for some silly old woman with arthritis.

I think I'd better write to Stephen first. What is his address? King Stephen Hotel, Thurlow-on-Sea. It doesn't say what county, but it must be Kent. Anyhow, that's the envelope done. It's such a bore, when you've written a letter, to find you've got the envelope still to do.

CARLICE ABBEY,
WILTSHIRE.
Thursday.

MY DEAR STEPHEN,

I was very sorry to hear what you say in your letter. You say you've got enough to carry you on till the end of August. Well, that is something.

He said "scrape along." I suppose I must send him something. Five pounds will do. After all, that will keep him nearly a fortnight. And I might spare something in July, after I get my next money. But I can't keep him altogether. I can't afford to do that.

I have heard from Don Rusper, and I think it's almost hopeless to try to make him change his mind. As you request, I am writing to him to-day, but I know him better than you do.

Oh dear! I won't say that. I'll cross out those five words.

But I know he takes a very strict view of his duties as your trustee. We've had this out before, and I dare say it's hardly worth while my saying it again. But you know perfectly well that Daddy would have left you your money outright, if he hadn't thought it necessary for you to be looked after. So far as that goes, he left four-fifty for you against my two-fifty, because he thought you needed it more than I did.

Perhaps it doesn't sound very nice reminding him of that, but it's quite true, and I'm going to leave it in. After all, if I'd made any kind of fuss, Daddy would have left the money differently, or even left it all to me. But I was set upon Stephen having most of it. That awful afternoon when Daddy was nearly dying, I told him so and stopped him sending for his solicitor to alter his will. "You see," he said, "I used to think you'd made this good marriage, and that it didn't matter to you any longer what you had from me." It was as if he knew Claude was only going to leave me five hundred a year. Perhaps dying people do somehow know these things. But I quietened him and let the money go to Stephen. I don't grudge it now, at all, but he should be a little grateful and not keep on at me about Don. Don must know best about a case like this.

So I feel it was Daddy's real wish that you should be guided by Don, and I can't go against it. Don tells me that the cure you had with Dr. Duparc was hardly any good. He's got to know this Dr. Ebermann, and has sent two or three patients to him, with excellent results. He says six months in his institute would make you a different man, in fact as well as you were before you were wounded.

And I wonder very much exactly what that means. The war's a very easy thing to blame. Other people were wounded and shell-shocked and are perfectly all right. Stephen never was quite normal, even before the war. I could see that. I don't know where he gets his weakness from. Certainly not from Daddy. Perhaps his mother had a poor strain in her. My mother used to say she had. But Daddy wouldn't let us talk about his first wife.

You've told Don that you won't go to Dr. Ebermann, and he thinks it's only kindness to you to make you go. The only way he can make you go is by stopping your allowance, which by Daddy's will he has every right to do. In fact, you and I know that Daddy would thoroughly have approved of what Don is doing.

Still, I am sorry for him.

Still, I am sorry for you, and send you the enclosed five pounds, which may be useful. It's all I can spare now. If, as you say, you are perfectly well, and have conquered your weakness, why not go to Don and let him examine you? If he finds you quite fit, I'm sure he'll only be too glad to continue your allowance as before.

Oh dear! Is that quite true? Anyway, I've got to end up by saying it, even if I think they're both deceiving themselves. Stephen hasn't really conquered his weakness, and Don is perhaps a little fond of interfering.

To-day it is pouring with rain, and this is a draughty cold house. I hope you are having better weather where you are.

Your affectionate sister,
DORA.

2

Now my letter to Don.

Dr. Donald Rusper,
95, Meridian Avenue,
South Mersley,
London, S.W.

I'm glad I can write to him quite easily now. I remember when writing to him was a marvellous treat, and how I planned the letters hours before I sat down at my desk. Because I wanted so much to write to him, I had the feeling that I mustn't do it. Or perhaps it was the other way round. The days when I decided to let myself write were the bright days in the week. I would slip down the lane to the pillar-box by Noakes' cottage, and as I heard my letter drop down inside it seemed as if a part of me had gone with it, and as if I wasn't complete when I walked home again. Whatever happened afterwards, and in spite of all the other things that were happening at the time, those were very lovely days ten years ago. I was a different person then, and he was different. Five amazing months, in spite of everything—June, July, August, September and part of October.

I hadn't been to Elmcroft for nearly two years, I think. Daddy used to write to me about every six weeks, and I wrote to him about once a fortnight. He only came here twice, and then none of us enjoyed it, not even Daddy. I could see he blamed me because he wasn't more of a success. I was terrified he'd suddenly say to Claude, "Young man, this isn't the way to behave to your father-in-law." Not that Claude was ever anything but polite. Still he couldn't ever bring himself to like Daddy slapping him on the back and calling him "old boy." He wasn't hearty enough. And there was the awful moment when Joan said, "Auntie Dora, who is that funny man?" and Daddy heard. He became huffy, as he always did when his dignity was attacked, and couldn't play up. "You ought to have sent the child upstairs to her room," he told me. "You'll fail in your duty if you don't give both children a taste of discipline." *Fail in your duty.* It was one of his favourite phrases. Don must have caught it from him, though it's come out more lately.

The telegram about Daddy's illness came when the General Strike had been over for three weeks—about the beginning of June, 1926, it must have been. Don had been Daddy's partner for eighteen months. He was living round the corner from Elmcroft, at 18, Portugal Road. But when I arrived I remember seeing his brass plate under Daddy's on the brick gate-post at Elmcroft. I'd almost forgotten that Daddy had taken a partner, and I don't think I'd seen Don since my marriage.

Don was out, visiting an urgent case, and Mrs. Greeg showed me in. She had grown quite plump, and I thought her dress rather flighty for a housekeeper. I thought, too, that she ought to have said "Dr. Payne," not "your poor father." "Your poor father's getting some sleep now," she said, "and Sister says he mustn't be disturbed.

Would you like to go to your room?" "But what *is* the matter with him?" I asked. The telegram and the letter I had had the week before had told me nothing definite. She didn't answer, but sniffed and led the way upstairs to the room I used to have before my marriage. It was just the same as when I lived in it, and still looked pretty, though very small after the big rooms at Carlice. "Dr. Rusper should be in any time now," Mrs. Greeg said. "You know, we now use the drawing-room as the patients' waiting-room. Your poor father used the dining-room as a living-room when he wasn't in his consulting-room." In my day the patients had waited in the dining-room. It was awkward for meals, sometimes, but it was nice to have the drawing-room free. The drawing-room used to be such an attractive room. I went down to it, when I had washed and unpacked some of my things, but found it spoilt with a big round table in the middle, covered with all the illustrated papers, and the chairs arranged against the walls. The door leading to the verandah was open, and I went out into the garden and walked round it. After the grounds at Carlice it seemed no size at all. I couldn't think how Stephen and I played our game of being "lost in the desert" there. But when you're a child you can imagine anything. The garden wasn't tidy, either, and there were weeds in the paths. It was seeing the weeds that made me realise that something serious must have happened to Daddy. He was always so particular that the garden should be kept neat.

I was still in the garden when Don came out to fetch me. Beyond having grown a little stouter in the four years since my marriage, he seemed hardly to have altered at all. If anything, he was hand-somer. Seeing him again brought back all the past to me—not, of course, that I had ever known him at all well. But his family had been friends of ours for a long time and it all goes so far back that I can't remember when I met them for the first time. I suddenly felt I wanted to cry, partly about Daddy, and partly because everything had become so different during the four years I had been away. He shook hands with me and gave me a look that he had never given me before—that searching "doctor's look" which always frightens me. He called me Mrs. Carlice and I called him Dr. Rusper. That shows how little we knew one another then. He didn't say anything about Daddy till we had gone indoors to the drawing-room. I suppose he was afraid of one of our neighbours hearing, or the maid might have been listening at a window upstairs. Then he told me the name of the disease Daddy was suffering from. They were going to operate the next day, to relieve the pain, though it was a disease they couldn't yet cure. I broke down, and he put his arm round me and put me in a big chair. Then he held my hand, while he told me the details about what had been done and the doctors who had been called in, and asked me whether I should like any further opinions taken. I said I should prefer to leave everything to him, and it came to me suddenly that I was going to rely on him tremendously, in a way I'd never thought of relying on Daddy or Stephen or Claude.

It can't have been that afternoon—no, it was next afternoon, when Daddy had been taken to the nursing-home and the operation was over, and I felt as if the day had lasted a month and anything could happen to me, I was so routed out—when I found myself leaning against Don by the round table in the middle of the drawing-room. It was one of those quick moments which seem to last for ever, because it was so vivid afterwards. It was a moment which I kept picturing and calling to mind at all times and places during the next few months. I was leaning against Don by the round table in the middle of the drawing-room when he suddenly caught both my wrists and drove me against the hard curve of the table, till it dug into my back, and made me face him. He drew away from me slowly, holding me there and stretching his arms out, and I could see the black hairs a long way up his arms under his wide stiff cuffs. Unconsciously I thought of how Dolly and I used to talk at school about hairy men, and the things we used to imagine together about them.

"You must pull yourself together and face this," he said. I remember well that the word *this* didn't only convey to me Daddy's illness and operation, but something very different. For me, and for him too, there was a double meaning in everything he said.

"We have to grow up," he went on, while I blushed, but didn't speak. "When we're young we imagine that these things only happen in books, or only happen to strangers and people we don't know very well. But they do happen. They happen to us. I want to see you happy again. I'm going to make you happy."

He let go of my left wrist and put his hand on my arm, slid it down to the elbow and then put it inside my arm, under my left breast. I felt something I'd never felt before, and we stood like that, looking at one another, till there was a step in the passage—Mrs. Greeg going into the dining-room. Then he came closer to me, and took me to the settee and sat down by me.

"Your father told me he wanted to get back home as soon as possible," he said. "I don't see why he shouldn't be moved here next week, in an ambulance. As soon as he comes, I shall come and sleep here. It'll be useful to have a doctor in the house. I've only got my rooms at Portugal Road by the week. As I shall have to do all your father's work, it'll be handier my being here—if you approve."

I nodded. Already, it seemed absurd to think that I might not approve.

Then perhaps because we heard Mrs. Greeg's step again, conversation became more discreet. Don talked of Stephen, who had thrown up his job as a solicitor the autumn before, and was at the time acting as tutor to a rich Japanese boy, whom he was escorting to Tokyo. Even if we wired for Stephen to hurry back he couldn't reach England before mid-July. And Don said it would be silly to wire. He'd seen a good deal of Daddy's relations with Stephen and felt there was no point having Stephen hanging around. "I think it's really better that Stephen is away," he said. "He might upset your father. And there's little danger that he won't be back in time. This is not going to be a short illness."

I shuddered and he put his left arm right round me. "And what about you?" he asked. "I'm afraid you won't be able to stay here the whole time, will you?" I told him that I ought to get back to Carlice for the week-end, when we were expecting visitors. He agreed that I should have to go backwards and forwards a good deal.

"If you had married me," he said, "you would have been here the whole time."

"You never asked me," I replied. "You *can't* have asked me."

"I did, at the Boswell's fancy-dress party."

"That was a joke. Three people asked me that night. Besides, you were practising in Luton then, and everyone said you were engaged to a Luton girl."

"I was half engaged, but when I saw you that night I knew I had made a mistake. I broke off the engagement the next week."

"For my sake?" I asked.

"You were partly the cause."

"But you didn't write to me, you didn't try to see me. You did nothing, till you turned up at my wedding with your mother and sisters."

He laughed.

"You wouldn't have married me then. Your father wouldn't have let you marry me. I was tied to my practice in Luton and you were a tennis star, meeting all sorts of suitable husbands. You soon found one. But he shan't have the last word."

3

I went back to Carlice for the week-end, and we had a large party. I felt as if I was acting, and only pretending to be mistress of the place and Claude's wife. I was on edge, but the shocks I'd had during the week seemed to have stirred up something in me and given me a new force. I was quicker in the uptake and brighter, as you are when you're in love. I noticed then, and still more later, that some of Claude's men friends, who had never bothered about me before, began to notice me. I was glad they did, as it showed me that there was something for Don to notice in me.

Meanwhile, Daddy was going on as well as one can with that kind of illness, and he'd been back at Elmcroft a few days when I next went there. There were two nurses in the house. They shared the big spare room next to Daddy's bedroom. Don had a little room on the next floor, just across the passage from mine. At supper, the first night, one of the nurses was with us and afterwards Don had some work to do in the consulting-room. I went to bed before he had finished. I lay awake for a long time listening for his footsteps. It was midnight before he came upstairs. Then from time to time I heard the floor-boards creak as he moved about in his room. There were moments when I felt I couldn't bear it if he didn't come to my room. I got very hot and threw the bedclothes on the floor, and imagined every little sound was his footstep. It didn't seem to matter to me at all that the house was full of people. But there was

only the maid sleeping on our floor, and she was right at the end
of the passage round a corner. Mrs. Greeg had a small room on
the floor below, which used to belong to Stephen. I was glad she
was so far away, though I thought it rather funny that she wasn't
in Don's room and Don in hers. I mentioned it to Don later, and he
said that she'd had the room done up and had filled it with her own
things and Daddy had refused to let her be disturbed.

Next morning I felt rather ashamed of myself and the state
I'd got into during the night. I was almost glad not to see Don at
breakfast. And at lunch I only saw him for ten minutes, and one of
the nurses was there. But as the afternoon wore on I began to get
worked up again and to wonder how I was going to get through
the next night—my last night that visit; for I had only come to
Elmcroft for two days. I thought about Don the whole time, even
when I went up to sit with Daddy.

After supper the nurse who'd had her meal with us went out
for a little walk, and Don and I had coffee together in the drawing-
room. It was funny to see the coffee things dumped down among
the illustrated papers on the big round table. I sat on the settee and
he came and sat beside me. It was the first time we'd been properly
alone together since I had arrived.

"You're tired," he said, and the way he said it made me know
that everything was all right between us. "It is a strain," he went on,
"being in a house where somebody is so ill." He took my hand, and
I said, "You know, I'm going back to-morrow morning." "Then,"
he said, "we must make the most of to-night," and he put his arms
round me and kissed me. Then he got up and walked round the
room and said, "It's too dangerous in here. Can I come and talk to
you later, in your bedroom?" I nodded, and he went on, "We shall
be quite safe there. But I shall be very late. Go to sleep first, and I'll
come in and wake you and we'll watch the moon together, through
your window." That was almost the only time he said anything
romantic to me. In the ordinary way, that kind of thing—I mean
the conversational side of love-making and the kind of talks lovers
have together in novels—never entered his life at all. But I didn't
mind. I didn't want pretty speeches from him.

He went to the consulting-room, and I went upstairs to say
good-night to Daddy, and came down again and went into the

garden, and then, when it was dark, sat in the drawing-room with a book, trying to pass the time. Then I went to bed and lay awake. I had pulled up the blind and the moonlight streamed on to my bed. And I remember being glad to think that it was in the room which I'd had as a child and a schoolgirl and young woman—the room where I'd imagined so many wonderful things happening to me—that I was going to meet my real lover. The night was so hot that I lay with only the sheet on top of me.

It seemed an age before I heard his step on the stairs. He trod rather heavily, as if the whole world might hear, and he was simply a tired doctor going ordinarily to bed. Daddy had been given something to make him sleep. Then a long time passed by, but I didn't mind it. I felt quite different from what I had been the night before—quite different from what I had ever been. It was as if I was asleep, or in a trance, and yet very wide awake. My body seemed to disappear and become part of the sheets and the mattress, even of the bedstead and the whole fabric of the house. I was so utterly at peace and so happily bewildered by the strange thing that had happened in my life. I forgot to think of time. I might have been lying there, flat on my back without moving, for a whole week or a few minutes. Minutes and weeks had become the same.

From time to time I heard little noises coming from his room— the click of an electric switch as he turned it on, the creak of the wardrobe door, the water running into his wash-basin—we had them in all the bedrooms—and running out again. Then another click of the electric switch. "He's turned out the centre light," I thought, "or turned on the lamp by his bed." Then silence. An owl hooted in the garden and a big moth flapped against the window. A motor-car went down the road. An engine whistled in the distance. The house was absolutely still. My room was over the bathroom and a piece of the lower landing, and I couldn't in any case have heard anything happening in Daddy's room.

Then, very slowly, and almost without sound, my door opened and Don came in. I lay just as I was, without moving or speaking, while he shut the door and sat down at the foot of my bed, with his thigh touching my toes. He was wearing one of those thin silk dressing-gowns with a Paisley pattern. Then he stretched forward and took my hand, which was outside the sheet, and kissed it, brushing his moustache against the back of it and right up my arm to my shoulder. There was no need for either of us to say anything.

4

I thought then, of course, that it was love, and I still think it was. Love, they say, can take many forms. It must have been love, or I should have felt guilty next morning when I went into Daddy's room to see how he was—and guiltier still when I went back to Carlice for the week-end. This time, Claude and I were alone, without visitors. Joan and Ronnie were both away at school. The weather was very fine and warm, and before lunch on Sunday I went for a walk—the big circle we used to call it—with Claude, through the park and some of the fields. The green of the trees was still quite fresh, and the fields were covered with long waving grass. I felt uplifted and excited and very happy, stronger and more important, more attractive than I had been before. Claude seemed pleased to have me alone with him. When I was getting over the stile into Herbert's meadow he gave me a kiss on the forehead as he helped me down, and I gave him a kiss back. It was just a kind of high spirits, and had nothing to do with what was between me and Don—nothing to do with love. And it didn't enter my head that I was "deceiving" Claude. Everything had seemed so natural that I couldn't believe Claude would mind even if he knew. Claude had become an elder brother, another Stephen. He never had been much more than that to me.

I was so sure of myself that I didn't even wonder if people mightn't be a little surprised that I had come back from my father's illness in such good form. I ought, I suppose, to have been pale and exhausted and worried. I simply couldn't pretend to be that, at least when only Claude was there. If Isabel had been staying with us, I might have been more careful, or felt that I ought to be more careful. But it didn't occur to me then, in those early days, that Claude would notice anything that mattered. He noticed so few things. He always seemed somehow shortsighted. You had to point everything out to him in the garden before he saw it. Isabel used to say that if the big cedar in the main lawn were struck by lightning to the ground Claude would only notice it when he tripped over the fallen trunk. I used to think she said things like that because he didn't appreciate all she'd done for the place. And why should he? Nobody asked her to do anything for the place. But she was quite right. He was detached from everything—even the people round him. And his not noticing things made him seem less real. But I did feel that, being so happy myself, I ought to be specially kind to him. I wanted to be kind to everyone.

Thinking of myself as I was then, I seem now, these ten years afterwards, to have slipped down into a rut, to have become something less alive, just a fidgeting rather lazy person who finds it a bore to run a big house, and wants her little comforts and the thrill of a new dress or a new chintz, a day at the races or a party every now and then. It must have been love that made me so different then. Not a very "spiritual" love, as they say, but still, love. And that is not the same as affection or devotion. I wasn't devoted to Don. I didn't worship him. I don't know that I ever really liked him. But I did love him. He gave me something that did me an enormous amount of good.

Daddy was asking to see me next week, and I went back to South Mersley on the Thursday, for two days. Daddy was better, and Don said that for a time he would get much better. "After a week or two you won't have the excuse for coming here so much," Don said. "We must make the most of the time we have together." At first I didn't think of the future at all, and just lived for the hours I could be with Don. But he was quite right. By the middle of July there was really no reason for me to keep slipping away from Carlice, where we were busy with visitors, and I realised that there was a difficult time ahead. Those were the weeks when I had to content myself with writing to Don, and would walk down the lane to the pillar-box by Noakes' cottage and post my letters secretly. It was a new stage in my love-affair—a less happy stage. If people had been watching me, they would have seen that I was less happy than when Daddy was really ill. Someone did suggest to Claude that I was in low spirits and he said, "Oh, it's only the reaction from what she went through earlier in the summer. She'll be all right again soon." My friend Dolly Headford was staying with us, and heard the conversation and told me about it.

I spent the first fortnight of August with Claude in Deauville.

It wasn't Claude's kind of place, but he thought the gaiety would do me good. When we got back I had a letter from Don telling me that Daddy wasn't so well. My visits to South Mersley began again—the third stage in my love-affair, like the first in some ways, but with a new background. I felt myself just as much in love with Don, but it wasn't the light-hearted love I'd known before. There was something more desperate about it, as if I was having a love-affair during a war or a revolution. Daddy soon became really ill again, and Don told me that the end would come sooner than the doctors had expected when they operated. He said it would be a merciful release. I suffered a good deal. I found myself fonder of Daddy than I thought I was. Besides, one would have been miserable seeing anybody going through so much. But Daddy was drugged most of the time, and there was no use in my sitting by the bedside all day. When he was conscious, I used to think he was more pleased to see Mrs. Greeg than to see me. Don used to take me for motor-drives in the evening, if he could spare the time. During the day he was very busy with Daddy's practice. At night we thought it safer for me to go to his room than for him to come to mine. Although Daddy had another doctor, there was no knowing that Don wouldn't be needed to do something in an emergency. If the nurse came up to fetch him it wouldn't matter if he was in his own room. That did happen once. I was terrified, though Don went and talked to the nurse by the door, and she didn't attempt to come in. And yet I got a kind of thrill out of the risk.

Don was different. Though he seemed to be just as fond of me physically, as time went on he became more cautious, and I think there were moments when he would rather have had me out of the house. I see now that he was already thinking of the future. The moment our love-making was over, he'd turn to some practical subject, such as what would become of Elmcroft. I said it would be nice if he could take it on with the practice. It had been my home for sixteen years, and despite Daddy's illness we had had such happy times there. It seemed a pity to sell it. But Don said it was much too expensive a house for him to buy and too big for him to keep up. He had his eye on a nice little house in Lillah Gardens. I didn't like talking about these things, but he said that the future had to be faced. One night I got angry with him—I had had two painful hours in Daddy's room, and my nerves were all on edge—and I said I thought he'd begun to prefer the pretty nurse to me. It was very silly of me. He told me not to be a little fool and didn't come near me the next day. The day after that I had to go back to Carlice. Ronnie had caught a chill bathing in the lake and had to be looked after. I wrote Don a long letter begging him to forgive me, but tore it up, and sent him quite a short one in which I said nothing very much. I hardly knew if I loved or hated him.

When I next went to Elmcroft Don was very kind, but not quite in the same way. He treated me a little as if I was a rich patient of his. The pretty nurse had gone, and we had a very ugly one instead, but something in Don seemed to have disappeared, and I couldn't recover it again.

Daddy died very suddenly. It must have been while I was in the train on my way to Carlice. The doctors had thought he would certainly live another week. Claude brought me the telegram when I was just starting to dress for dinner. It said: "Your dear father died peacefully this afternoon. Funeral Tuesday. Am making all arrangements. Writing. Rusper." The letter came by the afternoon post next day. It was full of the various legal things which had to be done.

Claude of course came with me to the funeral. He was pale and nervy, and said very little. We spent the Monday night in London with Isabel, and motored to South Mersley the next morning. Stephen was still abroad. He'd caught some kind of fever in Marseilles and was in hospital there. We hadn't wanted him at Elmcroft during Daddy's illness, but it would have been a comfort to have him at the funeral. It was a very beautiful day in mid-October, sunny but cold. The trees in the cemetery were coloured with autumn tints, and some brown leaves fluttered down into the open grave. When the coffin was lowered, I felt as if something in my own life were being buried. Don was very black and official and kept away from Claude and me. When we were looking at the wreaths arranged at the grave-side I broke down. Claude stood beside me, but didn't try to comfort me at all. He had forgotten to bring his thick overcoat and was shivering. It may have been then that he caught the cold which led to his influenza.

As for me, I went on crying into my crumpled handkerchief, and nobody seemed to care.

5

Dr. Donald Rusper,
95, Meridian Avenue,
South Mersley,
London, S.W.

Bother! That's the second envelope I've addressed to him. That's what comes of mooning over the past. But it was such a wonderful past. Even in spite of everything, I would not have had it.

CARLICE ABBEY,
WILTSHIRE.
Thursday.

DEAR DON,

I've had a letter from Stephen, who's very upset at the idea that you may be stopping his allowance. I told him that I'm sure you know best, and that Daddy would have wished him to follow your advice. Still, I think we ought to look at things from his point of view. He seems to be getting on fairly well now, and says there is no fear of his exceeding again. "Exceeding" was his word. He naturally feels it hard that he hasn't control of his money, and it makes him obstinate and specially suspicious of you. I think you ought to make allowances for this. Could you suggest that he puts himself in the hands of some other person for observation?

How do they observe you, I wonder? Do they surround you with bottles and watch through a skylight to see how much you drink?

I'm so afraid that if you insist on your plan, something frightful may happen. He's so set upon not going to the home, he might try to kill himself. Or he might turn up here and make a scene. He says he has enough money to carry on till the end of August. Don't you think you might let him know that if he goes on all right till then, you might alter your views? Surely you could get the local doctor to keep an eye on him. At present he's staying at Thurlow-on-Sea, and seems to like the place very much.

I really can't say any more than that. I'm not going to beg Don to let him off on bended knees. Don's probably quite right. Stephen might be better in every way for going to the home. He'd probably come out quite cured and get some work that would interest him. He might marry and settle down. What a pity that it should have been Don, of all people, who married the one girl who ever seemed to interest him. But Catherine could never have cared for Stephen. If she had, she could never have married Don.

Still, it's not too late for him to find someone else. Suppose he could make three hundred a year, with his four-fifty he'd be as well off as I shall be—when I leave here.

I hope Catherine and the children are well. It is pouring with rain here, and this is a draughty cold house. I hope you are having better weather where you are.

Yours very sincerely,
DORA CARLICE.

6

Still too wet to go out. At this rate the grass won't be fit to walk on for days. I can't bring myself to wear those thick rubber things Isabel wears. She's always dressed so *suitably* for the country, and I never am, although I live in it. But I'm better dressed for London than she is. She always looks dowdy there. I suppose it's county to look like that.

What shall I do this afternoon, if it goes on raining? Oh, there are plenty of things I ought to do. I ought to have the car out and see how Mrs. Grainger is getting on. Or I might take those things round to the Vicarage for their sale. No, I can send Flora round with them. Or I could drive in to Risely and go to a cinema. Joan might like to come. No, she wouldn't. And I always think it's a bit funny the lady of Carlice Abbey going to a little local cinema alone. Oh, the afternoon will pass somehow. With all these visitors coming, I shan't have many more to myself for a while. That reminds me, I ought to write to Dolly too.

> *Mrs. Headford,*
> *25, Occident Court,*
> *Paddington, W.*

I wonder what her flat really is like. It'll be very modern and labour-saving with all sorts of gadgets we've never heard of here. But I suppose there would be no room for one's things. It would be a change after living here. I suppose one would get used to it quickly, though it wouldn't seem like home. If it comes to that, Carlice doesn't seem like home to me—after fourteen years of it. Elmcroft was my real home. And God knows who's living at Elmcroft now. When we were at school, Dolly and I were quite sure we should marry Londoners with houses in London. She chose Carlton House Terrace and I chose Belgrave Square. And she married 80, Royal Avenue, South Mersley, and I married Carlice Abbey, and now we're both widows. It's funny how things move round in circles.

> CARLICE ABBEY,
> WILTSHIRE.
> *Thursday.*

DARLING DOLLY,

How exciting it must be! I quite understand that you wanted to get away from South Mersley, and I don't disapprove at all that you're not living with your mother and Frances, though naturally they would have liked having you there. But it would have been difficult for you to go back to them, after having had a house of your own.

And I should love to have what you call a *pied-à-terre* with you in London, though it's quite impossible just now. Frankly, I couldn't afford it. It's difficult to explain, but there's less pocket-money here than there was at Elmcroft—or, for that matter, at your mother's place. I even feel I oughtn't to spend my own money on myself, apart from my allowance from the estate. The estate income seems to get less every year, and it gets more and more of a struggle to keep things going. And this is a house in which it's difficult to economise. But you saw all that, when you came here.

It's funny how little she seemed to enjoy her visit. Perhaps she was a bit ashamed of Tom. I ought to have had them alone without other guests. But when I did ask them alone, they made some excuse for not coming. It must have been Tom. I wonder if she told him that I called him the Rough Diamond. When your friends marry, it often becomes very difficult. I can't help being glad that she's on her own again.

You know Ronnie comes of age next September. What will happen then, I can't say. If he wants me to stay on and house-keep, I suppose I shall have to do it. Of course there's Joan—you never met her, I think. She's a nice capable girl, but her great friend has just divorced her husband in South Africa, and when she comes back, I dare say Joan will start farming or market-gardening with her. They kept poultry together for a time, and did fairly well.

Of course, Ronnie will marry sooner or later. His Aunt Isabel says he's probably playing Tristan to a tobacconist's daughter in Oxford, when any ordinary undergraduate would be content with being Don Juan. (I hope I've got it right. They're characters from operas, aren't they?) He doesn't seem interested in any of the girls who live in these parts or in Joan's friends—though of course they're older than he is. But even if I stay on, pending his marriage, I think I should like to be able to get away a bit from time to time, especially if he lives at home. He would probably want the place to himself and his friends a good deal. So I shall go on thinking of your spare room with great excitement, and it is just possible that I could run up to see it for a few days in May.

How I wish it was May now.

Do I? Yes. I don't mind if it does bring the "crisis" nearer. I'm getting over all that silly worry, except sometimes when I get worked up in bed. Even if things go as badly as I imagine, they can't eat me. I shall simply say, "Well, there it is. I'm very sorry. I didn't mean it to happen."

There's a heavy April in prospect. Ronnie's now on a reading-party, as they call it, at a rectory not very far from Oxford. He comes back for Easter, of course, and Isabel Carlice and her friend Gwen Rashdall and other friends of theirs are coming down. Then, when they go, I've got Maud, Gladys and Lionel coming. I wish you'd come here then and help me to entertain them, though I know you don't care for Maud or Gladys much.

That was Tom again, I suppose, who made that awkwardness. He thought everybody was "putting on airs."

And then Ronnie is entertaining some undergraduate friends till the beginning of the summer term. Then I think I shall have to ask Isabel down again. She does so adore the garden at the beginning of May. She almost measures the plants and trees to see how much they grow each day. So you see, so far from being a lady of independent means, I'm really a kind of hotel-keeper. After that, though, there should be a little peace, and I do hope you'll come here for a few days, or let me come to you.

I've been very worried lately about Stephen, who's at logger-heads with Don Rusper. I think you know that Daddy made Don Stephen's trustee. I've been trying to keep the peace between them, which isn't easy.

Well, lunch is nearly ready, and I must stop. Besides, it's simply freezing in here. The central heating is on, but it's not strong enough for this big room—the drawing-room—which is my favourite place in the house. I'm too stingy to have the fire lit here before lunch, when there's one in the morning-room. That shows you a thing or two, doesn't it? I picture you snuggling cosily in Occident Court, and envy you. Really, the spring is hopeless in the country. Year after year it's the same. Lovely daffodils and lovely almond blossom and it's too wet or too cold to go outside and enjoy them. It's pouring now, with

great sheets of rain flapping at me from over the lawn. And
my nit-wit maid left the window open, and the rain has ruined
one of my nice new curtains. I don't suppose they'll be able to
repeat the stuff either. Write soon. And I'll try to fix something
up as soon as I can.

With love,

Your affec. DORA.

Chapter IV: STEPHEN PAYNE

I

In the name of the Father and of the Son and of the Holy Ghost. Amen.

HE kisses the Cross in the middle of his stole. Prettily done. I like to see that. It carries me back years ago to my High-Church phase which used to annoy my father so much. I could have slipped out before the sermon, but the preacher seems to have his eye on me now. After all, this is a pleasant place. I like these clean white pillars, and the shaft of sun striking through the New Jerusalem in that window. "In memory of Elias Topping who departed this life on 1st August, 1934." How different modern stained glass is from the Victorian stuff which kept all the light out. Thank God my feet are more comfortable now. I won't economise in shoes again. This afternoon I must put on my old pair, even though they're as crinkled as a nurse's face. If I can't afford good ones, I'll wrap my feet in newspaper.

And so, to-day, I am going to speak to you of prayer. The crudest form of prayer, and that with which, alas, you are probably most familiar, is the request for a material personal benefit. I know a young lady, who admitted that, when taking up her hand at bridge, she always prayed that God would give her four aces in it. And this, mark you, after the cards had been dealt. While we applaud this lady's faith in the omnipotence of the Deity, who, if He was to grant her wish, must miraculously transform a two of hearts into, let us say, an ace of clubs and *vice versa*, we cannot help wishing that her faith had been enlightened by a more spiritual vision. But, you will say, there is no need to suppose that God had to perform such a vulgar conjuring trick as I describe. With His infinite foreknowledge, He knew of the young lady's prayer before it was uttered, and, being disposed to grant it, so directed the fingers of the persons

71

who shuffled and cut the cards, that the four aces fell into the required position. Do not think, please, that I have chosen this illustration, which may to some of you seem almost profane, merely in order to amuse you or gain your attention cheaply. It is a forcible illustration at the root of a big problem, and the prayer that one may find four aces in a hand already dealt, is only an extreme example of the private prayers which many of you have already uttered to yourselves this morning, in this Church. For what, then, you will ask me, shall we pray? And is it safe or possible to limit the objects of prayer?

How full of lovely questions all this is. My feet are certainly hurting less. I wonder if society will ever become so harried by organisation that its greatest pleasure will be going quietly to Church? Or won't one be safe even there? Will they instal a psycho-detector to see if one is thinking an anti-social or improper thought? And will the concentration-camp be waiting as one steps out of the main door past the font?

Oh, I thank God for my momentary freedom—my freedom to leave now in the middle of this excellent parson's period, if I want to, and slip down to the harbour and watch the good people of the port cluster round the Seven Anchors, enjoying this late April sunshine and the glass that cheers.

Nothing for you this morning, old boy. You're a remittance man now, thanks to Doctor Donald Rusper. You must go thirsty to lunch at King Stephen's Hotel, and make your little go a long way.

The sun flows through the New Jerusalem in the stained glass window erected in memory of Elias Topping. It flows like free whisky from a cask—a pure whisky that does nothing to the guts, the liver or the head. I was never born a type to be a drunkard. Rusper might know that. I value the essential *me* far too highly to let it be impaired by systematic toping. I happen to have attacks of imprudence. That's all. Like old gentlemen with disordered glands who assault housemaids in the park. That's why no "cure" would be any use for me. And I don't want myself changed. They'd kill the complex that lays the golden eggs. (Somebody else said that, but it's good.) The great advantage of living near a volcano is that one discovers such peculiar beauties on the edge. If I had ten thousand a year and a handsome wife, I couldn't think life as lovely as I now do. This liberty to come and go—to slip in and out of the crowd, unknown and irresponsible—this liberty to merge my soul, and sometimes almost my physical body, into the material world which surrounds me—is so godlike that I should be insane to ask for anything more. That is why I cling to the past—like a fading rose-petal clinging to the stalk. Any change for me must be a change for the worse. Even "certainty of tenure," to quote a phrase from Daly's office where I used to work, might destroy these keen perceptions. But I shall win this battle against Rusper and his professional pomposity. Having twice his brain and fewer scruples—— Now we must all stand up. I should like to have gone out. My feet feel perfect. If I had ten thousand a year I should have gone out, and damned the collection. But as every shilling is important to me, I feel it would be mean to go without paying for my seat. Threepence will do. I have threepence, unbudgeted for, in my left trouser-pocket. How pleasantly the coins jingle as they fall into the bag.

I shall remember the sunshine through the New Jerusalem. I shall come here again. "Excuse me, Madam."

Now for the steep hill leading down to the harbour. Twelve strikes from the church tower, and the clock bears the motto: *Trifle not: thy time is short.* My time is short. That is why I trifle. Or rather, I don't trifle. I live. Those who don't trifle, don't live—in my sense of trifling and in my sense of living.

No drink for you, old boy, this bright summer morning. Lance, the boatman, waves, all got up in his Sunday best. Let him go in with his pals. I won't join them now. This seat will do for me. With any luck, that dirty old man sprawling at the other end will keep people away. The seat smells slightly of paint in the hot sunshine. The smells here alone are worth a week's contemplation—the salt in the air and the stagnant salt of these molluscs on the ironwork, where only the highest tide reaches. Beyond this little basin the waters of the harbour swell lazily, and rub a scummy fringe on the seawall. What are the secrets of that slimy ridge? The boats move with the same motion—up and down, up and down—and the sails, too, flap rhythmically. I can smell salted rope. No, nobody's ready for a sail to-day. It's too early for the sailing season. Besides, we should still be up there, finishing up the service. I'd go for a sail, I think, if I had half a crown. No, I wouldn't, I'd join Lance in the Seven Anchors.

It would be a waste of time to fall asleep here—while I've still got a bed at night. Those few moments of slipping down into nothing aren't worth the time I should lose. That nursemaid wasn't told to bring her charge down here, I'll bet. I wonder whom she's after. One of those sailors, I suppose, who hang about and always look very well. I should have thought she'd prefer the band on the upper parade. It'll be a job getting the pram up the hill. Oh, but she'll have help. There comes the sailor. I suppose the baby is too young to talk. I wonder if this stores up a complex for it, when it sees them kissing or cuddling and can't tell Mamma. If those dogs fight I shall pretend to be asleep. Otherwise I should get bitten and have to get Mrs. Temperley to bind me up and put on the iodine. I'm sure she has it in her medicine-chest. Already she's given me quinine, cinnamon, vaseline, pills, glyco-thymoline and boracic ointment—in less than six weeks.

I chose the King Stephen Hotel because it was called after me. And it gives me a little bedroom with morning sun at the top of the top flight of stairs, and three meals a day for thirty-eight shillings a week. A lucky choice. I hate none of my fellow-guests, and I adore Mrs. Temperley, who allows me not to see her when I would rather not. O admirable British matron—Kipling almost—economising at the King Stephen Hotel to keep her son at Harrow. How practical, unamorous and kind. I'll stay on at the King Stephen till I die. Already, on this May morning, I find myself praying that I shall stroll round this harbour in the mist of a November afternoon. (The very prayer the parson was talking about—for a material personal benefit.) But that is my four aces in one hand. I must have them. I must see this harbour in a November mist, while boys throw squibs at the boatmen, and dodge behind the barrels on the quay. I must hear the water lapping under the mist, and all that creaking which will be louder for the silence of that afternoon. I must still be smelling these smells which, however, will be different, staler, and impregnated with the long clamminess of autumn. I must be here—six months ahead in November, when even this Sunday's newspaper posters would cease to terrify.

2

Why do they have these posters down here by the harbour? *Victory—defeat—bombardment—warning—crisis.* For some months now, I've been living—at intervals only, thank God—twenty-one years ago, passing the dates of that period one by one and experiencing all their nastiness once more. And as I've formed the habit of casting my memory back, like a narrow searchlight, exactly twenty-one years, I've developed a superstition, that as each anniversary passes, as it comes of age, that precise horror at least can't hurt me again. Unfortunately, there are still so many of them I shall have to live through. That day near Laventie when I was really a coward, and might have been shot, if anyone had noticed. My return from leave—next November. Trench fever, and dreary convalescence at the Base, March, April and part of May next year. My "Company Commander's Course" at Monchy la Fontaine, which I hated with a strange venom, July next year. Then the Somme in October next year, and another go of trench fever. And still nine months of beastliness after that, with my wound in June the year after next, when the war will be over for me.

The worst is still to come. No, not quite the worst. I've done my enlistment, and all those timid heroics of mine. I've done that hideous camp at Bramfort Moor. The bayonet-fighting instructor has given me his last lecture. I mean the instructor there; for the lectures we had when I was an officer were never quite so bad. I've seen the last of that odious Sergeant Cleame. Last January that was, about the fourteenth or fifteenth. And twenty-one years ago to-day, after breakfast, I "entrained"—how the words stick—for the front for the first time. It was a Tuesday—after a little burst of unsatisfying leave. They had told us that officers ought to have revolvers, but we hadn't been shown how to fire them. The war was still amateurish in those days. It was only on Monday, the day before, I remember, when I went and bought mine. I really must learn how to fire it, I thought, and I pegged a sheet of newspaper on to a clothes-line between two apple-trees in the garden at Elmcroft, and fired desperately. I didn't realise how dangerous it was. To have shot an inhabitant of South Mersley would have been a monstrous crime, even though we were in the middle of a war. Then my father shouted through the window that he had a patient with him. "All right," I thought, "if I'm killed through not knowing how to shoot, it'll be your fault." But I was glad to stop practising. Then I went out alone for a walk on the common, and thought all kinds of beautiful things to myself. Dora was doing war-work most of the day, and there was no one else to go out with. Then dinner with the Boswells, and Pa Boswell's heavy fun about it all. "Of course you'll come back, my young fellow, as fit as a flea." (But he was to die very painfully before I came back, and two of his sons—though what is two out of five?—were not to come back at all.) The Ruspers were there, but not Donald, who was serving his country in Devonshire. But beware of bitterness about those who had an easy war. Didn't they do what I hope to do next time? Besides, Don Rusper in Devonshire was probably a good deal more useful to King and Country than I was in Flanders.

I awoke next morning, feeling slightly sick. The day had come. Breakfast, half-eaten, with father looking down his nose at me. He had a busy morning in prospect, and it was left to Dora to go with me as far as was allowed. I remember the click of the white gate at Elmcroft as it shut behind me. "Now I have really left home," I thought. It was the same click as Dora's mother must have heard the year before, when she was taken to hospital for the operation which killed her. The same click as my father was to hear, eleven years later, when he was taken to the nursing-home for his operation. Good-bye to Elmcroft—home, such as it was, and life, such as it was. The honeysuckle was early that year, and smelt very fragrant as it sprawled lazily over the wooden fence.

Dora saw me bravely to the last barrier at Waterloo. I kept saying, "Surely it would be better if you left me now," but she wouldn't go. As she walked up the platform she dabbed her eyes —not, I think, because it was I who was going, but because all leave-taking in those days was sad. And, in a generic way, treading daintily, dancing almost, through the packs and haversacks left on the platform, while their owners were crowding to the buffet and singing idiotic songs, she was seeing off a soldier-brother.

That was about midday, twenty-one years ago. The sun, which

shines now, shone through the railway-carriage window as we went to Southampton. The carriage smelt of sweat, but there are worse smells than that. Then comes the channel crossing—that'll be twenty-one years ago to-night—when I slept on the floor under a table in the smoking-room. But my superstition won't let me look ahead. Twenty-one years and I've finished with it all. But anything that isn't twenty-one years old is still a danger.

When the next war comes, I have a feeling I shall be fit enough to go, in spite of Rusper. If one's fit enough to enjoy oneself, as I most certainly am, one would surely be fit enough to do something unpleasant. Too old perhaps? Well, that depends on what breathing-space we have. These newspaper posters don't give one much hope.

But I am spoiling my morning—my meditation after church. "O Lord, give us peace in our time." Is that prayer taboo, as being too much a request for a personal benefit? I should like to talk to that parson—for one evening only, and on my own terms, so that there could be no chance of his trying to "reclaim" me. Reclaim me from what? From trifling, from sucking the very essence out of life, from penetrating its most full intention, if it has one, or giving it an intention, if it hasn't one? No, it isn't I who should be reclaimed.

Meanwhile there is lunch, for which they don't like you to be late at the King Stephen. I must face the hill and bear with my detestable shoes. Perhaps I shall overtake the sailor and the nursemaid. She too should be hurrying home to lunch by now. I have never fallen in love with a nursemaid yet. As well perhaps; for if I did, Rusper would come here for a medical conference and seduce her. No, he'd be too careful for that. Rusper *never* seduces. (I like the sound of that.) He simply picks the woman you want to marry and marries her himself. And she has two children.

3

If I had been more like Dora I should have made a successful marriage. But I'm unlike her in every way, except that she's quite a nice person and I suppose I'm really quite nice too. We ought to have something in common, although we had different mothers.

But I can see little trace of my father in myself. I must take entirely after that mysterious mother of mine, that girl of good family (as it was hinted to me), who quarrelled with it and went on the stage and became a pantomime fairy. "Your mother was an unsuccessful actress," my father once said to me, "but I need hardly say she did not come from that stratum of society." All South Mersley— such as it was thirty years ago—was speaking in the words "that stratum." "What was her maiden name?" I asked him once, and he didn't tell me. I suppose I could have found out, but I didn't. After all, she only lived three days after I was born.

It makes me rather a romantic figure, this—not merely the son of a clever little suburban doctor. Sometimes I wonder if I am his son at all. It is possible, I suppose, that I'm not—with the stage-door ever open. But *he* couldn't have known. He'd have turned her out, and me too. Even if his vanity might have prevented him from suspecting, however obvious it was, someone would have told him. And I have his utterly undistinguished hair. No, I must rule out that myth, though it's a pleasant fancy. Observe, that I give him no credit for having been passionately in love with my mother. And yet he must have been, or he'd never have married a girl who quarrelled with her family. Or did he think the family would reconcile itself to her and become his patients? "My father-in-law the baronet whom I am treating for gout." I remember his unctuous manner when baronets called. "Dora girl, just make sure that the hall and vestibule are thoroughly tidy." And Dora girl did. Rusper, I suppose, gives the same order, and Catherine girl has to see to the tidying.

Time. I must go.

4

It's easy for me to relive the war again, and pass its twenty-one-year-old landmarks one by one. But after the war I find it much harder to recapture myself. A dreary and long convalescence, then six years in Daly's office, which have left me with nothing but little muddled memories of law. And they are fading, and the law has all been altered, so that I couldn't go back there. Then my breakaway at the chance of going to Japan. Stephen Payne, private tutor, bear-leader with such a distinguished young charge. The pay was good, and the journey long and interesting. Ten years ago. And while I was away news of my father's illness. Ought I to have hurried back? He seldom if ever enjoyed seeing me. His death, while I was ill with fever at Marseilles, among the benign French nuns. Then my enfeebled return to find Rusper my trustee and my excellent income dependent upon his whim.

And still, I thought, I must get a job again. Barling House School. An academy for young gentlemen, where I taught classics and English literature with a mechanical competence which surprised me. A misty morbid period of misery without reason. I feared the future (not as I fear it now, because it may destroy the present), but because the present held nothing. I wanted to die, painlessly and romantically. A few months among the pine trees of Switzerland and then a tranquil ending. There was a boy called Napier who was supposed to have a tendency to consumption. I used to lean over him as I corrected his work, hoping to catch his breath and his disease. The feeblest attempt at suicide ever made. In course of time, Napier did go to a sanatorium and did die—and I didn't.

But that was some months after I had met Catherine Bain. I remember, the first day, before I had drifted into being in love with her, I thought we could never marry. Our names were too much alike. "Mr. Payne marries Miss Bain." The announcement would have sounded too absurd. But fancy my thinking of marrying her that first day—a tea-party given by the headmaster's wife. We had tea in the private garden by the big medlar tree. There was a strong smell of new-mown hay from the field beyond the iron fence. Her parents were there, nice people, and newcomers to the South Mersley district. They had enough, I gathered, but not much to live on. Catherine kept house for them. She had been to London University and was still disappointed at not having got an intellectual job. She was twenty-seven—ten years younger than I. Was the difference in age too big? That evening, when Howard, the games-master, said that she was attractive without being pretty, I blushed and went out of the room.

Two Sundays later, her mother asked me to tea. To reach their house one had to pass Elmcroft, which Dora and Rusper had sold to a prosperous sanitary engineer. Three noisy children were playing with a ball on the little front lawn, and the honeysuckle, which has a long flowering season, was still sprawling on the fence by the white gate. As I passed it, I thought, "That was my old life. Perhaps I am walking to a new one."

But here is the King Stephen Hotel, with the dinner-bell calling me in.

5

Mrs. Temperley has asked me to join her and Mrs. Adams on a motor-ride to visit some friends in the hinterland of the county. The friends, who must be rich, have sent their car. "Mr. Payne, you don't want to talk to two stout old ladies all the afternoon. Wouldn't you like to sit in front?" So I do. A fine car, but not broad enough in the beam. The driver is taciturn, which is a good thing. I must keep my nervous force for new contacts at tea-time. I wonder what they will think of my old shoes. The only thing that matters is not to do Mrs. Temperley any discredit, especially as la belle Adams is a bit of a snob.

All through lunch—or dinner, as one should call it on Sundays at the King Stephen—I have been thinking of Catherine in my second layer of thoughts, and walking my walk past Elmcroft to the Bains' new house, on the fringe of what is now the Garden City. It was neat, tidy and bare. There were intellectual books in the drawing-room. I felt suddenly intellectual myself, and exalted to a higher spiritual plane. Why had I let my gifts grow rusty? At school, I had always been "very promising." Where now was my performance? Was I destined, at last, to have a flowering season? (To think that all this is only five years ago.) Catherine talked to me, when she could, as if she were starved for someone like me to talk to. A conversation without back-chat. There was about her no touch of the bright young thing, as there was about her elder and married sister. Mrs. Bain listened, and joined in sometimes with just the right word—or so it seemed to me then. I gathered that Mrs. Bain had a brother who was a very brilliant doctor in London. This was an ingredient in my undoing, though I didn't know it then. That evening I prepared a letter asking Catherine if we could meet again. I allowed four days to elapse before posting it. She wrote back at once saying that she would be very glad to see me. And the whole thing began.

It was too deliberate, too ethereal on my side. I see it now. I was a poor lover. I had such high notions, and was too eager to make myself mentally fit, and do something worthy of her. I should have done better to develop my muscles and grow a strong moustache. That was what she wanted, though I give her full credit for not knowing it at the time. The first months were the happiest, when we met on the intellectual plane, tacitly resolving to leave the physical alone, until our souls had merged. In those ecstatic periods I wrote my novel. I read her passages from it and she flattered me about them. Our mathematics master, whom I always liked, had a brother-in-law who was a publisher. It may have been his influence which got the book accepted. I still think it was a good book, but it required a reader with patience and a certain attitude of mind which is not usual.

I had now known Catherine nearly two years. I was thirty-nine. She was twenty-nine, and it was high time we married. Yet when I asked her, she, who at first had been disappointed—so I imagined—at my backwardness, gave me a half refusal. I was dazed, but not shattered. We were meeting once or twice a week, went to concerts, exhibitions of pictures, lectures and high-brow plays together. Sometimes we even danced. As I now see it, there was too little dancing in the programme for her taste—which had changed somewhat from the taste she had when we first knew one another. Perhaps, I thought, she is ambitious for me. She wants a husband who will make his mark. My book must be a success. The inspiration was Catherine's and, as such, couldn't fail me. Desperately I polished up my proofs, making so many corrections, interpolations and excisions that my publishers complained. And almost the very day—yes, it was the very day—when I had sent back the last proof with its final revision, and had met Catherine and told her that the great work was completed for better or for worse—she said, with that careful indifference which is so ominous in a love-affair, "I met a great friend of yours last night, a Doctor Rusper."

My feelings for Rusper were not then what they are now. So far he had never thrown his weight about in my direction. I was only too glad to leave the business side of the trust to him and Dora, who seemed to have the knack of getting on well with him, and he for his part paid out my allowance without cavil. I didn't like him. In the early days he had been too fond of giving me semi-medical advice, often accompanied by jocular innuendo. "You look a bit washed out, young fellow. Can't go on burning the candle at both ends for ever, you know." And so on, like a mild school-bully. He had done quite well since taking over my father's practice, and was already one of the leading doctors in South Mersley. I was content to let him well alone, and avoided the houses to which he went. I couldn't understand how anybody could find pleasure in his society. Yet people did—and Catherine among them. "Why haven't you let us meet before?" she asked me. I answered that I had never wished to bore her. "But he isn't boring," she said. I asked her what he had said that was so remarkable—a foolish question. How slowly my wits were working! She laughed and said that he hadn't said anything remarkable. None the less, she hadn't found him a bore. "There are evenings when even you say nothing remarkable," she told me. "And I never find you boring." I probed further. Where had she met him, and how did she find out that he was connected with my family? She answered without reservation, and asked me why I was so interested in the meeting. "Because you seem to have been interested in it," I said. "Oh, well," she replied, "we've rather exhausted the interest of it now, haven't we?" Then, for the hundredth time, we talked about my book.

The next Sunday but one I went to tea at Mrs. Bain's and found Rusper there. "Mother asked him," Catherine whispered to me. "I think she's hoping he can cure Daddy's sciatica." It was the first afternoon I really loathed him. He seemed to make himself at home much too quickly—almost to hold the floor. He was at his best—talking well for him—and I was at my worst. He flattered Mrs. Bain about her brother the eminent London doctor, played up to the brightness of Catherine's married sister, and a couple of bright young things who had come with her to the house, and to Catherine herself he was quietly deferential. When he spoke to me, it was in a hearty manner which made me tongue-tied. Once or twice I caught Catherine watching him out of the corner of her eye. I went away full of woe.

The next four months have almost as bleak a record as the war. A bleaker record, in a way, though now, in my changed mood, I see that they didn't leave such a scar behind them. Catherine was in love with Rusper. I made appalling scenes which I had no right to make. I even thought she was his mistress. But Rusper *never* seduces. He decided to marry her—to marry into the family of the famous London doctor—and I might have known it would happen. To do Catherine justice, she wanted to be perfectly frank with me, as soon as she knew her own mind. It was I, really, who wouldn't let her be frank and tried to postpone a crisis. At all costs, I thought, I must keep her from committing herself till my book comes out. Somehow I thought of my book as a last desperate defence of our relationship. If it were a real success, surely it would bind us indissolubly together. I must have been more stupid then than I am now.

The book came out. Reviews were slow to appear and not very numerous. On the whole, they were unfavourable. The kindest remark was, "Mr. Payne has just failed to create a prose-poem," and the unkindest, "Mr. Payne's cult of the ego would be nauseating if it were skilfully portrayed. As it is, we can dismiss it as a piece of irrelevant tediousness." I was aghast at the injustice. This was the reward of all those hours of mental conflict, this the fruit of all that mingled ecstasy and despair, this the attention given to a sincere and sensitive view of life. I felt it all as keenly as if I had been nineteen and had published a volume of undergraduate poetry. Perhaps my development was arrested, and I was going through a phase which normal people do go through at nineteen.

Catherine was very kind. I really believe she delayed her formal engagement to Rusper for a few weeks on my behalf. She wrote me a long letter, and told me that, much as she liked the book herself, she had feared it would never have a popular appeal. To get good notices for a first novel one must belong to a literary coterie, or else one must be very young and startling. I wrote back with bitter agreement. "Yes," I said, "I suppose it is inevitable that a middle-aged schoolmaster who suddenly writes a novel should be as much a failure at that as at everything else. If I had been a murderer, everyone would have been eager to know what I had to say. But as I happen to have a fairly cultivated mind, and have tried to enlarge the scope of human sensitiveness and to create a thing of beauty, instead of exposing a scandal or howling at some supposed abuse, I am unreadable." I wrote a great deal more in this vein, which Catherine must have found tedious. It was a relief to write, and I took pains with the letter. I suppose that is why some of its phrases still remain in my memory.

She wrote back. We met. A dreary lamentable meeting. The games-master introduced me to whisky, and I developed a new accomplishment.

The fact that there was no crisis in my life when Catherine became engaged to Rusper, and no crisis even when she married him, amazed me. There was I, a failure in love, a failure in literature, still teaching at Barling House School, and likely to teach there for ever. One half of me looked at the other half with astonishment. I really think my personality did split in two at that time. I used to have staccato dialogues with myself. It seemed a pleasure—or if not that, a relief—to do things with one side of my character which should bewilder the other side. "Now, Stephen," I would say, "in ten minutes you've got to go into classroom number three and teach fifteen little boys *The Ancient Mariner*. Are you going to do it? I can't believe you're going to do it. Aren't you too bored?" And the other half would answer, "I'm going to do it, and I want to be bored. I hope I'm very bored indeed, and I hope *you* are bored stiff too." I began to enjoy watching myself as an automaton, and almost encouraged the rift between my two selves. Without knowing it, I was preparing for the salvation which I have now gained. But a crisis had to come first—a delayed crisis, quite a long time after Catherine's marriage, when she was already nursing her first baby.

It was six o'clock on a Thursday afternoon in November, and I was taking the usual lesson—not *The Ancient Mariner* this time, but Tennyson's *Dream of Fair Women*. The poem was an old favourite of mine, and many memories of my own schooldays were bound up with it—the sound of someone practising on the chapel organ, the heavy and dirty carving round the classroom door, and the smell of our evening meal cooking below stairs. I had already told myself that not one of my pupils would appreciate the work— that their *libidos* would be fluttering round motor-bicycles and wireless-sets, however inspired my interpretation of the poem's beauties. And the right-minded half of me had already said to the wrong-minded half, "Why don't you do something about it? Stage a demonstration. Don't take their indifference lying down." In vain my wrong-minded half had urged that if my pupils were indifferent, the fault was mine—that I should teach better. I was in a mood to be exasperated—perhaps a little stimulant had helped— and I soon had cause. The boy was called Tipples—a not inappropriate name. He was sitting where Napier—the consumptive who had failed to kill me—used to sit before he went away, and perhaps a burst of fatuity coming from that rather romantic corner of the room had a specially potent effect on me. At all events, when it came, I stood up on my little dais, and said, "You foolish boy!" There was a titter at this—an expected titter which nerved me to do my stuff in grand style. "This is the fifth time, Tipples," I went on, "that you've been inattentive. This is the fifth time that you've been impertinent in your answer. Do you suppose there's any pleasure in teaching a bloody little brat like you?" I paused, and the boy—I give him marks for that—said, "No, sir!" Then I took up the huge stone ink-bottle on my desk—it was full of ink—walked slowly to where Tipples was sitting, emptied it over his head and suddenly threw it at the window. There was a crash of broken glass behind the blind. I went up to my dais again, in a horrified silence, and after looking at the wretched boy, with ink dripping down his nose into his open mouth, I said, still very quietly, "You will spend the remainder of this lesson just as you are. I hope the ink tastes good." Then I fainted. I don't see quite what else I could have done.

When I revived, I was in my bedroom, on my bed. I stirred my eyelids cautiously and saw the headmaster, the matron and the games-master standing by. The games-master was a hefty brute. No doubt they had brought him there in case I was violent. I nearly laughed. Instead, I simulated a decorous return to consciousness. The games-master took my arm and said, "Steady on, old man." The headmaster, with a querulous dignity, said, "Sir, you've been drinking. You smell vilely of drink." The games-master said, "Sir!" (to the headmaster, not me); the matron said, also to the headmaster, "Don't you think, Mr. Elder——" and I interrupted them both by saying, "Mr. Elder, I wish to give immediate notice to leave your Academy." Then I did laugh, with big rolling hysterical laughter. The games-master said, "Steady on, old man. We've telephoned for Dr. Rusper and he'll be here any minute now." I replied, "I don't want a doctor," but the matron said, "Oh, yes, you do, Mr. Payne," and I thought I had better leave it at that. For some minutes there was a silence. Then the headmaster coughed and said to the games-master, "Keep an eye on him, will you?" and walked out of the room. I told the games-master that his presence was unnecessary, but he didn't move. Then I asked the matron why, if I must have a doctor, they had sent for Rusper instead of the school doctor. "Well, he's a relation of yours, isn't he?" she said. I protested that he wasn't, though I couldn't deny, to the games-master, that Rusper had taken over my father's practice. There was another silence. I got up, with the games-master's eye very closely upon me, took a book from a table by the window, settled down on the bed and began to read. This seemed to relieve them. The matron murmured that she had something to do, and went out. The games-master sat down on a flimsy cane chair. The seat creaked a little under his weight and he got up. "You'd be safer in the armchair," I said. Those were the last words I ever spoke to him.

Rusper arrived about an hour later. I judged at once that he was afraid of a scandal—almost as if he had married a Payne and not a Bain. For this reason, he was on his best behaviour, even with me. When we were left alone together, he said how frightfully sorry he was to hear of my breakdown. He realised how painful the associations of the school must be for me. Wouldn't I like to get away at once? He knew of a home managed by a medical friend of his, a Dr. Duparc, where I could have the rest and change of which I was in need. It was not far from Worthing. Would I consent to let him motor me there that very night? I said I should be delighted, and thereafter resolved only to speak to Rusper in words of one syllable.

The matron came to pack my things. I gave her a picture of a ship, which she had once admired, and she shed a quick tear. I felt very happy but tired. During the journey to Worthing I slept or pretended to sleep most of the time. Rusper asked me no questions, and on arrival at the home a nurse took me in charge, gave me some hot milk, and sent me straight to bed. It was a dilapidated house in big grounds, and reminded me of private asylums in detective-stories in which the heroine is nearly ravished by a maniac doctor. I wondered if Dr. Duparc would be a maniac. I was quite sure I was not.

I met Dr. Duparc the next morning, and found him most agreeable. He was half French, and a pleasant change from the people I'd been meeting. He asked me several questions and I answered them truthfully and intelligently. "I take it," I said, "that I'm under observation here?" He spread out his hands in an absurd gesture and said, "But of course!" and laughed loudly. I laughed too, rather nervously. "How long will the observation take?" I asked him. He shrugged his shoulders and said, "I cannot say yet. A month. Six weeks . . ." "And how much does it cost?" I continued. "Ten guineas a week," he said. "Our usual fees are of course much higher, but I am only too willing to make a concession to Dr. Rusper, and to you." "All right," I replied, "I'll stay here for six weeks."

I did, and really the time passed very pleasantly, in spite of the oddness of some of my fellow-patients. Duparc was an interesting man, and won my esteem by admitting that he found Rusper unsympathetic. I had long talks with him in French, a language which I was glad to brush up. He listened to me with close attention, and I began to feel that I was enlarging his mental outlook— almost as if I were a senior partner in his establishment. In fact, the interlude was so agreeable that I was sorry to leave. If only Duparc were still alive, and Rusper wanted to send me back to him for a few weeks I might almost give way. But Ebermann, the psychoanalyst, is a very different person. I've read some of his articles in the papers, and loathed the tone of them. His mission is to root out man's "illusion-complex"—which is his name for my scheme of realities. I well see what a pitiably drab creature I should turn into, if I went to his clinic. Besides, there is no possible ground for my being sent there. I will not go just to gratify Rusper's vanity.

I must admit that when I left Barling House School, Rusper behaved fairly well. But he wasn't pleased that I got on so well with Duparc, nor at the glowing testimonial Duparc gave me. He was less pleased when I refused to submit myself to periodical observation by him, and declared that I was going to live my own life and form my own contact with the core of life, in my own way, wherever I chose. And I don't suppose he was pleased when I walked out of his consulting-room in the middle of one of his sentences.

Perhaps that's why my second lapse—an accident, really, and not a lapse at all—goaded him into declaring war on me. Yes, it was a most unlucky accident that Catherine should come to Bos-church in March to give her influenzal children some sea air. It might have been better if she had come to my hotel—though it would have been too small and cheap for her. Then I should have met her in the ordinary way, said a hurried how-do-you-do and moved on somewhere else the next day. But finding her in the lounge of the Grand, among all those people, wearing a shoddy suburban evening dress, was too much of a shock.

The bar had just closed and instead of going out by the proper door—bad luck again—I had got into a long shame-faced passage which led deviously to the hotel. I had been treating myself to a night-out, and perhaps I was a little elated. I was far from drunk. If I did misbehave, it was through shock, not drunkenness. But really, I don't think I did. I came out of the twisting passage straight into the lounge. I was in shabby flannel trousers and a blue jersey. The people in the lounge were in evening dress, reading the paper, playing bridge and talking in whispers. Catherine was bang opposite me, making some sort of woollen garment, I suppose for one of her children. When she saw me lurch in—though I didn't lurch much—she shrank back as if I were a snake. I held a palm tree gently in my left hand and said, "My God! It's Catherine." I admit I spoke too loudly, but that again was the contrast between the bar and the lounge. In the bar you had to shout to make yourself heard. The lounge was as quiet as a Sunday school.

I repeated, "My God! It's Catherine." Then she made her mis-take, and pretended not to know me. In a flash I pictured Rusper saying to her, "You will realise that further contact with that person is undesirable," and the thought made me determined that she should know me. I advanced two paces from the door, unfor-tunately still holding the palm which balanced dangerously in its brass pot, and said, "I'm not going to allow you not to know me,

Mrs. Rusper." By this time two old ladies had edged away, and a stout bald youngish man had constituted himself Catherine's protector. "I think you've come to the wrong door," he said. "I advise you to clear out quickly, or I shall have to call the porter." Then he turned and shouted to someone further down the room, "Call the porter, will you? There's going to be trouble here." "There is going to be trouble," I said, "if you are going to interrupt my conversation with this lady. Catherine, will you ask your friend to go away?" I spoke in my educated schoolmaster's voice, and the champion of beauty in distress was rather taken aback. Catherine could have saved the whole situation if she had said, "Why, yes, this is an old friend of mine," or something of the sort. But she didn't. She turned away from me and said, "I think, Mr. Dudeney, you had better call the porter. I don't want to speak to this gentleman." Then I made a mistake and tried to justify myself. "You see," I said to Mr. Dudeney, "she doesn't deny she knows me. I can tell you her name and all about her. She used to be a Miss Bain, and lived at ——." Then the porter arrived, an undersized oily-haired youth. He too lost his head. (We were like the great powers on the outbreak of a war.) Making himself as truculent as he could, he said, "Look 'ere, you 'op out of this quick!" and advanced till his brass buttons were almost touching my jersey. I drew back with an attempt at dignity, and pulled the palm, which I was still holding, sideways so that it overbalanced and fell on the floor, with its brass pot rolling to Catherine's horrified feet. This was too much for the porter and Mr. Dudeney, the knight-errant, and each seized one of my arms and marched me through the assembled visitors to the door. It was too much also for me, and I let myself be led away quietly. "This matter will, of course, be reported to the management," Mr. Dudeney said, "and no doubt they'll take action." "They'd better not," I replied. "I can afford a solicitor, and I warn you we shall all look pretty silly. I did know the lady very well. She ought to have spoken to me." "That's her affair," Dudeney said. "Where do you live?" I told him I was staying at the Brigantine at the cheap end of the town. The porter sniffed with contempt on hearing the name of my inn and, turning to Dudeney, he said: "I can see him there, sir. He's not going to give any more trouble to-night." "I shall walk home alone," I said, and began to do so before they could protest. I didn't turn round to see if the porter was following me, but there was no sign of him when I reached my lodging.

There the silly little episode should have ended. But it didn't. I was having a cup of tea in bed the next morning about nine o'clock when the maid came up and said there was a Dr. Rusper to see me. I said that I was sorry I couldn't see him. She came up again almost immediately and said that Dr. Rusper insisted on seeing me. He had to catch a train back to London at twenty to ten and couldn't wait. "Tell Dr. Rusper," I said, "that I don't want to see him. Tell him I refuse to see him." When she had gone I nipped out of bed and bolted the door. In a minute or two I heard Rusper's heavy footsteps on the stairs and an imperious knock on the door. I whistled loudly. It was the most irritating thing I could think of doing. Then, after another bang on the door, he said, "I strongly advise you to see me, Payne." I whistled as loudly as I could. He went on, "I'm not here to waste my time, or yours either. If you don't open the door within two minutes I shall have to take other steps." "Take them," I thought, and continued to whistle breathlessly till I heard him go away. I dressed and came downstairs about an hour later, and the landlord, who had been waiting for me, took me aside and said apologetically that he must ask me to leave that day. I told him I should be glad to go, and should have gone in any case when my week was up. And so I left Boschurch two months ago, under a cloud, and came to the King Stephen Hotel, Thurlow-on-Sea, which I like much better than Boschurch. But I felt something would happen as soon as I gave Dora my new address, and sure enough Rusper's ultimatum came within four days of my writing to her—poisoning the whole future and making the present seem so incredibly sweet that I cannot bear to think of its ending. It shan't end. I'll blackmail Dora at Carlice Abbey, if necessary.

6

"The afternoon passed like a beautiful bird flying across a blue and white streaked sky." A phrase from my novel, of which I was thinking earlier in the day, during the motor-drive. Yes, it did pass like that. A house in the remote country with long drive guarded by a lodge, as the house-agents say. Mrs. Temperley and Mrs. Adams were greatly impressed. So was I. And I was glad that only the old lady and two children were at home. I could sit without talking and watch while she poured out tea—flash of sunlight on the silver tea-pot and rings glittering delicately on her lithe tapered fingers. Smell of pot-pourri from the carved wooden mantelpiece. Thick, white panelled walls, with the windows so deeply recessed that the world seemed utterly shut out.

A happy image this, to fall asleep on. The glittering of those rings upon those fingers, now raised, now dropped, but each time with appropriateness, fascinated me. I was reminded of Dora's sister-in-law, Miss Isabel Carlice, whom I met twice at Carlice Abbey. She had the same fingers, and the same leisure in her voice. Younger, of course, than the lady who entertained us to-day. And more alarming, I suppose. At least Dora seemed frightened of her. But full of an assurance of peace and effortless perfection. (How foolishly we have exalted effort into an ideal, forgetting it can never be more than a means to an end.)

I shall write and ask for one of the photographs the child with the new camera took to-day and send it to Dora. "You see where I go visiting," I shall say—leading up to it carefully. "A house which reminded me of yours, though less venerable. If you come and see me here, I'm sure Lady Evans would let me take you over to tea." Surely that will make Dora understand that I'm respectable and responsible and whatever else she and Rusper want me to be. The photograph was a very happy thought. And, as I stood behind that little balustrade, my shabby shoes were hidden. "Mrs. Temperley, Mrs. Adams and Mr. Stephen Payne visiting the home of Lady Evans." It's really worth passing it on to Rusper. "Stephen is at last making good," Dora will be able to say to him. "He's mixing with nice people. Perhaps some day he'll write another novel which won't be such a flop. Hadn't we better give him time?"

No use. She won't move Rusper like that. I've insulted his wife and, worse, insulted him. And he has the whip-hand over my allowance, and knows that I can't get work because secretly I don't want what they would call work. I suppose if I was actually starving I should want it—but not if there was any easier way out—petty theft, blackmail, cadging. People who don't know me would think worse of me for this than they need. And who does know me, really?

The full moon now is opposite my window, looking at me as it looked at Faust, at the beginning of Goethe's play. The moon which they can't yet think of spoiling, as they can spoil the earth, making it into an ant-hill with ant-inhabitants—the moon which will be increasingly unimportant for *them*, just as it will become increasingly important for me. The unproductive moon. I size *them* up in that adjective. But reality is not productive, and my grip on it is surer than *theirs*.

There will be moonlight over the little harbour now, and moonlight over it again in October, when I have got over the crisis. *They* can't stop moonlight, even if there are bombing aeroplanes fluttering in its indifferent rays—even if, like the man in Dowson's poem, I am beating delicate mad hands against the bars of Dr. Ebermann's clinic. If it doesn't matter what happens to me, then nothing matters. A lifetime of philosophy has taught me this. But I have a strength which can let a good many things happen to me without my being shattered. I can be sick with fear, and yet happy in a remote and sidelong way. I must cling to that remoteness, and look at life—by which they mean life's biological and mechanical appearance—in my own peculiar sidelong fashion. A curse on the head of the man who invented the word "escapist"—a word as dangerously misleading as the schoolboy words "swot" and "pi," coinage of the herd endeavouring to do down its betters. I was called both—"swot" when I was working for a scholarship, and "pi" when I refused to—but that's no image on which to fall asleep.

I will fall asleep enchanted by the glitter of rings on tapered fingers—Miss Carlice's, Lady Evans', and those of all other ladies whose existences I value. Their soft voices, unhurried but clear, shall lull me to sleep, while the rays of the sun, and, after the sun, of the moon, fall like notes of music on their raised rings and silver ornaments. Come, wave black veils in the moonlight, lovely ladies. Come, sing me to sleep with a lapping of harbour waters, with comfort and the peace of a long dream. . . .

Chapter V: ISABEL CARLICE

JOAN is spending the night with me in London. To-morrow she is flying to the South of France to meet her great friend Mrs. Benson, with whom she used to breed poultry. Mrs. Benson has divorced her bounder of a husband in South Africa and is coming back to Joan and England via the Suez Canal. Joan will bring her home from Cannes and they will start some kind of farming again. She is excited and very happy.

We are in full opera season. Lady Mawnan has lent me her box and her car, complete with chauffeur and footman. She does things handsomely. I had thought of asking a young man to join us, but Joan did not seem to want one. After all, a box is more comfortable with two in it than with three. It is insufferable with four. So we dined together here tête-à-tête and set off at leisure. Luckily it was one of those Italian operas that don't spoil one's dinner. I had the old red carpet put over the front steps. I wanted to see how much dignity it would give Joan as she got into the motor, but she just bundled herself in as if she were catching a bus in the Edgware Road.

While we were driving to Covent Garden, I said, hoping for a reaction, "I think it's so much pleasanter to see opera in a half-empty box than to pig it in the stalls." Ronnie would have exploded, and reminded me of the queues of musical devotees who waited hours for a seat in the gallery, while there was I, a lazy, well-fed woman, caring very little for music, etc., etc. But Joan delivered no such tirade. She merely said "Yes," and looked appraisingly at the crates of vegetables in Long Acre. A dull girl.

She was dull, too, when I introduced her to people in the intervals. Sir Thomas Hill was there, with his sister and a very handsome nephew, and there were some agreeable youngish men in a large party which included Gwen Rashdall. I chatted with everyone I knew, trying deliberately to make the evening like a page from a "society paper." Wasted effort. Joan hadn't improved at all since the "season" she spent with me. But what does that matter?

When we got back—she had refused all suggestions of supper—we sat in the drawing-room and talked for a long time. Dora, it seems, had done her best to make Joan promise to go to the Riviera by boat and train, and not to fly. Unless Joan flew, she would be too late to meet Mrs. Benson's ship. She had got her aeroplane ticket, but perhaps she could get the money refunded. She wanted to fly very much. What did I think?

"Well, my dear Joan, I think it's entirely a matter for you. You're well over twenty-one. Auntie Dora didn't *forbid* you to fly?"

"Oh no."

She laughed a little. Dora has never been successful at forbidding.

"She asked you not to fly, as a favour?"

"I suppose so. She said, 'Oh, Joan dear, I'd so much rather you didn't fly.'"

"But you got your ticket for the aeroplane?"

"Yes."

She looked shamefaced, like a school-girl reprimanded by her mistress.

"I'm not blaming you," I said.

"Don't you think Auntie Dora was being rather stupid?" she asked me. "Don't you think it is really for me to decide?"

"Yes. So long as I'm not responsible, if anything should go wrong. You've been born into this mechanical age, and sooner or later you'll be forced to enjoy its so-called blessings. Have you ever flown before?"

"Once, for a few minutes for five shillings. I don't feel any nervousness myself. I'm looking forward to the trip. Why, old women fly to India and Cape Town every week. It's ridiculous to hesitate. So far as Auntie Dora goes, we might be living at the time when Blériot was trying to fly the Channel."

She had worked herself up into a quick mood of anger, which I was glad to see.

"Well, then, fly," I said.

"You really mean that?" she asked gratefully.

I said I did mean it, and she sighed with relief.

"If you'd objected, too, I shouldn't have done it," she said.

There was a pause, while I urged her to mix herself a gin and barley-water. She did so, awkwardly, making a mess on the tray.

"And what about this farming of yours?" I asked her, when she had settled down again. "What have you arranged?"

"Only the vague plan."

"But you're bent on trying it again?"

"Oh, absolutely. After all, my last effort wasn't too bad, and we shall have more capital this time. You don't disapprove, Aunt Isabel?"

"Oh, not for the world."

"—or think it unwise?"

"Well, I should have to know a good deal more about it, before I could give you my views as to the wisdom of it. Why exactly are you doing it? Because you like it, or to make a living? Or both?"

"Both—and, oh well, there's a third reason."

I had often heard that kind of "Oh well" from young women on the stage. Evidently the expression is really used. It may have spread from the stage to normal conversation. Generally it is a prelude to an important line of thought.

"What is your third reason?" I asked.

"It's a bit difficult to explain to you," she began.

("It must be some kind of complex," I thought.)

"But I do feel," she went on, "that I can't only live for myself. I should like to feel that I am really doing something. Of course, you will say that I've been influenced by Ronnie. Perhaps I have, though I don't agree with him entirely. I know that a lot of what he says is simply undergraduate nonsense. But some of it sticks."

"You mean," I said, trying to make my voice sound amiable, "you want to do something for humanity in general?"

"That's putting it too priggishly, Aunt Isabel."

"I'm sorry. That's my fault. But it is rather what you mean, isn't it?"

"Yes, up to a point. It must be a good thing if there are more chickens and eggs in the world—and in England, especially—if we're going to have a war."

I agreed, though I forbore to tell her, that if such was her chief motive, she ought to join some large organisation where poultry farming is carried on with scientific economy. Being joint-boss with Mrs. Benson was indulging in a personal luxury of which she ought to have disapproved. But I hadn't the heart to make her be too logical.

"You feel," I said, "that the personal life—for your own spiritual and material gain, and that of your friends—is impossible. Yet most of the people whom we admire have lived it. This community-urge is quite a mushroom phase."

"What do you feel, Aunt Isabel?" she asked.

"Why should you suppose I have ever thought about such things?"

"Ronnie says you are dangerously intelligent."

"Why dangerously? Because I don't agree with him, I suppose. Well, I have thought about it, and, on the whole, I think his view is all nonsense. It would take me a long time to tell you why."

I paused, realising I had got to make some attempt at it, and she said, "I wish you would."

"I can only give you some of my reasons," I said. "Others will occur to me when I'm in bed to-night, or in my bath to-morrow morning. I shall be so eloquent to myself when you're not here—when you're flying over France to meet Mrs. Benson."

Her eyes lit up with joy at the thought of it.

"In the first place," I went on, "—and this is a piece of my inner philosophy, which I shall never be able to set down altogether in print—I don't see why anybody should have to 'justify his existence,' as the saying goes. We've been born without being consulted. It's for the universe to justify itself to me, not the other way round. In practice, of course, one compromises. But I won't waste time asking you to bother with this. There's my outer philosophy for you to deal with—the philosophy one has to invent when people like Ronnie—or you—say that the individual isn't automatically his own justification."

"Mind, I don't say that," she interrupted me.

"No, but I dare say you sometimes think it. And when you do, this is what I answer.

"It is a good thing for the world that people like me exist. Don't be shocked. I know one doesn't often hear people saying it, though I suspect they think it pretty often. It is a good thing for the world that people like me exist—even if we don't consciously go about trying to make the world a better place. It's a good thing that some people have the leisure to stand a little outside the struggle—developing a spirit of mellow and kindly scepticism with which to oppose cruel enthusiasms—developing standards of taste, which are, I believe, if not absolutely good, at any rate indications of an ideal. And we spread this kindly scepticism and these standards of taste—in dress and food and house decoration and art and manners—by just living our own lives and avoiding anything that savours of propaganda."

She laughed and said, "Tell that to someone with an empty stomach. I'm quoting Ronnie."

"I quite agree," I answered. "If my stomach were empty, I shouldn't think as I do. If I were in great bodily pain I shouldn't think as I do. We want to fill empty stomachs—and I gather they are being filled—but it doesn't follow that we must judge life only from that standpoint. After all, I may not have suffered from hunger, but I have from tooth-ache. At the time, I thought nothing else mattered but my tooth-ache, but when it was over I thought differently, and realised that my tooth-ache didn't justify a social revolution."

"But social revolution isn't a cure for tooth-ache."

"Nor is it, I'm afraid, for an empty stomach."

"Well, people differ over that."

"I know. And here's a concession. Don't tell Ronnie, but, up to a point, I'm prepared to give something away. I was going to say, before you broke in with your obvious comment, that if I believe anything, I believe that life must have a drawing-room if it's to be civilised. We've built up the drawing-room by centuries of struggle, and to destroy it, just because it doesn't hold everybody, is to my mind a reversion to savagery. I admit, we may have underrated the bathroom. (If you like, you can call the bathroom the needs of the community, and the drawing-room the needs of the individual—his sensual and æsthetic needs.) It may quite well turn out that the drawing-room has been too big and the bathroom too small. I dare say we can cut off part of the drawing-room and turn it into an extra bathroom and be all the better for it. But there's no point in having a bath, if there's no drawing-room to go into afterwards. A house without a drawing-room isn't a gentleman's house, and personally I don't want to live in it."

As if she had been taking me literally, she looked slowly round the room in which we were sitting, and said, "The trouble is, Aunt Isabel, that most people haven't got a drawing-room like yours."

"Good heavens!" I said, "it would be rather awful if our drawing-rooms were all alike. I haven't got one like Lady Mawnan's. (You remember, it was she who lent us her box at the opera to-night.) Happiness is relative after all. A great many people get as much thrill out of buying a new cheese-dish at the sixpenny bazaar as I do from buying a Rockingham china poodle, waving its little behind in the air. You'll see a pair of them on the mantelpiece over there. I love their insolent attitudes, don't you?"

She looked round painstakingly, and said, "I can't say they mean very much to me. But I think I'm following your argument. Happiness is relative—until you get to the empty stomach or tooth-ache level."

"Yes," I repeated, "it's relative. Only, there's this snag. Once you've bought a Rockingham poodle, you can't get any thrill from buying a sixpenny cheese-dish. The social revolution may not make anyone happy, but it's certainly going to make me miserable. So I prefer not to risk it."

"Ronnie would say that you're one of the few who should be sacrificed for the many."

"Why should you count by numbers in this way?"

She said nothing, and I went on: "You see, I believe that the happiness of one person is just as important as the happiness of a million people. The judge of importance is in each case one individual, and you can't multiply the individual, because—but I really am beginning to bore you now. Do you ever have this kind of conversation with Auntie Dora?"

"Oh no."

"I know the question sounded absurd. What I meant was, do you ever ask her what you've been asking me? Or does Ronnie?"

"Ronnie lets things slip out in front of her sometimes, but she doesn't seem to hear or understand."

"He doesn't bully her?"

I was glad to see that my question seemed to suggest a new train of thought to her. I wanted news from Carlice, though I was far from realising what news I was to receive.

"May I get another drink?" Joan asked me. "And can't I get you one, too?"

"Yes, do. Just a little gin with barley water and soda. And a ginger biscuit. Be careful of that syphon. It splutters. Shall I light the fire?"

I didn't want it myself, or I should have lit it before, but I suddenly thought Joan looked chilly. She was evidently going to tell me something, and I was anxious that she shouldn't hurry off to bed through feeling cold. I was prepared to sit up all night, if necessary, however cold the room. There are advantages in preferring luxury to comfort—which Ronnie says is one of my characteristics.

When Joan had settled herself again in her armchair, she said, "I wanted to talk to you about Auntie Dora to-night."

"Are you worried about her?"

"No—well, yes, a little. She's got so nervy."

"Do you think it's sheer boredom?"

"Why should she——"

"Well, she isn't like either of us. I shouldn't be bored living there. But from her point of view—— We were worried about her, you know, after your father died. Thomas Hill thought she'd never stick it, though I think she felt it was her duty to bring up you and Ronnie. How far has she become fond of the place, do you think, in these ten years?"

Again I found myself talking too much, in the hope of getting Joan to talk.

"I don't know if she's really fond of it at all," Joan said. "She likes her drawing-room"—we sniggered—"which she has had done up in that ghastly cretonne, or whatever it calls itself. But she'd really like something bijou and cosy and full of comfortable gadgets, not too far from the cinemas and the shops, with a pretty view of somebody else's geraniums."

"That's what I thought," I said. "Then I don't see any reason for her to be upset at the thought of any changes which may occur in September, when Ronnie comes of age, and takes possession. Not, of course, that he would necessarily want to get rid of her then."

"But she is upset about next September."

"About possibly having to leave?"

Joan laughed nervously. "It's really too silly," she said, "but I feel as if I were betraying Auntie Dora's confidence in telling you. And it's all rather painful, too."

"I'm sorry," I answered. "Has Dora really told you a secret? How long ago was that?"

"About a fortnight. She'd been very jumpy for a few days and I felt I ought to do something about it, just in case I could help. So I took special care to be sympathetic, and give her chances to open out to me, if that was what she needed. You know what I mean. Ronnie had gone back to Oxford, and we had the house to ourselves. In the end, it came out one night, when I was sitting with her in her drawing-room. She said quite suddenly, 'Joan, there's something I must tell you, but you're not to tell anyone else!'"

"Did you promise?" I asked.

"No, I didn't actually promise, though I dare say she thought I did. She was a long time nerving herself to tell me what the trouble was, and when she did tell me, it seemed so absurd, and yet, in a way, so nasty, that I didn't know what to say, except, 'I shouldn't worry, if I were you,' and that sort of useless stuff."

"What was it?"

She took a gulp at her drink, and went on, "It seems that a few days after Daddy died, Auntie Dora was going through his things and found a kind of tin box—quite a small one——"

"A cash-box, was it? About six inches long and, say, two or three deep?"

"Yes."

"I remember his buying it for a shilling on his tenth birthday, to keep treasures in. Go on."

"It was done up with string and sealing-wax, and had a label on it in Daddy's writing, saying, 'For my son Ronald Carlice. To be given to him on his twenty-first birthday.'"

"How very extraordinary! You say Auntie Dora found the box a few days after your father died. Where has it been since then? And why didn't she tell someone about it? No doubt you asked her that."

"Yes, I did. She says she has kept it locked up in the bottom drawer of her bureau. She opened the drawer and showed me the box. She seemed almost afraid to touch it, as if it might explode or contained a snake. 'If it's been worrying you,' I asked her, 'why ever didn't you show me it before? Or hand it over to the solicitors? Or let Aunt Isabel see it?'"

"How did she react to that suggestion?"

"Not very well, I'm afraid. She said that the box had obviously been put where she should find it, and that it was her responsibility to pass it on to Ronnie when he was twenty-one. I asked her if that was all that had been worrying her. Then she surprised me by saying, 'Well, wouldn't you think it enough to worry about, remembering everything?' In a way, I couldn't help agreeing."

I thought for a few moments before I spoke next, while Joan herself was silent, as if her talk with Dora had been a shock and she were feeling the shock of it again. There were so many things I wanted to know—things which Joan didn't know and probably had never thought of.

"In the first place," I said, "is there anything to show that this box was in any way connected with your father's death? He might have done it up years before, as a kind of joke. It may contain a present—the remains of a stamp-collection, or some sovereigns——"

"In that case, he was cheating the Estate Duty people."

"Nonsense. He never thought he was going to die, like that."

She looked at me indignantly, and said, "You must remember, Aunt Isabel, I was old enough to *know*. I wasn't like Ronnie."

"Oh!" I said, "I know you heard what the Coroner's verdict was. I meant that when your father tied and labelled this box, there's no need to suppose that he had anything—like that—in his mind. Was there a date on the label?"

"No."

"You see, you jumped to poor Dora's conclusion. She found the box just after your father had died, and assumed that it must be connected with his death. I don't see that at all."

"But if it were connected with his death—and Auntie Dora seemed quite sure that it was——"

"Why?"

"I—I don't know. I didn't ask her. I suppose I was a bit upset myself."

"That's very natural," I said soothingly. "I feel rather upset too. And you must remember that poor Auntie Dora was still more upset when she saw the box for the first time. The inquest only just over. It was quite natural that she should connect the box with your father's death. But she should have taken a more sensible view later. I wish you had told her that. Poor thing, the idea has probably become a mania with her. These secret worries can."

"I wish you had been there, Aunt Isabel."

"If I had, I don't think she would have told me."

Again I pondered, this time deciding what I intended not to say to Joan. Then she interrupted my thoughts by saying suddenly:

"Aunt Isabel, what do you really think is inside that box?"

"Quite probably, some sovereigns."

"It didn't rattle, and wasn't at all heavy."

"Or some stamps. Or perhaps a family heirloom. I believe we once had a letter from Queen Anne to some ancestor of ours, which seems to have disappeared."

"If it was something valuable, it ought to have been kept in a safe. Would Daddy have left it about like that—if he had been in his right mind?"

"I know what you're thinking of," I said. "You're going back to the Coroner's silly verdict. You must remember it was ten years ago and they didn't know then what the after-effects of influenza could be. It isn't a happy subject, but I think we ought to face it for a minute or two. There have been three famous suicides last year, all put down to 'flu. There was an opera singer, you may remember, a barrister and—who was the other one?—oh, a Bishop. In each case no known worry. I'm perfectly sure that if the inquest on your father were held now, the verdict would be 'suicide while the balance of his mind was disturbed by the after-effects of influenza.'"

"But he had such a slight attack."

"You mean he only had a slight temperature. It may, in other ways, have been a very severe attack. I'm sure it was."

"I know you're thinking that I'm worried in case there's insanity in the family. I'm not at all—so far as I'm concerned. And it isn't really what we were talking about. The point is, was it a sane action on Daddy's part to put something valuable into a flimsy little tin box and leave it about?"

"Not if it was something really valuable," I was forced to agree.

"Was it a sane action to put anything in a box and tie it up and address it like that?"

I admitted that it seemed rather fantastic, and she went on: "What I'm frightened of, and what I think Aunt Dora is frightened of, is that there's something in that box which is going to upset Ronnie. I'm quite prepared to believe with you that Daddy was perfectly sane till the balance of his mind was upset by influenza—but we can't get away from the fact that the balance of his mind *was* upset. And as the cash-box business is fantastic, to say the least of it, it seems almost a certainty that it dates from the 'unbalanced' period in Daddy's life—those two or three days before he died, when we were all at Leamington seeing Ronnie."

"Well—if it does?"

"If it does, there's no knowing what Daddy may have put into the cash-box. Suppose he told Ronnie that he had some hereditary disease——"

"But he hadn't anything of the sort."

"He may have thought he had. Or there may be something in the family which has been kept from you, Aunt Isabel."

There was nothing for me to do but to smile with grim incredulity at this. I was a little surprised to find how pertinacious Joan was, now that she was aroused. I had never thought her a fool, but she was revealing herself in a new light to me. My assumed scepticism had clearly provoked her, but I didn't want her to do anything dramatic—at all events, before I had evolved my own theory. For this reason I adopted a more conciliatory tone.

"I must admit," I said after a pause, "that it is puzzling and disturbing. What's the position now? Where is the box? Did Dora put it back in the drawer?"

"Yes. I told her to, and said I'd think what we ought to do. I suggested asking your advice, but——"

"But what?"

"It seemed to frighten her."

"And what did you say to her the next day—or when you'd thought things over?"

"I said she ought to open the box herself."

"What did she say to that?"

"She didn't want to talk about it at all. I couldn't even get the subject going. I think she regretted confiding in me. I suppose the attack of nerves, or whatever it was, had passed and she saw things differently. In the end, she said that there was plenty of time and that she'd probably speak to you about it, next time you came to Carlice. We just left it at that—on the understanding that I should do nothing and say nothing to you. I shouldn't have, perhaps, but I'm worried about Ronnie and the shock he may get, if she suddenly produces the box on his twenty-first birthday. I'm afraid Auntie Dora doesn't count, compared with him."

"But Ronnie is such a very modern young man. Even if it is a guilty secret of your father's, Ronnie isn't likely to be upset much."

"You think he knows——"

"He must, by now."

"I don't see why. You did everything you could to prevent his knowing. You were splendid. And he's never given the smallest sign to me."

"Probably because he thinks you don't know."

"You know, he's really terribly highly strung."

"Still? I thought his new political creed forbade that luxury."

She looked at me with anger, and then, thinking better of it, she got up and kissed me inoffensively on the forehead.

"Good-night!" I said. "Sweet dreams, and a safe journey to-morrow."

Yes, to-morrow she is flying across Europe. That ought to seem a great achievement to me, who have never flown at all. But it seems nothing. It would have been absurd for her to listen to Dora. I was quite right to urge her to fly.

But this mysterious box is another matter. I'll think that out to-morrow. When Joan comes back, she'll be so busy with Mrs. Benson and the poultry farm that it'll be left to me to decide what ought to be done. Perhaps the farm is a wise move after all. Poor girl. We need never try her out at the Opera again. But if she likes farming and finds peace that way. . . .

Chapter VI: RONALD CARLICE

THE cemetery. I *would* notice that to-day. I remember when I was coming up to Oxford to try for the scholarship which I didn't get, my house-master said, "The first thing you'll see of Oxford, as you arrive by train, will be the cemetery." What a paradox that seemed, as one entered the City of Dreaming Spires. The first thing—and the last thing as you leave the town.

I once had thoughts of being buried there. But we can't tell where we shall fall—least of all in these days—and they mayn't be able to bring one back, as they're bringing Joan back.

Poor Joan.

That's the bridge over the railway, leading up to Boar's Hill. Now Kennington with its villas. Perhaps we shall stop at Radley. What's the matter with me? It might be my last journey from Oxford to Didcot. I'm not even going down yet. There'll be time for all this attitudinising in another three weeks when I've taken Schools. And then I shall have to come up again for my *viva*. And my degree. I suppose I must have a degree. It'll be a nuisance paying for it. By the way, I'm now five hundred a year better off.

There isn't any conscious purpose in things. If there were, I should have gone, not Joan. She was always worth three of me. I couldn't release a bird from the strawberry nets. She used to do that. I couldn't climb a ladder. When Mildon cut his hand with a pruning-knife, I fainted. She bound it up and telephoned for the doctor.

Do these things count, or not?

I should have got her on my side, too, in the end. No, not really. I'm thinking about her differently because I shan't see her again.

A stupid accident on the way to the aerodrome. A collision with a lorry—not even an accident in the air. Two passengers slightly injured and only one killed—the head crushed by a heavy piece of metal. And that passenger was Joan.

I hope to God it was as quick as they say. But there are worse deaths—there are many worse deaths than that. We don't very often think that we've got to die. Quite right too. It's waste of time and makes us feel too important. How they loved death in the eighteenth century, with its urns and wreaths and cracked marble. It's all rather like one aspect of Carlice. Carlice must go. Somehow this business makes that more definite. I might almost tell them my decision after the funeral service, instead of letting them wait for my precious twenty-first birthday.

"This is the last funeral," I might say, "that'll be staged by our family from this house." They'd think me utterly heartless, and it wouldn't do any good. I suppose one may as well be kind rather than unkind, if unkindness doesn't serve any social purpose. There are times, of course, when one has to be unkind. It doesn't come easily. That's perhaps why we go about practising it—forging the social weapon. I must put that to Dan Cruttley. He'd laugh.

What I'm dreading, of course, is the thought of meeting them all.

I wonder if Aunt Isabel will arrive to-day or to-morrow. I hope to-morrow, though it means I shall have a night alone with Dora. Whenever Isabel arrives, she'll do the correct thing. Perhaps she'll escort a party. Is she conscious of being one stage nearer the ownership of Carlice? Probably. It's funny to think of myself as the one person in her way—till I'm twenty-one. After that, she's out of it, unless I forget to make a will. But I shan't forget.

Sir Thomas Hill will be there—not till to-morrow, I hope—and he'll bring his sister. And we shall have the pleasure of Gwen Rashdall's company, and the Callitons, those friends of father's whom we've never been able to shake off. And about two dozen "county" friends—Heaven preserve me from them. One or two of Joan's friends may have heard and want to come. Dora and I seem rather left out of it. Perhaps she'll have someone along, her co-trustee, Rusper, or the half-brother who's gone to the bad, or some of her "dreadfully common" London friends. Poor thing, I dare say she'll be nervous of standing alone. I shall be nervous too, and that won't help.

And now the train's stopping at Didcot, where I must change.

In the days when I was frightened of the world, and wanted to get home, home seemed to begin at Didcot. This was our own line, marking a safety-zone. Beyond it, by those other platforms which we're leaving, began the perilous unknown, containing everything that appalled me—school, my career, my death. What a thorough little egotist I was! No wonder I wasn't "converted" without tears. And still I backslide, and shall go on backsliding as people will, until we've remodelled the nursery and education. "Master Ronnie, won't you be glad to have a bedroom of your *own*?" It was my nurse, when she was moved out of my room. At the time, I didn't want her to go, and was frightened of sleeping alone. But I soon got over that and became proud of my *own* bedroom, already full of a jealous possessiveness, which, instead of eradicating, they rubbed in at every turn. "This little plot of garden shall be *yours*. I wonder what flowers *you* will grow, dear Ronnie." *My* stamp-album, *my* kitten, *my* cupboard which I could lock with my own key. And soon, perhaps, *my* house, in Gothic letters on the map, *my* garden, *my* fields and cottages. No, it won't do.

I think I can say I've nearly outgrown all that. But there are other pitfalls, and temptations which may be stronger than I bargain for. A tendency to have love-affairs—for instance last Tuesday afternoon. It hurts me to rationalise it like that, which shows my danger. I should like to go on mooning over Tuesday afternoon, as I mooned over it in bed on Tuesday night—till I found myself on my knees beside the bed and praying, "O God, grant I may never let Rose down." What a story that would be to tell to Brench—the most convincing atheist I know.

I know exactly what I was thinking of. I had raced ahead in my mind to my marriage with Rose—I was twenty-one and no one could stop me—and Rose was with me at Carlice settling things up and turning the place into a centre for social service. I became full of what we could do there together, then suddenly I wondered if she would see eye to eye with me about it all. Would she want her own drawing-room, for instance, or a bit of garden railed off, to sit in alone? And I pictured myself riding the high horse and telling her that that sort of thing had no place in our programme—

educating her and correcting the faults of her upbringing, and perhaps smiling over them to some of my clever friends. I saw in myself the failure of a husband. It hurt—exquisitely. I can use that overworked adverb, because there was a sort of *recherché* pleasure in my pain.

So I prayed, and got back to bed and felt happy again, and fell asleep dreaming about the afternoon. It was Dan Cruttley who had proposed the expedition. "I know a farm where we can get a decent tea," he said. "There are three streams round it, with willows. It's such a fine day, would you like to come if I can borrow Tony's car?" And later, as we drove through the flat fields north of Oxford, he told me that the farmer—a man named Cleetham—had two pretty daughters. The elder one, Marjorie, was just twenty, and the younger one, whose name he'd forgotten—yet what an easy name it is to remember!—was two years younger. He confessed that Marjorie interested him a good deal. He'd been to see her three times already that term, but there was nothing doing. He wasn't the first undergraduate she'd met. Last time she'd produced some poems by Day Lewis. She wouldn't say who had given them to her, but it would hardly be one of the locals. So the soil was already prepared for the planting of good seed.

We arrived, said how-do-you-do to Mrs. Cleetham, and Marjorie brought in tea. Had we heard of Auden? Yes, we told her, we had. And who'd been telling her, Cruttley asked, about Auden's work? She wouldn't say, but promised to walk in the woods with us after tea. Rose was in, if anyone else turned up.

Then Rose came into the room and bowled me over.

"You two go out for your walk," I said. "I'll stay here and look at the farm. Perhaps Rose will show me round, if she has time."

My boldness amazed me and exhilarated me. They seemed to notice nothing and went away gratefully, while I sat, looking down at my jammy plate, feeling all of a sudden as if the Infinite had stretched down a finger towards me, saying, "All this has been specially planned for you, Ronald Carlice."

And, for those hours, I did believe that it had been. Rose came and stood in the doorway smiling. I couldn't bring myself to interrupt that smile. "What would you like to see?" she asked. "The hens or the pigs? They're mowing in one of the fields, and I ought to take them some beer."

"Let me help with the hay," I said. "I know what you do."

"Have you lived on a farm?" she asked.

I told her that my home was surrounded by fields, and suddenly she seemed to become a part of Carlice, bringing new life to it and a new joy. I longed desperately to know if I should ever see her there.

We saw the hens and the pigs and joined in the haymaking. All that Rose said seemed natural and inevitable—neither too simple nor sophisticated. The leaves of the willows by the stream were greener for her presence, the hay was more golden and smelt sweeter. The men kept their distance, allowing us to do as we liked. Of one of them she said, "That's my brother over there." He was a huge fellow with a sunburnt chest. He made me feel puny and lamentably out of training. For the most part they were still mowing, and there was only one small field of hay ready to be stacked. That was why, perhaps, they didn't think us in the way. I asked if she had to do much work on the farm. She said she hadn't, except to help with the fowls. Teas paid better than farming. I asked if I could help her to wash up the tea-things, and she laughed and said, "Don't you think it's nicer out here?" So we stayed out, talking of nothing for a long time, till Cruttley and Marjorie waved to us from a bend in the stream and joined us.

"I suppose," Cruttley said, "we ought to be getting back."

"Why shouldn't we all have supper at the inn?" I suggested. "An early supper. Do you think your mother would mind?"

"We could ask her," Marjorie said.

We walked back to the farm. Mrs. Cleetham suddenly became an authority in my life—a being whom I must propitiate, a goddess.

"I don't see any harm in it, and it's very kind of these gentlemen, I'm sure," the goddess answered. "But you must be back by eight at the latest."

We assured her that we had to start back before eight.

The inn was only across the road from the farmhouse. We were shown into a kind of parlour. Marjorie giggled when Judith, her friend, began to lay the table. Rose said nothing, looking wide-eyed, like me, at the dark beams in the low ceiling. The windows

were small, and in that glimmering light the oldness of the wood
and its smooth but irregular surface seemed suddenly to acquire
a meaning for me, to carry me back to a quiet age before I or my
creed had come into being—an age when we were more closely
linked with the earth, and could still feel our kinship with it. And
this earth was our universe. No thought then of protons and elec-
trons. We were living in an age of magic, black as the oak, the
prey of forces that transcended us, yet impregnated us. It was a
most fantastic reverie. Humanity suddenly ceased to be an end,
and I myself became possessed of a dark force that was older than
mankind.

The mood lasted to our farewells to the two girls. Beyond my
saying, "I shall come and see you again soon," I don't know what
was said.

During the homeward journey Cruttley talked to me a little,
and I managed to reply. We said good-night and I went to bed still
full of ecstasy, and, thinking suddenly of Carlice, and how I would
bring Rose there, got out of bed and knelt down and prayed. "O
God, grant I may never let Rose down!"

Illusion.

And retribution came next day, with the telegram about Joan.
And here I am, in the train approaching Newbury, where the car
should be waiting for me. An extravagance this, because I could
have taken the slow train to Whitchurch.

2

James noticed I was wearing a pale green tie. Oh, I'll conform
all right, so far as I can. I haven't a morning coat, and won't commit
the folly of buying one. I've brought my black school suit with me
instead. It's a bit shiny and tight. If Joan were here, she'd manage
to find my black tie. I wonder if Dora has unearthed some black
for herself. But I'm forgetting, women can't suddenly wear something ten years old.

James is driving very slowly. We might be following a hearse.
Perhaps he really feels that this is a sorrowful journey. I ought to
be sitting in front, with him, instead of lolling in the back of the

car. Joan would have sat in front. So would my father. That shows I'm not really fitted to be a country squire.

If I can, I'll speak to Dora quietly and tell her what I intend to do. I'll tell her at once, quite frankly, that I may be marrying soon. I wonder how she'll take that. There was a time, after I'd been reading some French novels, when I wondered if she wasn't in love with me herself. I couldn't explain on any other grounds why she bothered about me so much, and was always so careful to see that I had little Benjamin's double portion. I underrated her sense of duty. Since my "conversion" I have tended to underrate the strength of middle-class sentiment.

I shall say that I may be marrying quite soon, and that, for this reason, it would relieve me if she could begin to make arrangements for her own future. And I shall tell her that even if I don't marry, I've no intention of living at Carlice as an exotic bachelor. Putting it bluntly, I shan't want Dora to keep house for me. After my birthday, of course. Till then, everything must go on as it has for the last ten years. It relieves me to think that the time till my birthday is so clearly mapped out. Schools, my *viva*, then a trip to Russia with Gievely and Brench. Then home, a few days before the great event. Then a meeting with my solicitors, who disgorge reluctantly, and I am free. Free, that is to say, to do what I ought to do—the only true freedom. As to this, Russia may clarify my mind. If I read myself aright, Russia will so convince me that I shall really take the plunge and put myself and Carlice at the disposal of the Communist party. This means losing more old friends, just as I've already lost Bunny Andrews. But it's a poor ideal that lets friendship stand in its way—or any other of the bourgeois virtues.

James drives more quickly now, like a horse with his nose turned to home. No doubt he wants his mid-day meal. As I do. "And when all physical needs are perfectly satisfied, what then?" That was the broadminded clergyman at our last meeting of the Labour Club. "Then," somebody said, "who knows, we may have the millennium. But they aren't satisfied yet, and you'll do more harm than good, Padre, by looking ahead too far." They reproach us on the score that our creed is materialistic. Yet we are formed of matter. My very feelings are matter—or if they're not (to quote the horrible old pun) they don't matter. They are irrelevant illusions, phantasms of escape from a reality you can't face. O harsh true creed!

I can say this, and yet know that I myself am the most pitiable prey of illusions. It only needs a fine afternoon in early June, a babbling brook studded with willow-trees, a pretty face, to make me forget all my doctrine, so laboriously acquired. A not unhealthy sign, some people might say. Illusions have a biological value, hence their origin. Yes, but if we *know* they're illusions, can we enjoy them? Can we let ourselves go? Isn't it precisely at such moments that one is most eager to convince oneself that here, at last, we are touching reality? Witness my absorption in the old oak beams of the pub, while Rose was sitting beside me, my certainty that the Infinite had me for once in His Mind. "This has been planned especially for you, Ronald Carlice." And later, my bedside prayer, "O God, grant that I may never let Rose down." I still blush at the thought of that prayer. I have prayed—or should have prayed, if I believed rationally in prayer—that I might never be false to what I knew to be right, that I might never let the party down. But never so instinctively, never so fervently. The truth is, I'm still hopelessly and utterly warped. I should start again, not on the first floor at Carlice, but in a communal crèche for children with no parents but the state. How they will laugh at me, these children of the future!

And I am weak enough to wish to add, "How, if they understood me, they could excuse me." But there won't be time for excuses, and why, anyway, should they bother to understand such a transient oddity as myself, while there are new metals to discover, new stars to weigh, new secrets in the electron to explore?

3

We have lived through luncheon, tea and dinner. Dora is wearing her black. When I came in, she made as if to kiss me and I wasn't quick enough to let her. She sniffles, this brilliant June day, as though she has got a cold. "Aunt Isabel will think the garden looking very lovely," she said. So it is, for those who like that sort of thing. I wandered round it after luncheon—a meal during which we said nothing to one another. The perennials are just reaching their climax, peonies in full flower, delphiniums growing while you wait, lupins covering the bank with massed spikes, iris-beds glittering in the heat-haze—and all the rest of the patter. And on the side of the house facing the drive, every blind has been tightly drawn down. Despite that—or was it because of that?—I had an impulse, after luncheon, to take that walk which we used grandiloquently to call the Big Circle—through the park by Herbert's field and Wicken's farm, across three fields, through a wood, out into the fields again past Mildon's cottage, through the spinney and into the Park again, approaching the garden through the lovers' walk. The hay was only half mown. They have stopped work, I supposed, in Joan's honour.

I walked slowly, wishing to be away from the house as long as I could, and glad to find that I felt no vestige of proprietary pride. Even the little memories that came up—here the site of a "fortress" that we built when I was twelve, this bank where, one year, five robins nested, the ditch into whose muddy water I fell one Christmas Day—meant little to me. I might have been reading about them in a prolix novel—one of those old-fashioned narratives which assume that small events, occurring to small personalities, are worthy of record. I was far more concerned with what lay before me—with bracing myself to face to-morrow's ceremony and to-morrow's company. Aunt Isabel doesn't come here till to-morrow. She is staying in London, supervising, by telephone, the arrival of Joan's body. I ought to have done that—if it really had to be done.

I came in late for tea. Dora insisted on having another pot made for me. I sat with her half an hour when they had cleared away. Small talk mostly, but she did say, "I begged her not to fly. She said she would ask Aunt Isabel what she thought." I answered, "But of course Aunt Isabel would tell her to fly. It was the sensible thing to do, if she could afford it." I had the feeling that, despite this accident, Aunt Isabel would tell me to fly to Russia, if it were possible. I ought to admire her for it.

Then I went out into the garden and read one of my textbooks for Schools. I had suggested that we needn't dress for dinner. Eames interrupted me three times by calling me to the telephone—two tedious condolences, and a message from Aunt Isabel, to say that

there was no hitch in her arrangements. Joan's body would arrive
to time. Isabel was sweet and kind, but I felt slightly sick after
talking to her. Then as I was going to wash, the undertaker called,
and asked me questions I couldn't answer. In the end, I gave him
Aunt Isabel's telephone number, and told him to ring her up, and
do as she said. It seemed a little unfair.

I don't think I've ever dared not to dress for dinner at home
before. What a confession! Eames didn't seem, however, to disapprove. Perhaps he regarded my day-clothes as part of the ritual.
I had found a black tie among my worn-out socks, and put it on.
Aunt Dora had altered her dress a little, but was still in black. I
wondered what finery she was cherishing for to-morrow. After
dinner, I took coffee with her in the morning-room. We sat in two
big chairs, either side of the gunroom door. I studied the carving,
scroll by scroll, wondering if it had any beauty. She studied her
foot, which tapped irritatingly on the carpet.

"Ronnie!" she said suddenly in a peculiar voice. And then, not
quite knowing what I was saying, I burst out:

"Auntie Dora, I have been wanting to talk to you for some time."

She looked at me like a frightened hen, her head on one side.

"You know I'm twenty-one on September the eighth," I went
on. "We both know what's to happen then. Well, I'm afraid it isn't
going to be quite as my father intended."

She looked so scared, that I hurried on with, "I mean, when I
come into the place, I shan't just live here as he lived here. I shall
use it for some political purpose I think important. If I marry—
and I have met someone, as a matter of fact—Aunt Isabel wouldn't
approve and I dare say you wouldn't——"

Here she broke in with, "Oh, Ronnie, I do hope you'll be happy."

Her eyes filled with embarrassing tears.

"I don't expect to be happy," I said. "It isn't what I'm here for."

Bunny Andrews would have pulled me to pieces over that
remark, but Dora only sat dangerously still, as if she were waiting
for some frightful news. Then the sunset struck my face, and I
moved to another chair, where she couldn't see me, unless she
altered her attitude.

"Whether I marry or not," I continued, "I don't want this house
to go on any longer in the old way—surviving, like a period-piece,

from an age which had different social values. In other words—I hate to say it, Auntie Dora—this house will be no place for you. I do hope that doesn't upset you very much."

I paused with conscious feebleness. She drew herself together, as if in desperate search for a dignity which made her slightly ridiculous, and said, "Oh, but of course, I've been expecting that. I've never thought I should always be wanted here."

I almost demurred at the word "wanted," but thought better of it. Our conversation might too easily slip on to a sentimental plane, full of endearments and veiled reproach.

Instead, I said, "I think it's been frightfully good of you to stick it for ten years. I've never imagined this house meant much to you."

For a moment she wondered how to take that. Then she said, "It *was* my duty to stay to begin with, wasn't it?"

"Well, yes. Some people might think so. Others might have said you were rather wasting your life. I don't want you to waste it any more."

(Why couldn't the woman say she'd be glad to go?)

"It has been dull," she said meditatively. "I had thought, during the last two or three years, specially after Joan gave up farming and came home again, of moving to London. Then I shouldn't have been in Joan's way, or in your way, and I should have been leading the kind of life I suppose I was intended for. Is that what you mean by 'not wasting my life'? I dare say it isn't, but it doesn't matter. But I felt somehow I ought to stay the time out. You may understand better some day——"

To my horror she dabbed at her eyes with an inanely small handkerchief.

"I know, and Joan knew," I said uncomfortably, "that you've been very good and kind to us the whole time. Just think what frightful rows we should have had if Aunt Isabel had taken your place here. She'd have driven us out—or we should have murdered her——"

Then an awful thing happened. Dora broke down into roaring tears and said, "She's murdered Joan. She's murdered Joan."

I got up, went over to her chair and uttered platitude after platitude. "You mustn't say things like this. You really mustn't. It's all my fault for starting this conversation to-night of all nights. But I thought it was such a good opportunity. Auntie Dora, do pull yourself together. It makes me so wretched." And so on.

While I spoke, she murmured incoherently about Aunt Isabel and me and having something to say to me, but she couldn't say it then. It was a real scene. I patted her hand mechanically, fearing that Eames would come in to draw the curtains. In the end, I did say, "Auntie Dora, I'm sure I hear Eames in the hall." A lucky remark; for she dried her eyes at once and said she would go to bed. I told her that I should also go to bed early, but would take one turn in the garden first. And I said good-night, and added—out of sheer weakness—"Please do forget what I've said to-night, if it hurts you." She looked at me with surprise and said, "Oh, Ronnie, it isn't that."

For a moment I thought she was going to have another attack of hysteria, but then Eames really did come in, and we both scuttled away like rabbits—she into the hall and I through the French window out into the garden, where the real rabbits scuttled away at my approach.

And so we have lived through lunch and tea and dinner. We've still got to live through to-morrow. To-morrow I shall come down late and work myself up into a whirl of inefficiency, concentrating on the arrangements and getting them all wrong, always being in the way and never to be found when I'm wanted, disappearing when I ought to be saying good-bye to someone and going to fetch more sherry without having the cellar-key. Do I tip the under-takers? Or does somebody do it for me? Or isn't it my place to do it at all, as I'm still a minor?

I don't understand how people get through these things and cope with all the paraphernalia of gentility. Perhaps my poli-tics have something to do with this incompetence of mine—this shrinking. "Poor Ronnie, he's so hopeless in a crisis." But this isn't a real crisis. It's only make-believe—a pandering to a superannu-ated code. I would have stopped it if I could, but they took it out of my hands. Well, let them see to it. This show is their last chance here—the last of the big parades from Carlice Abbey.

If Joan were here, she'd laugh and agree with me.

Chapter VII: DORA CARLICE

THE house is very full of noises to-night. That must be a big moth flapping over there by the window. Tan has clumped downstairs again. Whatever for? Why can't he settle in his basket? Poor Tan, if I do get a little flat, how he will hate it. But Ronnie won't want him, and he seems to think he belongs to me. I suppose that's because I'm here nearly all the time.

That noise didn't come from the stairs. That was the morning-room, or even the gunroom. I used to think you couldn't hear noises in old houses, but you can. We had noises in Elmcroft, of course, but they were different. You knew what and where they were. There is one thing, this furniture doesn't creak. I suppose it's too old. The dressing-table I chose for my twenty-first birthday present used to scare me terribly at Elmcroft, till I found out that it was the fitting of the mirror. Cheap new wood. I wonder who's got that dressing-table now. It fetched twenty-six shillings in the sale, and Daddy paid eighteen pounds. It just shows you.

It's silly to think we're going to be burgled, just because it's after midnight. We were burgled once here, and it happened when the house was full of people, all dressing for dinner. And our two burglaries at Elmcroft weren't at night either. One was in the morning, about ten o'clock, and the other—if you can call it a burglary—he just ran in and took the silver tray from the hall-table—at three in the afternoon. The silly maid had left the front door open.

I shall never get to sleep if I go on thinking like this. But I can't stop thinking. And reading seems to tire my eyes now. I suppose I ought to see an oculist and get glasses. Oh dear! The things one has to do as one gets older. And I ought to go to the dentist again soon. I know he'll want me to have those two out, and begin hinting at a small plate which will screw my mouth into a funny shape. I wish I hadn't such a tiny mouth. There's no advantage in it, and people don't admire them nowadays.

Perhaps the reason I've been sleeping badly is because I take a

nap in the afternoon. But I feel so sleepy after lunch. I can't help
dozing off. And I like it. When I'm alone here, there's nothing to
do but go to bed early. But even when I'm not alone and go to
bed late I often don't sleep either. Would it be any good seeing a
doctor, I wonder? He'd only give me some feeble little powders
and say I ought to have a change of air.

They can't help you with nerves. You've got to fight them alone.
I must be getting to a nervy age. I've been feeling lately that I was
in for a crisis—that some crash is bound to come soon. Well, there
will be a crash—when Ronnie's twenty-one, the month after next.
I don't care if there is. I've gone over all that so many times, there's
no use going over it again to-night.

There's Tan again. Was that a growl he gave? It couldn't be.
That would mean he's heard something. People have often asked
me if I wasn't afraid of sleeping here alone, and I always laughed
and said I wasn't. That was untrue. I used to be terribly afraid, after
Claude——, but then I got used to it. And when Tan was given to
Ronnie six years ago and he slept up here, I didn't think I should
ever be bothered again.

I shan't get off to sleep at this rate. It really would be better to
get up and see if there's anyone about. I know what I'm thinking
of really, but I won't give in to it. I've settled all that, come what
may. I shall simply say, "Here you are, Ronnie," give him the box
and have my suitcases brought down. When I've done that, I
needn't see any of them again.

Only one more week here, thank God, before my cruise to
the Northern Capitals. That ought to do me good. I'll have dancing lessons on board. And play all the deck-games. We'll have a
splendid time. When she's in the right mood, Dolly Headford is an
awfully good companion. Perhaps I'll be able to decide whether I
could share a flat with her, though I don't think it would answer,
really. I've got too accustomed to having a place of my own—well,
not my own exactly—but it certainly gives me a good deal of space
to myself. I shall miss all these drawers and cupboards. But that's
about all. Of course, it's nice to have the garden to walk in, but
that's never been my own. That belongs to Isabel. I've always felt
it's kept up for her benefit. I wonder what she'll say if Ronnie does

as he threatened, and turns the place into—what was it?—a political school. She won't like that at all. But he doesn't care what she likes. I really think he would take my side against her. I don't know, though. Blood does tell. It's no use counting on him.

I won't stay here for them to hiss me out of the house. I'll be gone before they can do it, bag and baggage. I needn't meet them or their set ever again. There, I'm hammering away at it once more. Well, I've got to go through with it. Even if I don't sleep to-night, I can rest all to-morrow. I've nothing to do to-morrow. Oh, yes, Miss Eagre, about the church fête—but I can put her off. It's funny how these moods take me, and how differently you feel about the same thing at different times. Until this year, that box seemed nothing to worry about. Well, this year seemed so far off. Ronnie seemed to go on being at school for ever. When he first went up to Oxford, it did give me rather a turn. It showed time was passing. But even then, you didn't think of him as ever being twenty-one. No, I've been much worse lately. Not so bad as at first, of course. My word, I did go through it then! I ought to have talked to somebody, but I just couldn't. The damp hand on the landing, that's what did it.

Before that visit to Leamington, ten years ago, how lovely and simple life seemed. Of course, I was ten years younger. I'd had my love-affair. Was that wrong, as I knew I couldn't have a baby? Whether it was wrong or not, I'd had it, and it was over without anything terrible happening. Of course, I was melancholy at the thought of its being over. It was the day of my father's funeral that I knew, really, that it was ended. But it was an easy, pleasant kind of sadness, as I see it now—something romantic to look back upon, not shattering to the nerves like what happened later. I remember that as we were going to Leamington, while Isabel, oh, so carefully, was giving me advice as to how to behave when I saw Ronnie at school, I was thinking to myself, "Now, Dora, you've had your fling. You must settle down—for a good while, anyhow. You've learnt a lot lately, and you must use it properly. You've got a nice husband and a lovely home. You must live up to your position and make something of it for yourself. Settle down, be a good wife, and take your proper place." I was thinking like that even during the Sunday afternoon when Ronnie and his friend came to see us in our hotel, and let off those smelly fireworks and ruined the drawing-room grate. I was thinking like that when they'd gone and the page-boy came in and said I was wanted for a trunk call. And then—the tone of Eames' voice was enough to break me up. I knew in a flash that it wasn't an ordinary accident—that it was something which *I* should have to pay for. That's why I sent Joan running for Isabel, and nearly collapsed when the telephone call was over. I remember Isabel saying, "If you faint, I shan't come with you." I suppose she meant to be kind. After all, it was her own brother. But I thought, "You poor fool! You don't know what I know."

What an awful journey back we had together, with Joan crying and asking awkward questions, and Isabel being so considerate to me. Then those long talks with the solicitors and the doctors and the police-inspector, and those newspaper men. I don't know how I lived through it. Then the inquest. And the night of the inquest— it was before dinner, I think—I couldn't stay downstairs with Isabel any longer, and came up to my room—it had been Claude's and my room—and began to go through Claude's things, in case they were untidy when the Probate people came. I hadn't the heart to go to his dressing-room where he kept things he usually wore, but I thought I'd look through the tallboy of his in here, where he kept his overflow stuff. And there I found the box, in the bottom drawer where he kept his old tennis clothes. I remember seeing the tennis clothes made me cry. It reminded me so of the time I first met him at the Grangeleigh tournament, and of all the games we had together that year, and the thrill of staying here for the first time. There the box was, humping up a pile of flannel shirts, a kind they don't often wear now. What's this, I wondered? As I took it out, I thought it must contain old studs, or broken links or the bits of whale-bone he stiffened his best collars with. Then I read the label: "For my son Ronald Carlice. To be given to him on his twenty-first birthday." The writing was Claude's, rather more spidery than usual. And I read the date too: "November 7th, 1926"—the day we left for Leamington and two days before Claude's death.

At first I was just frightened without knowing why. I put the box in a drawer full of my own things and locked it up. It was not till the middle of dinner that it dawned on me what the box really meant. I felt suddenly sick and asked them to excuse me, and went to lie down upstairs. I knew now that I'd been right in thinking that Claude had killed himself because he had found out about me and Don Rusper. The box was his punishment for me, and he'd put it where I should find it, or at any rate where someone would find it and tell me about it. On the other hand, I thought, if he was so sure that I should understand what he meant, how could he be sure I shouldn't destroy the hateful thing? I could take it to London and drop it into the Thames, or go to France and drop it over the side of the steamer. Would it have floated and followed me round the world? Or I could open it—and really see——

The idea of opening it didn't come to me till Isabel and Joan had been up to say good-night to me, urging me to have the doctor and hoping I was better and so on. When they had left me, and I felt safely alone, I got up and took the box out of its hiding-place and looked at it for about an hour. I must have read the label, and the date, a hundred times. I felt Claude was there, watching me and daring me to open the box or destroy it. And I couldn't do either. But some extraordinary instinct made me tear off the date, and burn it in the ashtray by my bed. It was ever so neatly written, "7.xi.26," right in the top corner, away from the rest of the writing. I don't suppose I had to tear off more than an inch by half an inch. In any case, the label was an old one and ragged at the edges. No one, except a detective, would have known. And if anyone saw the box he would have thought that the label had been written at any time—perhaps when Ronnie was born, before Claude had ever heard of me. There was no outward connection, once the date had gone, between the box and Claude's death—no connection between the box and me. That is to say, until the box was opened.

Why didn't I open it that night, and find out the worst? I was too upset and too frightened. I put it in the drawer where I kept my jewels and locked the drawer.

I didn't have any dreams that night. It was the next night, when Isabel was already talking of going back to her London house, that I had the dream.

I dreamt that Claude and I were in our bedroom, but instead of being in bed we were in two coffins, side by side. I knew his mouth and face were shattered by the wound and felt I couldn't bear to see him. If I counted a hundred before he spoke, I knew that he couldn't speak or look at me. I got to eighty-seven, when he suddenly said, "Dora, you've found that box!" I said, "Yes," and he went on, "And you've begun to destroy it. You've torn the date off the corner of the label. That's as far as you'll go. Swear that you'll go no farther." I said nothing, and then, very slowly he got up—or rather, the coffin he was in stood slowly up on its end and turned round towards me. "You will swear," he said, "or I shall make love to you." His face was jagged and bleeding, and his thin little moustache was dripping blood. A drop fell on my face as he leant over me in his coffin. I tried to put up my hands, but they wouldn't move. "You'll swear," he said, still closer to me, "to guard this box till Ronnie's twenty-one, and to give it to him yourself." I said nothing, and Claude's coffin slowly lowered itself towards mine till it was only six inches away. Then it moved back a little, and Claude said, "I shall do this three times, but the third time my coffin will rest on yours. They fit exactly, and you'll never escape again. The worms in me are longing to eat you." As he spoke, a horrible black worm with one yellow eye came out of Claude's mouth and dangled over my breast. "That's what I mean by love-making," he said. Then I shut my eyes and swore, time after time, eighty-seven times, without knowing what I was swearing, and Claude's coffin stood upright again and Claude said, "I've got your oath, here. If you break it, I'll come again. Beware the damp hand on the landing as you turn out the light by your bedroom door. The damp hand over yours. . . ." Then I don't know what happened.

When I was nineteen I read *Dracula* all one night at Elmcroft, and the book became a mania with me. By day, it didn't bother me at all. I went about in the ordinary way, and even laughed at the story when I thought of it. But at night I felt quite different and would lie still in bed, listening for the flapping of a bat's wings against my window-pane. I was afraid to sleep in case the vampire broke in and sucked my blood. After about a week, Daddy noticed that I was looking ill and dragged it all out of me. He gave me a long talking to in his consulting-room and made me feel such a silly little fool that I was cured.

But I daren't talk to anyone about my dream of Claude. It gripped me like *Dracula*. In the daytime, I thought very little about it, but every night, when I went to bed, I hardly dared go to sleep for fear of dreaming it again. I did dream something of the kind again, but not so vividly as the first time. And then came the evening when Isabel went back to London. Joan had returned to her school and I was alone in the house, except for the servants. When I went to bed and turned out the landing light, I distinctly felt a damp hand closing softly over mine. It passed in a flash, but I went to my jewel-drawer, took out the box and went downstairs with it and put it in the bottom drawer of my writing-desk in the drawing-room, and hid it under a large piece of embroidery that I'd begun when I was expecting my baby, and knew I should never finish. I didn't make any actual vows, as I put the box there, but I felt somehow committed to guarding it and carrying out the instructions on the label.

Then gradually life became normal and cheerful again. It went on, and nothing terrible seemed to happen. Nice things even began to happen. I went to London for a few days and saw some of my friends, the shops and the shows. Friends began to come to Carlice. Major Inchley and his sister took me to the races—a lovely day, I remember. I got three winners. I began to get the hang of running the house. I saw to it that Joan had pretty dresses and that Ronnie had all the things he needed for school. He began to bring his school-friends back here, and Joan brought hers sometimes. A year went by, and another and another. You can't go on worrying about anything for ever. I began to forget about 1926 and all its troubles. They'd come back at night sometimes, if I was nervy or out of sorts, but by day they disappeared completely. I was able to look in the bottom drawer of my writing-desk and make sure the box was still there without upsetting myself.

"Oh, I'll give it to Ronnie all right," I used to say to myself, "but I really can't bother my head now about what's inside it. There are still—seven, six, five, four—years to go before I've got to do anything. And even if Claude did leave a writing behind telling Ronnie that he killed himself because of my love-affair with Don, what could any of them do? What would they want to do? It would be so long after Claude's death. Isabel might be dead by then. So might I, or even Ronnie."

And so on, except for little passing bursts of worry, till Ronnie's last birthday—when he was twenty, and there was such a lot of talk of his next birthday, and guessing as to what would happen then. At Isabel's suggestion, I had asked some of our neighbours in—"Ronnie ought to be getting to know them," she said—and I imagined them saying things about me when my back was turned and wondering what I'd do. As luck would have it, there was a big scandal in the papers round that time. Some woman was supposed to have been got hold of by a negro in a London night-club and her husband made an awful scene and smashed the place up. Most of the people I had invited to Ronnie's birthday party knew the husband fairly well, as he used to visit one of the big houses in our neighbourhood. For nearly the whole of dinner, I had to listen to our men guests saying that he must have been a poorer creature than they'd supposed, ever to let his wife start such a beastly business, while the women guests blamed the wife and said they'd never liked her. And all the time both the women and the men were enjoying it.

I felt quite sick when I got to bed that night. "In another year," I thought, "they'll all be talking about me like that, and Joan and Ronnie will have to bear it. And how Isabel will hate me!"

I went over everything again, making my part out to be as bad as I could. *"And while her father was dying!"* It had never occurred to me before that my father's illness made it worse, but I invented that little sentence and every time I put it into our friends' mouths it sounded worse. *"And while her father was dying!"* I fitted it to each of their voices in turn. And I began to think that I shouldn't only have to leave Carlice in a hurry—I was already more or less prepared for that—but that even my London friends wouldn't have anything more to do with me, and that nobody would want to know me once they knew who I was. Even emigrating might be no use. My story would follow me.

Then for some weeks I got back my old calm. What did it matter if people did talk about me? It needed more than anything I'd done to shock people nowadays. I might be pointed at for a week or so, but then I'd be allowed to live in peace. (And it was all so unjust —to be punished for what had happened ten years before. It was like being punished for a sin committed in a previous life.)

I reminded myself of the stories I used to hear of the gay days before the war, all the scandals about grand country-house parties and the intrigues that went on. Nobody seemed to mind very much what happened then. Why should we all be so much more prudish now?

(But it's I who am prudish really. It is I who am shocked with myself. That's why I did so frightfully enjoy my love-affair with Don—my love-affair—*while my father was dying*.)

I've thought this over so often, and given myself so many different answers to the same questions. But I've been getting worse lately. Each month that goes by makes me worse. And I've got a new fear—a more sensible one, I dare say some people would think. It's the fear that I shall get so worked up suddenly, that I shall do something really silly—tell the whole story in public, or have hysterics as I nearly did with Ronnie, the night before Joan's funeral.

There are times when you feel you can't go on any longer, when there are too many things against you, each one getting you down just when you've begun to recover from the last. I *did* nerve myself to speak to Joan. I'd decided some time ago that she was the only person I could possibly talk to, if ever a time came when I felt I simply must talk to somebody. Don, of course, is the obvious person, but for some reason it's utterly impossible for me to talk to him. If it was to be anyone, it was Joan. And I did speak to her and show her the box. She touched it with her own hands and saw where I kept it.

I thought, that evening, that somehow she'd take the responsibility from me—break the box open, perhaps, or throw it away. But she didn't. She didn't know what to make of it. (Why couldn't she have guessed what must be inside it?) She was very kind and told me not to worry, but beyond that she didn't help at all.

Still I had talked to her. I had broken the ice. If ever I felt too wretched, I could talk to her again—straight out, with no beating about the bush. "Joan, dear," I could have said, "I'm afraid I'm still very worried. You know what about." And sooner or later she would have taken the lead. I could have forced her into taking it. She'd have dragged the whole story out of me and been bound to forgive me and to help. I could have made her an ally, and I counted on her.

And then she says she must fly to France to meet Mrs. Benson's boat. I begged her not to. I was frightened of what might happen to her—for my sake, I'm afraid, more than for hers. She said she'd ask Isabel, and I might have known that Isabel would go against me—and do it, as she always does, by seeming to be ever so sensible and rational. Isabel said "Fly," and Joan set out for the aerodrome and was killed on the way. Of course, she might have been killed anyhow. There might have been an accident to her taxi on the way to Victoria, if she'd done as I wanted, and gone by train and boat. There might—but there wouldn't have been. She'd have been alive in England now, and I could have gone over any day to see her at her farm, or asked her to come over here and see me. And sooner or later she'd have found a way out of all my troubles.

Perhaps it was Claude, taking revenge on me—and sending another warning. Oh, God, how awful! I hadn't looked at it like that before. This rather stuns me. . . .

I can't go on lying here doing nothing but think, think, think. I'll get up and walk about the room—or go out on the landing and talk to Tan—or go down to the drawing-room and take out the wretched box, and smash it open. That's a new idea! Quick, before I think about it too much, and find I can't do it. There'll be no damp hand if I leave the landing light on all night. I spoke to Flora yesterday about leaving the stillroom light on. Well, I don't care. Fancy thinking of that now.

There. I'll leave my bedroom light burning—and now the switch on the landing. I don't care if something does touch me. I don't care. I don't care. It'll only be like a smelly sponge, if it does. There you are. There's the landing a blaze of light for you. Those shades need cleaning. The flies have made them filthy. The maids have been getting slack lately. I suppose it's really my fault.

"All right, Tan, dear little doggie. Where have you been, prowling about the house at this hour of the night? Come along then, and pad downstairs with Auntie Dora. Auntie Dora's going into the drawing-room, and you shall come too and see what Auntie Dora's going to do. Come, Tan."

And now I've forgotten the key of the drawer. Fool that I am. I was thinking so much about the landing light. Come, Tan, Auntie Dora must go upstairs again. She's forgotten her key. No, it isn't bedtime yet. We've lots to do before bedtime. There now, Tan, up we go again. . . . Down we go again, right through the hall—your Aunt Isabel's hall—*she* spent the money on having it made historical again—and into the drawing-room, which, as you know, is your Auntie Dora's room. . . ."

It isn't here. It's gone.

There's the piece of embroidery and all that mess of tangled wool. Eight kinds of pink you needed for that big rose to get the proper shading. It was the rose that finished me. I hadn't the patience to go on with it.

And the box was here, underneath. I've kept it here for nearly ten years. It must be here. No, that's the box of old photographs from Elmcroft. And that's more wool which I never unwrapped even. But Claude's box isn't here.

I must be mad. I must have been so excited after showing it to Joan that I put it back in the wrong drawer. Perhaps the drawer above. But it couldn't be there. I put an old cheque-book in there yesterday. No, of course it isn't there. It was hardly worth looking to see.

Oh, what shall I do? Where else shall I look? What shall I do if I never find it? Oh, Tan, tell me what I ought to do now.

Let me see. Joan looked at the label—she didn't notice I'd torn the date off—and felt the box to see how heavy it was. Then she gave it back to me, and said, "Put it away now, Auntie Dora. It's upsetting you too much. Do put it away." She saw me put it away, underneath the piece of embroidery with the half-finished pink rose. She saw me lock the drawer with this key, and put the key in my bag.

That was, how many days before she went to London and got killed? Monday to Monday, Tuesday, nine days. She was here nine days, knowing all about it. I was hoping she'd speak to me about it again, or persuade me to tell her more. But she didn't. Except once, and then I felt I couldn't bear to talk to her. She seemed to forget about it. She was so full of meeting Mrs. Benson again. She thought of nothing but that journey to the South of France, and writing to the aeroplane people. She hardly mentioned Ronnie or her family—or this house. If she'd opened the box and found out what was in it, she couldn't have been so detached like that. She would have been bound to speak to me, or let me know, somehow, that she'd had a shock. And if, by any chance, contrary to what I've always believed, the box contained something quite harmless— something that had no connection with me—love-letters written to Claude by Ronnie's mother, for instance—Joan would have been bound to tell me, so as to relieve my mind. There was nothing nasty about Joan, poor girl.

Suppose she took the box, intending to open it later—when she'd come back from her trip to France. Then I should have seen it among her things, when I had to sort them out for the Probate people. I should have found it in her room, just as I first found it in Claude's and my bedroom. The awful thing! It always seems to be connected with death. But I didn't find it in Joan's room, and I went through everything she had—even her locked cupboard. Almost any key fitted that cupboard, just as, I suppose, almost any key would fit my drawer. I ought to have kept the box in a safe, but I never thought anyone would rummage through my writing-desk.

Suppose Joan took the box and simply destroyed it without opening it—for my sake, and perhaps for Ronnie's, too, in case there was anything inside it which would hurt him too much. She might have done that. It would have been rather a fine thing to do. But surely she'd have told me. She'd have said, "Auntie Dora, it's no use your worrying yourself any more about that box. I've——" How could she destroy it, though? At one time, in the early days, I used to wonder about that. I could only think of throwing it into the sea. And then it might have floated and been washed ashore, and picked up by some busy-body on the beach. Joan might have found another way. But she'd have told me. She seemed quite distressed to think I was so worried.

She was a dear kind girl, and she must have liked me more than I thought she did, leaving me her pearls and those two rings of her mother's. I wonder if I could afford to have the stones reset. If I had the little diamonds clustered round the sapphire it would be very effective.

"Tan, don't scratch. The box has gone, Tan, and Auntie Dora doesn't know what to do."

There's no use staying here. I must go to bed. Somehow, I feel much better. Isn't it extraordinary how differently you can feel about the same thing at different times? I can't do anything more, and I'm not responsible any longer. I don't care where the box is. I don't care who has it. If I'm blackmailed, I won't pay one single penny. I've done what I could to carry out Claude's wishes. He must see to it now. It's no use his bothering me any more about it.

(But when Ronnie is twenty-one, oughtn't I to say, "Ronnie, there *was* a box——" and he would ask me if I had any idea what was in it, and without lying I couldn't say I hadn't any idea. And so I shall start the whole thing over again.)

But not to-night. I'm too tired to worry any more to-night.

"Come, Tan, your Auntie Dora's going to bed again. And doggie should be sleeping in his basket, or he'll be too tired to go rabbiting with Auntie Dora to-morrow. There's a rabbit among the phloxes you've got to find. Come, doggie, upstairs. That's right. Now go to your basket. It'll be daylight very soon, but Auntie Dora is going to have a nice long sleep, with breakfast in bed to-morrow morning. Good-night, Tan. . . ."

I turned out the landing light without a thought of the damp hand. That's better. Much better. And soon I shall be away on a nice long cruise. I'll learn all the modern dances. . . .

Chapter VIII: STEPHEN PAYNE

L EAVING Thurlow-on-Sea, even though on a pleasant errand, reminded me somehow of leaving home for the front. My last days at Thurlow were like my last days of leave. My war-neurosis increased formidably. I began to relive the twenty-one-year-old past with new vividness. Twenty-one years ago to-day, I kept thinking, we left those horrid little huts at Merville, and moved to the line near Laventie. Twenty-one years ago to-day, I was first machine-gunned by an aeroplane. Twenty-one years ago to-morrow will be the day when I ought to have been shot—when I skulked, trembling and sweating in a big shell-hole, and left my platoon to look after itself for an hour. And Sergeant Ledward had his head blown off.

We left Thurlow early in the morning—the Hicksons wanted to be in London well before lunch. It was a bright day, like to-day. A heat-haze was preparing to steam up from the asphalt promenade, and there was a slight mist over the sea. We turned inland, and the fishy smell of the narrow streets, through which one has to go to reach the London road, filled me with nostalgia. I wished I were not going, and had refused the Hicksons' offer of transport. Cornwall, I thought, could never be so lovely, or mean so much to me as Thurlow. The chauffeur, beside me on the front seat, said that it looked like being a fine day, and would be very hot in London. He'd be glad to get into the West Country the next day. Mrs. Temperley, behind, tapped on the glass partition and pointed to our last view of the harbour from the top of the hill. I nodded and smiled. We left Thurlow, and began the crowded, character-less main road. Then Digby V. Hickson tapped on the glass partition and indicated that Mrs. Digby V. Hickson didn't like to go so fast, with so much traffic about. The chauffeur slowed down a little. In my mood of nervous apprehension, I should have liked him to drive as fast as he could.

I hadn't had time to read a paper before we started—in fact, I doubt if the papers had arrived—and as we approached the outer suburbs of London, I craned my neck to read the posters outside the dreary little newsagents' shops as we passed them. The first poster I saw seemed to bear the words, SPECIAL BOMBING REPORT, and the second, THREAT BY something DICTATOR. We had to go about two miles before I discovered that, for BOMBING, I should have read BOXING, and for something DICTATOR, COMPANY DIRECTOR. Even when I realised that my alarm was founded on a Boxing Report and a Company Director's threat, I was still shaken, and the mood persisted when I reached my cheap little hotel near Earl's Court—having said a temporary good-bye to Mrs. Temperley and the Hicksons at the Hyde Park Hotel—and unpacked my bag. Then, to my horror, I saw that my sponge-bag was wrapped in a sheet of newspaper which bore the headline GRAVEST HOUR SINCE 1914. I looked at the date, wondering if I had missed some terrible news the day before, and saw that the paper was issued ten months ago in October, 1935, and remembered that I had asked the maid to bring me some newspaper for my packing. While I had luncheon, I felt exasperated with myself, and with the world as a consequence.

The idea of visiting Rusper had occurred to me as soon as I knew that the Hicksons' programme was going to give me an afternoon and evening to myself in London. I decided that I would make no plans, but would go to South Mersley or not, as I felt inclined, when the time came. If I felt fairly serene, I would go. Otherwise, I wouldn't. I should do more harm than good if I saw Rusper and was unable to make a good show at the interview. Naturally, I went through a number of imaginary interviews with my enemy, and planned the opening conversation several times. The night before I left Thurlow, and during the drive to London, I felt that a meeting with him was out of the question. But by the end of my lunch—perhaps by way of a reaction from my absurd timidity of the morning—I felt bolder and resolved to go and see him. It was too ridiculous, I thought, to be afraid of facing a suburban doctor, when we might so soon have to face a European war. Even if our meeting ended in vulgar abuse, it couldn't make matters any worse than they were. And it might not end in vulgar abuse. Rusper might have recovered some of his sanity, so far as I was concerned. We might compromise. I might let him examine me—though it was odious to think even of his touching me, let alone that he might want me to strip. I would not go to Dr. Ebermann's clinic to be experimented on and run the risk of having my *self* disintegrated—that *self* of mine which, except on a few bad days when it lost control, was an instrument of such peculiar satisfaction to me. On the other hand, if Dr. Duparc's successor were an agreeable man, I might be willing to submit myself to him for a fortnight's observation, when my Cornish holiday was over.

When I had got into the train for South Mersley, I made an effort of will and refused to think of what might be in store, so as to be as calm as I could. I told myself that I was not committed to anything till I had rung the bell at Rusper's house—and even then I could run away before the servant had time to reach the front door. I concentrated my mind on the landmarks of the journey—those landmarks which I had created for myself at the time when I used to go up to London quite often. As I saw them, they came back to me—the house with the little conservatory on a balcony, the glass grimier than ever—the poplar tree growing out of the pavement by the chapel porch—the eight arches, each one slightly bigger than the last (or smaller, if you were going the other way), which carried the road over the adjoining railway—the extraordinary black little early Victorian house standing in a garden of about an acre, containing three enormous horse-chestnuts and a grotto of gigantic stones, and flanked by rows of five-hundred-pound villas. How I have loved certain aspects of the material world! That, I suppose, is why I fear Dr. Ebermann—in case he should make me hate or despise these passions—my identification of my *self* with a sunset over Thurlow Harbour, with the smells of the harbour and the sound of the little waves scrunching against the barnacles on the pier. But it wouldn't be *I* who hated or despised them. A new person would have come into the world, more useful, they might say, to society. But *I* should have lived, and I doubt whether the new person would ever really live at all.

The train reached South Mersley station and I got out, recovering from my reverie just in time. I remember the days when South Mersley was the terminus, and you couldn't inadvertently be carried any further. I took a bus from the station to the corner of York Road, and then walked slowly down Penelope Avenue. I had an impulse to make a detour and pass Elmcroft, but resisted it. Elmcroft was part of my past, and as such I must respect it. But its memories were not too happy. It was before I learnt the secret of happiness that I lived there.

Rusper's house—his second, since he had been practising on his own—was not unlike Elmcroft. Though he was a generation younger, he had been brought up in the Elmcroft tradition. He had the same little front garden, and the same honeysuckle sprawling over the fence by the road. The grass was better kept than ours used to be, despite the hours my father made me spend spudding out plantains. The paintwork of the house was an aggressive blue. There were blue curtains, of not quite the same shade, in the front windows.

For a moment I hovered by the gate, sniffing the honeysuckle— again I remarked what a long flowering season it has—and reading the brass plate, DR. DONALD RUSPER, M.D. It was magnifi- cently polished. I wondered how often Catherine had been told to see to it. Then I opened the gate and walked slowly up the stone path. It had a little kink to the left, about halfway, just as ours had at Elmcroft.

Before I had reached the porch, I heard the click of the gate behind me and heavy footsteps. I turned my head and saw that it was Rusper himself, top-hatted and morning-coated, carrying the usual little bag.

I said "Good afternoon," and at the same time he said, "Good God, man, what are *you* doing here?"

I began to explain nervously, but he cut me short and hustled me, almost physically, through the hall into his consulting-room— a room in much the same position as my father's, but larger and more expensively decorated. As he smoothed his hat irritably before putting it down on a chair, I caught him murmuring, "Anyone might have seen you!"

I sat down in the inevitable chair facing the light, and hoped that, as I did so, my muscles didn't betray any unfortunate symptoms. "I wanted to have a talk with you, Rusper," I said, "and as I found myself in London this afternoon, rather unexpectedly, I thought

I'd run down here on the chance of finding you in."

He looked at me suspiciously, and said, "I'm rather surprised you didn't telephone. I suppose it didn't occur to you that I should probably be away in August."

"I'm afraid it didn't."

"As you know," he said pompously, "we always do go away in August, but this year it happens that I have three important cases on hand—important, I mean, from the medical as well as the social point of view—and I was disappointed in my *locum*. So Mrs. Rusper and I have arranged to postpone our holiday till the middle of September, when we shall probably go abroad. And now, what can I do for you, please? I'm afraid I can't allow this unexpected visit to last too long. Mrs. Carlice, in her last letter to me, told me that you were still at Thurlow-on-Sea."

I could see from the way he talked that he hadn't decided what line to take with me. He was more shocked at my arrival than I was by his running into me so suddenly. The thought gave me courage.

"I left Thurlow early this morning," I said. "I am motoring with an elderly lady I met there, and two American friends of hers. We are going on to Cornwall to-morrow. My friends are busy in London this afternoon, and it occurred to me that it was an excellent opportunity to discuss my affairs with you. I admit, I had overlooked the fact that you usually go away in August."

I sat back and watched for his reaction, which, when it came, was not favourable.

"I take it, you wish to discuss your financial affairs. You hope that you may induce me to reconsider my decision."

"Yes."

"On what grounds?"

I paused for a moment—sign of weakness, I fear. My real grounds, of course, were that in three weeks' time, if he didn't pay my annuity, I shouldn't have a single penny in my pocket. But I felt that if I told him this, I should simply be strengthening his hand. My game was to pretend that I had some resources, and not to make an appeal for pity, till everything else had failed.

"On what grounds?" he repeated. His eyes narrowed slightly, and his black coat seemed to emphasise the blackness of his moustache, and the hairs in his nostrils.

"On the ground that you see me here as a perfectly responsible and respectable member of society, and that there is no excuse—any longer, if ever there was one—for withholding my allowance."

"I see. As to that, I think you must expect me to come to my own conclusions. During the last few months—since March, in fact, when to my personal knowledge you were neither a responsible nor a respectable member of society—you have withdrawn yourself from observation by me. And you have declined so far as I know to submit yourself to the observation of any other—er—competent observer."

He gave no vestige of a smile as the silly sentence ended.

"I'm quite willing to talk about that incident in March," I replied. "In fact, I should like to. Perhaps I do owe you an explanation. Look here, Rusper, it is a thousand pities that the personal equation has been fated to crop up between us."

"What exactly does that mean?"

"I mean the fact that I was once—can't you help me out? You know I don't want to antagonise you."

"If you are alluding to Mrs. Rusper, I shall be glad if you will cease to do so."

"Can't you see that I'm bound to allude to her—to explain what happened in March?"

"No, I do not."

He sat back in his chair, and went on:

"I think you may have some idea in your mind that my attitude to you has been determined by the fact that you insulted my wife in a public place. Please disabuse yourself at once of that notion. The fact that the lady in the lounge whom you accosted, while you were drunk, happened to be my wife, is neither here nor there. The fact that it was my wife merely explained how your outrageous behaviour was brought so quickly to my notice. I have no personal feelings in the matter. I am glad it was my wife, because, otherwise, it might have been a long time before I heard of your condition. I am sorry it was my wife, because I dislike to think of her being insulted in a public place, and still more because you seem to think that my decision regarding you has been made through vindictiveness on my part."

"But, Rusper, haven't you considered——"

"What?"

"Haven't you considered what the effect of suddenly seeing your wife sitting there was on me? Do you suppose I should have behaved like that, if it had been any other woman?"

"You had every opportunity of explaining all this to me the next morning, when I called at your hotel. You refused to see me, and have given me no explanation since then."

"Well, will you let me give you one now?"

My moment had come. I began to talk, warming myself up to eloquence, and making deep inroads on my poor little stock of nervous energy. I wondered whether Rusper was listening. From time to time he drummed his hairy fingers on the mahogany desk, behind which he was sitting.

I gave him a short sketch of my career, enlarging on my difficulties, and disappointments—the handicaps of my sensitiveness and vivid imagination. I touched on my service in the army, my wound in the head and its after-effects, the hidden mental scars which the War left behind. I see now that it was a foolish line to have taken, but I forgot I was talking to Rusper and imagined I was pleading before a more sympathetic tribunal.

Then I passed on to my meeting with Catherine, saying nothing to her discredit and much to mine, and admitting that it was perhaps lucky for her that she had not married me. When describing the shock of her refusal, I was careful not to blame her in any way. But I was bound to describe my wretchedness, so as to explain the episode which led to my abrupt departure from Barling House School. Here I was able to pay a tribute to Rusper for his prompt and tactful handling of the situation. I reminded him of the "satisfaction" I had given while I was in the charge of Dr. Duparc, and how, on leaving, Dr. Duparc had declared me to be rather highly strung, but perfectly normal. I admitted that since then, I had not been teetotal, but maintained that I probably drank far less than the average business man—or professional man, for that matter. I insisted that I was in no sense drunk on the unlucky evening when I ran into Catherine in the hotel lounge at Boschurch. I begged him to try to realise the effect which that shock was bound to have upon me, and I added that it was quite clear that half the trouble had arisen from the silly conduct of the hotel-porter, and the man who had fetched him. It was with some difficulty that I refrained from calling Catherine's conduct silly, too. As for the next morning, I confessed that I had acted like an idiot in refusing to see Rusper, when he had taken the trouble to come down from South Mersley. I had regretted it a good deal afterwards, but hoped that Dora would act as peacemaker. Meanwhile, I had gone to Thurlow, and my life there had been in every way above reproach. I had made some nice friends—I mentioned the visit to Lady Evans' country house—some of whom were even then taking me with them to Cornwall. The party, I told him, consisted of a Colonel's widow, an American business-man and his wife who had been at school with a cousin of the Colonel's widow. None of them had any idea that my allowance had been stopped by my trustee on the ground that I wasn't a respectable or responsible person. Had they known, they would have been amazed and horrified at my trustee's action. (This remark was not very wise, I fear.)

And lastly, I went on, I had a written testimonial from the resident proprietor of the King Stephen Hotel at Thurlow to the effect that I had been a thoroughly satisfactory guest.

Here I tasted the last dregs of humiliation, as I stood up and handed Rusper the letter which I had got the proprietor to write. I felt like a street-corner cadger, who stops you and urges you to read a grubby and illegible doctor's certificate—rather than do which, you give him a shilling. I felt worse, because the cadger is used to it and knows all the moves of the game, and I was a novice. It had been distressing to ask the proprietor to write the letter, to cope with his surprise and to give some explanation of my strange request. But it was infinitely more distressing to give Rusper the letter. I had tried to keep it clean, but none the less it was a little dog-eared. As he read it, I felt full of shame, particularly at the thought of the word *gentlemanlike*. How I wished I had made the writer change it, but it had been such a strain to get the letter written at all, that I couldn't cavil at the phrasing.

As if to spare me nothing, Rusper read it aloud.

I have great pleasure in stating that Mr. Stephen Payne has resided at the King Stephen Hotel, Thurlow-on-Sea, from March 14th, 1936, to August 17th, 1936. During that time he has met all his obligations punctually, and has behaved both to his fellow-guests and the staff in a most gentlemanlike manner. I am extremely sorry he is leaving us and hope we shall soon have the pleasure of welcoming him here again.

E. BEAMISH,

Proprietor of the King Stephen Hotel,

Thurlow-on-Sea.

Rusper stood up and, as he gave me the letter back, said, "Thank you."

There was a pause, so long that I had to break it. "Well?" I said. He said, "Sit down."

I obeyed, and he went on:

"I am sorry to say, Payne, that everything you have told me to-day only confirms me in my opinion, that I am not justified, either as a medical man or as a friend of your family, in permitting you to be at large, until you have had a long course of treatment. I have listened to your account of yourself with more sympathy than you will give me credit for. A doctor, you know, shouldn't feel too much sympathy for a patient, because——"

I interrupted him by saying, "But I'm not your patient. I'm nobody's patient."

He frowned, but with an effort went on quietly:

"In a sense, you are my patient. It was your father's manifest intention that you should be. I owe your father a great debt of gratitude. He was kindness itself to me at the start of my career, and I intend to act up, as fully as I can, to the responsibilities which he entrusted to me. The chief of these responsibilities is you. I am afraid that, perhaps owing to the—er—friction which there was between your father and yourself, you have tended to under-rate the very real affection he had for you. Surely he showed this affection in leaving you the greater part of his fortune. Despite his knowledge that your sister was well provided for by her marriage, he might easily have divided his money equally between the two of you. As you know, you had the bigger share. But—and this is where we shall disagree—he also showed his affection for you by appointing me to be trustee of your fund. In other words, he was insisting that, in some sense, you should be my patient. As a medical man, he was far from blind to the perils of your unstable temperament. He realised, especially after your unfortunate experiences during the War, that you needed watching. He saw, as plainly as I do, that your mental health was not all it should be. He saw, as I do, the dangers that lie ahead of you—not the commonplace danger that you might be imprudent with your capital and land in the bankruptcy court—but the more subtle danger that your psychic traumatism would lead to a progressive dementia with lamentable consequences both for you and for society. It is for this reason that I insist—that I am bound most regretfully to insist that——"

"And when have I shown signs of this dementia?"

I asked the question almost perkily. The thought that Rusper imagined that he could impress me by his medico-parsonic lecture made me feel frivolous. I hadn't come to South Mersley to be lectured. I had come to claim my rights. If there was to be lecturing, it should be done by me.

"You show it now," he said.

"Rubbish."

"You will hardly deny that you showed it when you had to leave Barling House School, or last March when you insulted a lady— never mind if she happened to be my wife—in a hotel lounge."

"I do mind if she happened to be your wife. (a) If she hadn't been, you'd have heard nothing about the incident, and (b) if it hadn't been Catherine, the incident would never have occurred."

"If the lady you accosted hadn't been Mrs. Rusper, the scene might easily have been worse. She might have had hysterics. She might have——"

"I shouldn't have accosted her, as you call it."

There was a pause, and I went on: "Can't you see that ridiculous event in its true perspective? Can't you judge it like an impartial person?"

"I venture to think I do."

"And I venture to think you don't."

It was like playing noughts and crosses. It led us nowhere, but I felt bound to make my mark wherever I could.

"Well," he said, "so as to avoid personalities, let us consider the incident which led to your leaving Barling House School."

"We can't avoid personalities there, either," I said. "The trouble then was caused entirely by Catherine's—Mrs. Rusper's, perhaps I should say—rejection of me. It unnerved and unbalanced me."

"You see. Being crossed in love hasn't, normally, such an outrageous result."

One up to Rusper, but I parried the thrust.

"Perhaps it hasn't, but you whisked me off to your friend, Dr. Duparc, and he discharged me as cured a few weeks later. You, yourself, let me go free and paid my full allowance. That's all past history, you can't rake that up now."

"It becomes relevant in the light of what transpired later."

"What did transpire later?"

"The Boschurch incident."

Here, lamentably—though if I hadn't done so, it would have made no difference—I lost my temper.

"Haven't I explained to you," I shouted, with a thump on Rusper's desk, "one thousand times, that that was your damned wife's fault, and no one else's?"

The next pause was horrifying. I had leisure to watch all his reactions. I saw with an instantaneous clairvoyance that he was not in love with Catherine. I guessed that he had never been in love with her, as she, physically, had been in love with him. I guessed that in marrying her, he had married her uncle, the famous Harley Street specialist. But I saw that in insulting his wife, I had insulted—not his affections—but his vanity. This was unpardonable. I had done for myself, utterly, finally, and for ever. If I didn't say something quickly he would tell me to go to the gutter where I belonged.

So I said, "Where is my hat, please?"

"Before you go——" he said, taken slightly aback.

"I'm going now."

He gave me my hat, which was lying on a sofa by the wall. I raised it—it was a heavy brown Homburg, monstrously shabby—wondering whether I should give myself the pleasure of hitting him in the face with it, but refrained, and, consulting-room or no consulting-room, put it on my head, and walked out of the room rather slowly.

He followed, all agog.

When we reached the door—he was two paces behind me—I said, "Your hall needs doing up. The paper's filthy."

Then I went through the door and shut it in front of him. I had an impulse to run, as I walked down the little garden path, but mastered it. In fact, I put my nose to the honeysuckle before I shut the gate. But smell, for once, meant nothing to me.

2

Things like that produce a numbness. I was numb all the way back to London, too numb to eat my dinner—useful economy— and too numb to take in the plot of the film I went to see in the evening. When I went to bed, I slept pretty well.

I awoke feeling rather sick, as I do when my nerves have been strained, and I was still feeling rather sick when the Hicksons' grand car startled my shabby hotel by calling for me and my luggage, before collecting the party at the Hyde Park Hotel. Mrs. Temperley said I looked pale. Digby V. Hickson said she ought to be more discreet. When a young bachelor comes to London, he naturally makes a night of it. Or words to that effect. It was kindly meant and sounded quite funny in American.

I revived with every mile which separated us from London. Between Salisbury and Shaftesbury we had a roadside luncheon— hamper from Fortnum and Mason's and champagne. We all slept afterwards, in the car, except the chauffeur, and I missed Yeovil, Chard, Crewkerne, and Honiton. In Exeter we had a quick tea. The Hicksons were eager to dine at Falmouth. And I must be their guest, at any rate for one night. Oh, yes, I must. They had felt terribly upset that I hadn't gone with them to the Hyde Park Hotel.

We reached Falmouth about eight o'clock, and there was no room for me at the Hicksons' hotel. Hickson called himself a blamed fool for having omitted to make proper reservations. However, I must dine with them. During dinner, the porter should telephone around and get me accommodation for the night, and whatever it was, it should go on the Hicksons' bill. If I didn't allow them to make that little gesture they'd think I was a downright unfriendly person. Dinner was long and large, and we had more champagne. Mr. Hickson congratulated me at great length on living in such a beautiful country as England—a country with such great traditions, so steeped in all the splendour of the past, and still maintaining such equilibrium and poise. And it had been just too wonderful having me along. Mrs. Hickson, who was a bit of an invalid, complained of sleepiness and went to bed, taking her husband with her, and leaving Mrs. Temperley to make a private farewell. She did it with great sweetness. If I didn't write to her or come to visit Thurlow again, she'd search me out. She asked no questions, but showed that she had guessed a good deal. I felt a little maudlin, and called her "My good angel." Then rather hurriedly I said goodbye, and walked through the narrow streets of the town to my hotel. The Hicksons' chauffeur, I found, had taken my luggage there while we were having dinner. It was a relief not having to tip him.

So this was Cornwall.

3

It was still more Cornwall, next morning, when I found the room in the fisherman's house where I'm now staying.

It is still Cornwall, utterly, unbelievably, enchanting. And except for Dora—to whom I must now write—there is no one to whom I can write about it. And she, to be convinced, will want silly picture-postcard raptures, like those vivid views of Chillon our friends used to send us when holiday-making in Switzerland.

Before I write to Dora, perhaps it would be as well if I re-read her last letter to me:

> *Monday,*
> S.S. "DANCING UNICORN"
> (SOMEWHERE IN THE BALTIC).

MY DEAR STEPHEN,

Thank you very much for your letter, which arrived the morning I was leaving Carlice for this cruise. I ought to have answered before, only, as you can imagine, I've been seeing so many new people and new sights that I've hardly had a minute.

I'm having a lovely time and it's doing me no end of good. I had got nervy and run down before leaving home and this is just what I needed. Of course, a lot of the people aren't the class

I have been accustomed to, but some of them are very nice. There's a Lady Evans at our table. (I don't think she's anything to do with the Lady Evans whom you know.) And there's a Captain Edgbaston who is very attentive. He's giving a cocktail party in the private dining-room to-day. In fact I must go there as soon as I've finished this. He's a widower, travelling with his sister and brother-in-law. Oh, and do you know who else is here? Daphne Boswell. You must remember the Boswells in the old days. We dined with them, Daddy, you and I, the night before you went out to France for the first time. What ages ago that was! Twenty-one years, isn't it? Daphne must have been a little girl at school then. Now she's quite portly. She's here with her husband—not very exciting—who's had jaundice, and his doctor—Don Rusper!—recommended him a sea voyage. Daphne is full of South Mersley news. Some very common people have Elmcroft now. She says that Don Rusper is getting an enormous practice with some very distinguished patients— among them Sir William Smith, a millionaire who lives in the huge house in Mersley Park. (You remember we used to try to toboggan down that hill?) She says Don's wife's uncle is very high up in the profession and has recently got some kind of Royal appointment. She thinks that connection must have been very useful to Don.

I know you will be annoyed with me for talking about Don so much, but I do want to persuade you to go and see him. He's much too big a man to nourish any silly grievance against you, and I'm sure he'll overlook what happened in March, if only you'll apologise to him. Besides, it's the only thing you can do, unless you can make a living of your own.

That's nasty. She knows I could only write a book that wouldn't sell. Besides, why should I make a living, when the wherewithal is there? Surely, the fewer people who have to "make a living" in this world, the better the world is. Did her husband make a living? Does she make one? However——

I only felt a little sea-sick once, the second day. Since then everything has been delightful. I'm really rather dreading going home. I think I told you that my stepson Ronnie comes of age on September the 8th. I expect to arrive ten days before. I gather that when the Carlice heir came of age, they used to have a huge party with fireworks, and a beano for the village. This year, as we're in mourning for Joan—I told you she was killed in the aerodrome 'bus on her way to fly to the Mediterranean—everything will be very quiet. My sister-in-law, Isabel Carlice, will be there, of course, and the family solicitor, Sir Thomas Hill. And Ronnie may have a friend or two, but he's quite a little Bolshy and says he doesn't want any fuss. He's spending his summer holiday in Russia, and comes back three or four days after I do.

I've naturally been wondering what my own future is going to be after Ronnie's birthday. He has already let me know—quite nicely—that he won't want me at Carlice. I think he wants to turn the place into a Communist Club, or something of the sort. (Poor Isabel! What will she say!) I suppose I shall look for a little flat in London. I'm not sure that I shan't enjoy the change, though it's hard to tell, after so many years in the country. I think I should have liked the country better if I'd had a more ordinary kind of house—a house that I could really make my own.

Here's Dolly, saying that I must come along to the cocktail party. So I must stop. This ought to be posted in Stockholm to-morrow morning. I hope you're well. Let me hear from you again soon, and do go and see Don Rusper.

Your affec. sister,
DORA.

DEAR DORA,

Thank you very much for your letter from the Baltic. I'm in Cornwall, sitting on the rocks at the foot of a wooded hill which slopes down to a creek. Beyond the creek, I can see the white line made by the little ferry plying between——

What is the use of writing this to her? She couldn't enjoy it as I enjoy it, or understand it as I understand it. Nothing will make her realise that I have fallen in love with this county, and that people in love are justified in everything they do. Poor Dora, who, I gather, never had a love-affair. Well, I've tried falling in love with people, and I find it wiser and more satisfying now to fall in love with things and places. I had a passion for Thurlow, but I see now, it was too near London. It was a passion of adolescence, not, like this, the affair of a life-time.

"You wait," said Mrs. Tregisky, when I had wearied her with my raptures, "till we have real bad weather. You wait till the rainy winter months come, and see how you like it then. Year in, year out, with the wind howling down that chimney fit to blow your boots off."

But that's exactly the nucleus of my passion—to taste Cornwall in each varied mood, at each season of the year, in fair weather and in foul, in winter as well as early autumn, and in spring—that spring which they all agree is a miracle. Just as I felt an urgent longing to see Thurlow harbour in November—the harbour lapped in a mist which would mute its noises and make its smells more subtle—so now I crave for Cornwall in the spring. And at all times, and for ever, as one says "for ever" when one is in love.

It might have been so easy. If my interview with Rusper had passed off differently. "Go and see him," Dora says, as if it were an easy thing to do—but I have done it and failed. If he had been reasonable, or I had been forceful enough to master him, I should be singing a hymn of praise to Heaven. I should be *living* here, not staying like a visitor or a ticket-of-leave convict, not counting the hours and the money in my pocket which gives them to me. And yet how sweet, how peculiarly *my own*, are these hours that pass before my bankruptcy, like the last night before one goes to a war. How sweet are the hours while I can still sit here, by the water's edge, merging myself consciously now in the motion of the stream, now in the vibration of the trees behind me, now in the line between the light and the shadows, now in the smell of salt and seaweed which pervades everything and is a background to all other smells down here. It's funny, here, to think of the unknown me, the me of the future, cadging at street corners, selling newspapers perhaps—or could I mend broken chairs?—or stepping jauntily out of Dr. Ebermann's asylum, five hundred a year in my bank-book—and what in my brain after that probing, that demolition and reconstruction of myself? I should come out a new man. Yes, Stephen Payne would be dead, and somebody else would be born, somebody else who might do valuable work as assistant to a vivisector or inventor of poison-gas. A new man would come out, but it wouldn't be Stephen Payne, and Stephen Payne has no wish to die yet awhile. Better the street corner and the bundle of newspapers. "Special Boxing Report." "Gravest hour since 1914." "Sensation." (Down here you read "Ultimatum—*by Cornish Farmers!*")

If I could tell Dora all this, and bring it home to her, if I could make her feel as I feel, she'd have to do something for me. How far has she taken my side against Rusper? Has she threatened him with the law? Oh, yes, he's within his legal rights, but pressure can be brought to bear. Have *I* the money to pay a solicitor? We couldn't touch Rusper, but with Dora really at my back we might bluff. Trustee Act 1925. Gone, with the memory of all my other law—deliberately forgotten. Trustee Act 1925. There must be some section of it with which I could plague him, if only Dora would see me through, and be prepared to give evidence for me. It's the sort of case they might hear in chambers—an unsavoury family affair. After all, Rusper has a reputation now, and baronets in Mersley Park are touchy about such things. "An excellent doctor, no doubt, but, my dear, there is that nasty story about his behaviour to old Dr. Payne's son." That's the kind of whisper to threaten him with. It's there he's vulnerable.

This means I must see Dora, and the only way to see her is to take her by surprise. If warned, she would lock the gates and turn the bloodhounds loose in the park, rather than have the black sheep grazing there.

Yet, I daresay, she's fond of me and would like to see me settled, just as she would like to see everything settled, made comfortable, round and smooth. I must reassure her, so that the shock, when she has it, will be as small as I can make it. The Lady Evans line was good and right. It stuck, as I intended. "There's a Lady Evans," she says in her letter, "at our table, but I don't think she's anything to do with the Lady Evans whom you know." I must show her that I know more people than Lady Evans, that I'm moving in most respectable circles quite beyond the aspirations of South Mersley.

I am scheming like a house-maid who wants to make the greengrocer's assistant want to ravish her. It wasn't for that that I came all the way to Cornwall. This plotting poisons me. Yet Rusper has forced it on me. Touch pitch, etc. Well, I never wanted to touch him. Forgive me, trees and rocks. Ten minutes, and I'll be back with you again. And from that time, till the moment when I get into my third-class carriage in Falmouth station, I'll be the man that I intend to be.

How pitiable this difference between what I am and what, if I fail, they will make of me. The difference between the athlete leaping seven feet in the sunlight and the old man he'll become, lying motionless in bed while the impurities of his body are drained through a tangle of tubes to base receptacles, and even the nurse, on the sly, must hold her nose.

4

MY DEAR DORA,

Thank you very much for your letter from the Baltic. I am glad you are having such a good time. I suppose one needs a change, however perfect a home one has.

You'll be surprised to hear that I'm in Cornwall. Some American friends of Mrs. Temperley—she is the Colonel's wife who was so kind to me in Thurlow—gave me a lift down here via London. They are nice people, not very rich as Americans go. They only stayed at Falmouth one night, and, after I parted company from them, were going to Land's End and up the north coast through Devon, Somerset and Gloucestershire, into Wales. They seem to admire England very much, and want to see all the beauty-spots if they can.

Personally, I couldn't bring myself to stir beyond Cornwall. I should like to live here. I am lodging with a fisherman and his wife. Rather dear, as it's August, but I've no doubt their terms will come down as winter approaches. Mrs. Temperley said that if I stay here, she'll get me an introduction to the Tremartins. Commodore Edgar Tremartin is a very big landowner between Falmouth and the Helford River.

I've made friends with one or two people, and the other day a Cornish farmer took me out shooting rats and rabbits.

I feel I ought to tell you that while passing through London I did slip away from my friends and visit Dr. Rusper. I wish you could understand what the effort cost me. As always, I found him utterly unreasonable about me. I did everything I could, but it was no use. I don't want to bother you with details now, especially when you are still full of happy memories of your cruise. I'll tell you about it later, when we meet. It is an age since I have seen you. I am sure I shan't find you changed, though you may see a difference in me. A difference for the better, let us hope. Mrs. Temperley told me that spending this summer at Thurlow had made me look ten years younger. That only takes me back to thirty-two.

Unless I suddenly find I have the means to settle here, I shall be moving eastwards in a week or so. I am sufficiently in funds to get back to Thurlow, where my credit is good. What with the cares of household, and this birthday party in the offing, you will be too busy to send me a letter while I'm still here. I'll give you a new address as soon as I have one.

Your affectionate brother,
STEPHEN.

Chapter IX: ISABEL CARLICE

I

THE day before I set off for Carlice and Ronnie's twenty-first birthday party, I had a letter from my solicitor reminding me that I had to decide within a week whether or not I would extend the lease of my house for another seven years. I had not forgotten about it, but I had not yet made up my mind. As houses go in London, I shall find nothing better. I have tried a flat and loathed it. I have always preferred the country and still do. Why then hadn't I got rid of my house years ago, left London and settled in the country? I know the answer to that question. So does Gwen Rashdall, who didn't hesitate to tell me. And so, I suppose, do all my intelligent friends. I have been waiting to see what would turn up. There is only one house in which I should like to end my days.

I rambled on in this vein for quite a long time to Gwen Rashdall, when she came to see me the other day—cadging, I suspected, for an invitation to the birthday party at Carlice. As my "great friend," she ought to have been there. But Dora hadn't asked her, nor had Ronnie. It's true we're in mourning for Joan, but, through me, Gwen is almost one of the family. Perhaps not being asked—and for some reason her shooting friends haven't asked her to stay with them either, this year—made her a little sour. She was sour in her reply, when, mentioning the lease of my London house, I said, "Gwen, if you were in my place, what would you do?"

She said, "I should kill Ronnie, and give up the lease of your town house."

When I protested, she went on, "Well, you can't let a silly little undergraduate go giving Carlice to the Communist party, can you? With luck, you'll be able to enjoy it for another ten years, during which, if you're still more lucky, you will die. It seems to me, Carlice is quite worth a murder—especially after Joan."

I guessed what she would say, but I had to ask her what on earth she meant.

"Joan's death brought you one stage nearer," she said. "You don't regard it just as a coincidence, do you?"

"Of course I do—so far as I believe in coincidences at all. I don't really believe that anything is entirely purposeless. If I drop my bag and have to stoop to pick it up, I believe there's some purpose even in that. I mean a particular purpose relating to me—something quite beyond the mere working of the law of gravitation."

When she left me, she murmured, "Well, I think you'll get what you want. You're that kind of woman. If you will things to happen, they happen. So go on willing."

The immediate effect of my talk with Gwen was the realisation that I must give up the lease of my London house and buy Carlice from Ronnie, when he gets it on September the eighth, even if it beggars me to do so. I know he doesn't want me to have it, and will drive as hard a bargain as he can. Still, surely the Communist party would prefer a nice lump sum in cash to a house which, anyway, they think they'll confiscate in a year or two, if it isn't bombed first. I must put that point to him forcibly. I might even write to one of their officials. I suppose I could find out who deals with that sort of thing.

That's going to be the contest at the birthday party. That's why, two hours after I got the letter from my solicitor, I wrote telling him that I would give up my lease, and sat for hours at my desk, going through old papers and destroying what I could, and gazing round the room like the stranger that I shall make myself to it.

"I haven't really lived here," I thought. "It's been a waiting-room. There isn't a single memory glued to these pale blue walls that I want to carry away—except the memory of my waiting here. In a day or two I shall forget where the bells and the electric light switches are, while I shall always remember what stairs creak at Carlice."

I saw my pair of Rockingham poodles on the mantelpiece—those poodles to which I had drawn Joan's wandering attention the night before she was killed. If I died suddenly, some faint emanation of me might radiate from those poodles. I have, slightly, identified myself with them. But only because there is a mantelpiece at Carlice on which I know they would look well.

I sat for hours, till half past three in the morning, tearing up old papers and receipts. Each one brought something of the last fourteen years back to me, as if it had been a page in a diary. Yet it was not my real life which most of them recorded. My real life was barely documented at all. A receipt for three hundred English irises which I planted one autumn round a small may tree at Carlice, another for two garden chairs, another for twenty bales of Sorbex peat—these, and a few others like them, were the only emblems of my proper existence.

For the last fourteen years I have been the power behind Dora, and a thorn in Ronnie's flesh. Was that worth while? Did that give me a claim to immortality? There has also been a person called Miss Carlice who had quite an agreeable circle of London friends, gave parties for them and went to theirs, but this lady never set out as being one who would live for ever.

No, my claims to immortality go back further. I made my first when I stood enraptured, at the age of six, in front of a crimson-velvet salpiglossis. I made another claim that exquisite autumn day when Claude came back from his tennis tournament to tell me that he intended to marry Dora. And oddly enough—I say "oddly" because the scene, for once, was not laid at Carlice—I achieved quite a measure of reality on that November day which Dora, Joan and I spent at Leamington, when Ronnie and his friend let off fireworks in the hotel drawing-room, and, as soon as they had gone back to school, Eames telephoned to say that Claude had been found dead in the gunroom. Perhaps I thought that Dora would do the obvious thing, and leave the coast clear for me. I didn't know, then, what I know now about her. But her instinct was quite right. It was her duty to stay. Ronnie would have been miserable if I had been in charge. I daresay I should have been miserable too.

There and not there.

I have long reached the age of wanting to settle down. I have settled down all my life. Even when I was traipsing about Europe with my father I was always asking myself, "What on earth are we doing here? Why do we waste our time seeing all these tedious people? We could manage without the money." Then, mercifully, my father had to retire, without any great success, despite Lubinsky, Prince Osric, the Duchess of Malfi and the Emperor's telegram. Indeed, I suspect he rather muffed the Emperor's telegram, or they surely would have given him something more than a simple knighthood. It's amazing how our family has contrived to avoid titles. Perhaps they were all too like me—not public-spirited enough. There is no possible chance of my ever being made a Dame. Dame Dora Carlice even is more likely than Dame Isabel Carlice, and that's saying a good deal.

The happy idea that I might be able to buy Carlice from Ronnie, even if it ruined me and the funds all went to the Communist party, filled me with excitement as soon as I conceived it. I couldn't think of going to bed, or sleeping. I felt furious that the silly boy was still away—returning sadly from Russia. I should have liked to telephone to him, or to hire a car and visit him, and, late though it was, burst into his bedroom, shake him by the shoulder, and say, "Ronnie, how much will you take? Can you telegraph Stalin to-morrow?"

I began to work out ways and means. Suppose Ronnie asked so much. That would leave me—so much. I could live in three rooms. I could shut the east wing, and Dora's idiotic drawing-room. If Eames wanted to stay, he would have to accept smaller wages. Simmonds would stick to me. I reckon myself as equal to one and a half gardeners. It could be done. What matter even if the place does fall into rack and ruin—if I can't afford to have the roof repaired, or the wall of the coach-house cracks as it did last year? I shall be there, enjoying a bedroom which faces a line of copper beeches, a morning-room with a view of the salpiglossis beds, and the high vaulted hall which, in the days of my riches, I created out of what used to be the crypt of the Abbey. I shall be there. And when they come with their knives, or bombs, or gas, to drive me away, I shall be found—or not found—gibbering by the Elizabethan bed-posts in my bedroom—gibbering, but happy, one eye on the door, and the other on the window and the copper beeches at sunset—a real person, with every access to the wide door of immortality.

I awoke the next morning, full of a dream I had during the night.

The Communist party were holding a grand adjudication. They wore dresses like those seen in pictures of Spanish inquisitors.

Ronnie was there, but occupied a rather humble place. I could tell this, because his chair creaked, like one of the stairs at Carlice. The Dictator said, "Tell me about this woman."

Ronnie got up very nervously, as if ashamed of having me for a relation. "Of course, Sir, she is pleasure-loving and very worthless," he said.

The Dictator said, "We authorise you to accept eight million roubles."

I couldn't help shouting "Done," and opened my bag to pay. But, search as I would, I could only find one ten-shilling note. The Dictator ordered an instrument of torture to be brought in. I dropped my bag, and thought, "There is a purpose in this dropping of my bag."

2

I wonder if Ronnie, when he makes this journey from London, feels, as I do, that home begins after Basingstoke. Or perhaps Newbury, or Didcot, if he's travelling by the other line from Oxford. I can't believe that, despite all his new social theories, he can utterly root out that feeling of relief, which he used to have as a small boy on coming home. I remember meeting him once, the day after he had arrived for the Christmas holidays, walking through the leafless orchard, with his hands in his pockets and whistling loudly. I said, "You seem pleased with life to-day, Ronnie," and he said, "Oh, Auntie Isabel, I *am* glad to be here."

That reminds me, I haven't done anything about his birthday present. Dora is sure to have spent too much on something he won't want. But he'll manage to pretend he likes it, as it comes from her. If I gave him a gold watch or a gold pencil, he'd simply despise me, or suspect I was trying to insult him. If I give him anything at all, it had better be a cheque. Whatever his theories may be now, he always used to like postal-orders and cheques from me. Well, we shall see. Perhaps he'll drive so hard a bargain that I shan't even be able to spare him half a crown.

As the train neared Whitchurch, I thought, "I'm coming home. I must have this place as my home, even if I have to lose it soon after I get it. At least I shall have had it, and that will be an immortal fact in the history of the universe. Isabel Carlice once owned and lived at Carlice Abbey. That can't be abolished. The past is our own and untouchable. That's why it's worth fifty of the future."

Poor stunted gas-masked little ants who shall succeed us! . . .

But when I got home to Carlice there was no Ronnie to bargain with. He had telegraphed to say he wouldn't be back till Sunday the sixth—only two days before his birthday. The wire ended, "Bringing no one. Please have no party."

Dora said, "No doubt that's because of Joan," but I knew it wasn't.

"Very well," I thought, "we won't have a birthday party for you. We want the money for other things. But Thomas Hill will be here, and by Tuesday night everything should be settled. You'll go on the Wednesday, if you've any sense, and Dora will go too. And I shall stay."

Dora had only come back from her cruise a week before. She looked very well indeed and less like a blonde suet pudding than usual. I found her mood rather strange, almost as if she were expected to do something desperate and had decided to do it. She told me, under a little pressure, that Ronnie had given her notice. I said, "I think you're glad, really," and she said, "I shall be glad when I've gone. It's the going that's awkward"—a reply which showed a spirit I shouldn't have expected to find in her. I was on the verge of telling her my plan for a deal with Ronnie, but thought better of it. I was on the verge, too, of telling her that I knew her little secret—how easy it had been to find a key to fit that drawer—but an instinct warned me against it. I asked her about her plans, and she spoke of a flatlet in London. "And how will you get on there?" I asked. She tossed her head a little and said, "Oh, I shall just live and try to have a good time. At any rate, I shall be on my own."

3

On the Saturday, the day before Ronnie was to arrive, heir to Carlice and straight from the feet of Stalin, I sent Dora to the races. She has a suburban love of a gamble, which I, who play nothing for money, have always encouraged. "What matter if we are in mourning?" I had to say. "You're leaving here so soon—as I suppose I am. Major Inchley would love to take you. Do go with him, and enjoy yourself while you can." She let me fix it all up, and was glad to go.

That afternoon, Saturday, the fifth of September, when the Major had called in his noisy little sports car and relieved me of Dora, I sat down at the big marquetry desk in the morning-room—it's absurd that marquetry should be so out of fashion—and wrote to Thomas Hill, telling him my plan. "You'll take the view," I wrote, "that it's only a phase of Ronnie's. But it isn't a phase. Ronnie has been born too late to enjoy life. That's why I despise all young people. They're all miserable, and they doom themselves to misery. And every day, charming old people are dying, and horrible young ones are being born. Don't you feel this yourself? At all events, prepare a legal contract and bring it with you. The boy, in his present mood, is set upon making the place over to the Communist party. He'll probably regret it, but that'll be too late. I'm going to buy it from him and save him from such idiocy. I can always leave it back to him in my will—in case he gets older and wiser. (I've got to leave it to someone, I suppose.) So bring a contract with you, ready made out. There's something dramatic about a twenty-first birthday, and I should like the stage-properties to be at hand. The car will meet you at 12.50 on Tuesday at Whitchurch. I know lawyers take ages to prepare things, but you've got to get this job done by Monday. Anything to bind him. I can't leave it to chance. Of course, he may be obstinate. Then I shall have failed. . . ."

It was too important a letter to leave to a servant to post, and I walked myself down the lane to the post-box in the wall by Noakes' cottage. How many hundreds of letters had I posted there? Each step I took, every tree-trunk I passed—already the leaves were turning a faint brown—rooted me more firmly to that sacred soil. The letter fell in the box with a little "plop," reminding me of the "plops" of all the letters which I thought so important when I posted them there secretly as a girl. Perhaps Dora too had posted secret letters there.

I turned away from the post-box almost sadly, and the suspense caused by Ronnie's uncertain attitude came back to me, and made the intervening hours seem too long. It was an age since I had been so excited about anything. But this was more than an excitement. It was a climax.

As I walked slowly home, I passed a line of beeches under which I had once seen the tramp sitting. My feeling of kinship for that shabby unknown increased—despite the fact that I was hoping to buy one of the stately homes of England, and he was probably wondering if he had cheese enough for his bread. Our aspirations were the same. I was only doing what he would have wanted to do, if he had been in my shoes.

As I turned the corner before reaching the lodge, I heard footsteps behind me. I looked round and saw a little man carrying an old-fashioned leather suitcase with something of an effort. He had a straggly fair moustache and wore a misshapen Homburg hat. His shoes were covered with dust, as if he had walked a long way. He looked very vaguely familiar to me. Usually I feel a mild dislike of strangers who walk in our lane, but this little man reminded me so much of my tramp that I couldn't but wish him well.

I went in by the lodge gates, and walked up the drive still more slowly; for I was examining the collection of rhododendrons which my grandfather planted there, the year he died. As I feared, the seeds had not been picked off, and the buds for next year were fewer than they ought to have been. Some of the bushes were altogether overgrown by the trees behind. It wasn't a good place, really, in which to plant them, I thought, all in a row like that and so near the trees. Nowadays one would have them in big clumps in a special garden to themselves. I was beginning to wonder if any of them could be transplanted when, once more, I heard footsteps behind me. It was the dingy little man with the fair moustache and the suitcase. I turned towards him.

He stopped three feet from me, put down his suitcase, raised his hat and said, "I am right in thinking this is Carlice Abbey, and that you're Miss Carlice?"

I said, "Yes," and he went on:

"I'm paying a surprise visit to my sister, Mrs. Carlice. Can you tell me if she's at home? My name is Stephen Payne."

I became effusive at once.

"Why, of course. We have met two or three times, haven't we? But it seems so long ago. Dora is at the races this afternoon, but she ought to be home in an hour's time. Won't you leave that heavy case in the drive, and let me send someone to fetch it?"

He said he could manage quite well, and picked it up. I asked him if he had walked far. "From Busley station," he said.

"Good Heavens, that's nearly five miles. What a pity you didn't ring up from there. We could have sent for you."

He paused for a moment in his stride, and said, "I wasn't very sure that I should be welcome. It's only fair I should tell you that. I've come to talk business, family business—with Dora, and I don't think she wants to talk it. That's why I've made this dramatic, if undistinguished, entrance."

"Oh, I'm sure she'll be delighted to see you," I said, walking towards the house. "I am, even if she isn't. But we'll talk about that while you have some tea. Or perhaps you'd prefer a drink? I had my tea about half an hour ago. You must be thirsty after walking all the way from Busley with that heavy bag. We generally use Whitchurch station. The trains to Busley are so very slow."

I chatted till we reached the house, where I rang the front door bell. It was answered by Charles. "This is Mr. Stephen Payne," I said to him. "Will you take his bag to the room next the grey room? And tell Mrs. Sowerby that we shall be three for dinner."

As Stephen Payne followed me into the morning-room, he said, "But I can't stay the night. I can't even dine here. I haven't any evening things with me."

"We can send to Busley station in no time. I suppose you left your other luggage there?"

"I did leave one bag there," he replied, "but I'm afraid I haven't any evening things in that either. I've just come from Cornwall, where I didn't want them. Besides, I live in places where people don't dress. I had thought of spending to-night in the local pub. Isn't there one called the Carlice Arms?"

I laughed.

"They say it used to be called that, but now it's the Queen Adelaide. But we can't let you stay there. It's too uncomfortable. No, you must spend the night here, and it doesn't in the least matter about your evening clothes. Now here's the whisky and there's the syphon. Would you like some biscuits? They're in this box, if you would."

It was not till he had begun to sip his drink and look round the room, that I realised how impulsive I had been, and wondered why. I recalled the fragments I had heard about my visitor—the family ne'er-do-well, as Dora had described him in the early days, when she was trying to "keep her end up" with us. Earlier in the summer she had mentioned to me that there was trouble between her brother and his trustee. I hadn't been interested enough to ask what it was. I supposed it was that trouble which had brought him to Carlice. It was amusing to put a finger into the Paynes' pie—to dabble in Dora's family affairs. So far all the dabbling had been done by her. Perhaps this was why I enjoyed taking charge of the new arrival, and making myself his champion. He seemed to need one. Despite his nimbleness of tongue, there was something woe-begone about him which claimed my sympathy. He looked well but frail, with the frailty of my father and Claude. I might have added, with the frailty of Ronnie, but Ronnie had now become simply an adversary with whom I must fight. Perhaps Stephen Payne would prove an ally against him. As the crisis approached I was prepared to regard all events as full of meaning.

He broke the long lull in our conversation by saying: "How you must love living here."

"But I don't live here," I answered. "I kept house for my father, and for my brother, between his marriages. I live in London, or rather, I used to live in London, because I've broken the lease of my house there. So you see I'm not living anywhere at present."

"That's how I feel," he said. "I should like to live in Corn-wall."

"You've come here at rather an interesting time," I went on, feeling that I ought to get my explanations in before he began his. "Perhaps Dora told you in a letter. My nephew, Ronnie—that's her stepson—comes of age on Tuesday, and this place becomes his outright. We don't quite know what he intends to do with us then. I say us, because Dora has very kindly allowed me to spend a good deal of my time here, and I feel rather closely associated with this house. But my nephew, like so many Oxford undergraduates, is a Communist, and I believe he intends to turn this place into a kind of Communist school. If he does that, neither Dora nor I would fit in. If you're in touch with the young—which I'm not—perhaps you can understand him, and have a talk with him. He'll be here to-morrow for luncheon. Oh, look——"

I had suddenly seen, through the window, a huge rabbit calmly nibbling the leaves of a bed of salpiglossis.

"What?"

"That rabbit in the flower bed. The brute. And we spend pounds wiring the garden in. Do you shoot?"

"Hardly. I went out with a Cornish farmer last week and shot a couple of rats."

"Then shoot this rabbit. You can get it through the window. Quick, before it eats up the whole bed. This is the gunroom. Do you understand guns like this?"

I showed him an old-fashioned 12-bore gun which Claude had used as a boy—but only as a boy.

While I hustled him, he said, "I oughtn't to, really. I'm sure to miss."

"It doesn't matter. You'll frighten it away."

He loaded nervously.

"Come along," I urged him, "it's still there, eating.

"Now."

He crept up to the window-ledge, and rested the barrel on it, as if he were using a rifle. As he aimed, his left wrist trembled a little. Then he fired, and the rabbit tumbled head over heels.

"Well done. You've saved the salpiglossis and provided a fine supper for someone. Put the gun away and I'll get you another drink. Then we'll go out and look at the damage. Perhaps to-morrow you'll take the gun out with you and do some more shooting. They come from that little copse of birches over there on the right. We've put wire behind that hedge a foot into the ground, but they keep getting through somehow. Oh, I forgot, to-morrow's Sunday. You must try on Monday."

"But I shan't be here on Monday, or to-morrow."

"Oh yes, you will. You must stay for the birthday party."

"Does your nephew shoot?"

"No, he won't. I think he's still secretly afraid of the bang. He used to disapprove, rather, too."

"I was afraid of the bang till the last war."

"Ah, yes, that made a difference."

Before we went out, I rang the bell again, and told Charles that when Mrs. Carlice returned, he was to tell her that I was out in the garden with Mr. Payne.

"Neither of you would like to meet," I said, while we walked across the lawn to the bed of salpiglossis, "when Major Inchley is in attendance. Let Dora get rid of him first. I know you're nervous about meeting her, but you must let me help you over that stile. I know what these family reunions can be, particularly if there's business behind them."

"The trouble is," he said meditatively, "she doesn't want to see me at all, and least of all here. And she wouldn't approve of my meeting any of you."

"Aren't you making her into a bit of an ogre?" I asked. "One does when one doesn't see people often. The only reason she hasn't asked you here more was that——"

I was about to say "she didn't feel very sure of herself," but realised suddenly that despite the bond of the shot rabbit, I hardly knew him well enough to say that about his sister. However, he surprised me by finishing my sentence for me with the words, "I didn't want to come," and smiled at me sideways.

As he bent down over the rabbit, hesitating to pick it up in his hand, I wondered what his secret really was. A little wind blew across from the silver birches, and for one moment I felt very slightly cold, as if the first faint ripple of winter had touched me.

With an effort he lifted the rabbit up, and said, "I was afraid I should find I hadn't killed it. But it's dead all right."

"Let me show you the garden," I said. "We'll leave the rabbit here till we come back. I'll tell Charles about it, and he shall give it to one of the men."

We began our tour of the garden, but somehow I felt no inclination to show it off to the visitor. I never paused and said, "The house looks quite attractive seen from here," or, in Ruth Draper fashion, "This border was simply glorious in June." It came home to me, with the sudden chill of that burst of wind from the west, how much older I was than when I had been exiled to London by Claude's marriage to Dora. My winter was approaching. Every year now I should feel the cold more keenly. A time would come when I should be too feeble to do more than scratch the surface of that garden. I had been exiled too long—no, not too long—but I must waste no more time in waiting. The hour of my return was overdue.

It came home to me also during that walk, how, in spite of my "independence," and the way in which I had been allowed to domineer at Carlice, I had bottled up my hopes within myself. Hadn't the time come, at last, to shed the mask? The arrival of Stephen Payne, in whom I knew I could take a spiritual interest, though of course no more, excited me in a way he couldn't guess. It was a symbol of my coming fight—as desperate as the fight of which he was telling me. For, oblivious for once of the garden, and busy with my own thoughts, I had encouraged him to talk to me, and was hearing all that was uppermost in his mind—his quarrel with his trustee, Dr. Rusper, and the stoppage of his allowance.

"I came here," he said, "intending to sponge on Dora, and on you, if she wouldn't help. I wanted to show her my empty pockets, turning them inside out, with nothing falling out but bits of dirty fluff, and saying, 'Now, what are you going to do about me?' As a matter of fact, I still have one pound eight and six, but you needn't tell her."

"But what can Dora do?" I asked him. "She could, I daresay, give you a five-pound note. But would that help you?"

"It would delay the asylum for ten days. That's something."

"It isn't for that that you walked five miles from Busley station."

"Now what would you do about it, if you were my sister?"

"That depends on my relations with your trustee."

I watched his face carefully as I said this, but he showed no sign of reading a double meaning into my words. Evidently he knew nothing of that little secret.

He only replied, "She must have influence with him, if only she'd bother herself to use it. She could say she'd back me if I made some application to the court. Rusper would hardly dare to flout both members of the family. Between us, we could make a pretty good case for having him removed from the trusteeship. As it is, with Dora not caring twopence, or even being vaguely against me, I shouldn't carry any weight. He could rake up—oh, there have been times when I haven't behaved very wisely—and I think he'd get away with it. Could *you* talk her round?"

"I don't know," I said. "I might force her to agree with me, but, frankly, if I took your side, I'm not sure that I shouldn't be putting her against you."

"I must risk that."

"Besides," I went on, "she wouldn't like the way you've confided in me. If only we had time to take things more slowly——"

"If it hadn't been the eleventh hour, I should never have dared to come here, or talk to you like this. Do speak to Dora."

"Very well."

We walked in silence between the big yew hedges at the eastern side of the lawn. "We shall both be ashamed of ourselves later," I thought, "if we ever meet again. We shall feel shy at the thought of having undraped our selfishnesses so quickly. But I've been draping mine for so many years. It's a relief. He's too preoccupied now with his own concerns to sum me up. He'll do that afterwards, when he's got what he wants, or is behind the bars. Then he'll realise, as I do now, how very unlike both of us this meeting has been."

"I'm asking you for everything and giving you nothing," he said suddenly. "But that, I believe, is the way a request should be made."

I wondered quickly if he knew that my purse was longer than Dora's, and whether he was counting on me in that way too. Well, what if he was? It wasn't a time to resent that sort of thing.

"We've now gone right round the garden," I said, "and you haven't really seen anything. When we get to the end of this avenue, you'll find yourself at the side of the main lawn, with the house in full view. Dora should be back now. If you like, you can loiter down here, and I'll send her to you. Or we can advance boldly together. When Charles gives her my message, she'll get rid of Major Inchley quickly enough. At least, I gather she will, from what you've told me. Or I can stay with you here, and wait till she comes to find us. This is probably the first time anybody's ever been nervous about meeting Dora."

He laughed, a little too readily and too long.

"Oh, let's go and meet her. If Major Inchley is still there, what does it matter? It's part of my game to show myself in respectable company. I regard all acquaintances as possible witnesses for me in court."

We turned the corner of the hedge and looked across the lawn. Through the morning-room window I caught a glimpse of Dora's black dress against the white panelling. She was walking up and down, straightening a cushion perhaps or putting the biscuits away. Too nervous to come out and meet us. Well, there was no reason to spare her that little ordeal.

"She's there," I said. "We'll go closer and I'll call her to come out. Difficult meetings are easier in the open air. She won't have to ask you to sit down. And if you begin to talk—as you'll have to, as soon as I've slipped away—it won't seem quite so formal. Dora! Dora!"

I shouted gaily, like a child that has found a bird's nest. There was a flash of black across the window, and she came out by the side door on to the lawn, with quick steps.

"Did you have a good day?" I asked, when she was about three yards away.

She stopped suddenly, looked at her brother, hesitated, and then said, "Oh yes, quite good. Two winners, but they were favourites. Well—Stephen!"

I said, "Your brother's come to us for the birthday party. I told Charles to put his things in the room next the grey room. And now, I'm going to leave him in your charge."

Before either of them could speak, I went indoors and up to my bedroom.

4

If my window had looked over the front lawn, I might have been tempted to watch them, to see whether he kissed her, or took her arm, whether they wandered round the garden together, or whether she drove him indoors at once. But my window looked westwards over the little garden with the cherry trees towards the line of beeches that twisted round with the lane towards Noakes' cottage and the letter-box in the wall. I was in the room I had always had, where the setting sun about that time of the year struck through the top of the beeches on to my dressing-table and for a few moments filled the mirror with strange colours.

It was still an hour off sunset, and for some reason I felt too tired to sit and wait for it. Instead of remembering to deal with the shot rabbit, I did something I hardly ever do before dinner, and lay down on my bed and shut my eyes. "I'm here now," I thought, "and I won't be driven away. I'm here, in the innermost core of the place, in my own bed, where I want to die. Oh, gradually, when this crisis has passed, if it ever does pass, I shall find my debonair self coming back again. For the moment I've been jolted out of all that. I'm lying here, clutching the earth, and making it mine."

Indeed, it did seem to me, pressing my heels into the mattress, as if the mattress were earth—the essential earth of Carlice—and I were burrowing into it for such security as one could still hope to find.

Stephen Payne wished to live the life of his own mind. Cornwall—yes, for the moment. It was a caprice, a source of inspiration, but he carried his real world about with him in his head. I in my wishes was more materially bound. It wasn't the life of the mind that I wished to live, but a life which oozed from one particular place. Take me away, and I become nobody—a hyena with the mask of a gracious old lady.

Is this an ugly passion? Are passions ugly? And if I get what I want, what shall I give in return? I have passed the age of giving. I am here to take. It seems to me, I have been giving all my life—giving way to others.

Stephen Payne is no real kindred of mine. He's of a superior order. Certainly I shall do any little thing I can for him, if only to propitiate the unknown. But my real kindred is the tramp I saw, sitting under the beeches, eating his bread and cheese. When I saw him, I knew that he sat there, not because he was too infirm to move, or couldn't get work, or for any laudable reason of that sort, but because he liked the place, and for an hour in his wandering life had taken root in the roots of those old trees. And for once there was no policeman at hand to move him on.

Chapter X: RONALD CARLICE

I THOUGHT on the way back, "When I get home they'll look at
me curiously, as people look at someone who's been in prison
or had the most frightful of operations. They'll probe me in a
thousand gentle little ways, to see if I've changed again, or at least
have begun to waver. They'll have a specially lovely food served,
to remind me that food in Russia isn't so good as it is in an English country house. They'll put the best linen sheets on my bed to
remind me that people don't have linen sheets in Russia. They'll
have the garden neat and beautiful to remind me that in Russia
there are no gardens, as we understand them. They'll watch me
carefully, hoping for a sign that I'm relenting. They'll talk to me
circumspectly, as one talks to an invalid. They'll say I've got too
thin—even thinner than I usually am. They'll say, 'We must fatten
you up with good English fare—the good English fare of Carlice
Abbey.' And in spite of everything I've said, by word of mouth,
by letter and by telegram, they will have arranged some kind of a
birthday party for me."

Small wonder if I couldn't bring myself to arrive till two days
before my birthday!

And they'll nearly succeed in having their way with me. That's
why I feel so ashamed. Have I got to admit to such weakness—
to confess that my point of view was simply an undergraduate's
enthusiasm, or that, while I know that I was right and they were
wrong, my whole upbringing is too much for me and puts me,
ultimately, on their side and not on the side to which I should
belong? Will they find out, whatever I do or say, that I was miserable in Russia, and am really coming back like a convalescent to
a convalescent-home, tired and shocked and longing desperately
for the little bourgeois conventions, those decent curtains which
they hang between themselves and life in the raw—those pieces of
solicitude which are charming to me because they were ingrained

in me from the day of my comfortable birth? Will they guess that I can't help reminding myself that I'm committed to nothing, except the good opinion of a few friends? That I can still easily stage a come-back, and decide to enjoy life, concerts, first-nights, good food, race-meetings, yachting, witty society, poetry, fine linen, old china, old furniture, and all the rest of it? It may still be possible to go on like that for a dozen years or so. Shall I sell myself to the devil for the sake of those dozen years? And adopt the view of my class and say, "Oh well, if you destroy us, you destroy civilization, and there really isn't much point in surviving afterwards"? And there's this more subtle argument. I used the phrase, "Sell myself to the devil," but, according to my creed, my *self* is utterly unimportant to the scheme of things. And there isn't a devil. Personal salvation is, in no case, a legitimate ideal. So what does it matter what I do with my *self*—that self which my creed will hardly concede to me?

All this means that I must be more than usually on my guard. I must make no concession. I must be, if necessary, standoffish, awkward, churlish and offensive. I mustn't even allow myself to think. I must obey blindly the categorical imperative.

2

It was Aunt Dora who met the car as I drove in. Still in black. Of course, it's still the same year that my sister Joan was killed in.

"Well, Ronnie," she said, "I'm sure you have so much to tell us. But, my dear boy, how frightfully thin you've grown. You ought to have gone on a cruise like me. It did me so much good. We haven't arranged any party, but I'm afraid you'll find somebody here you never expected. It's my brother Stephen. My half-brother really. His mother died when he was born, and my father married mother only three years afterwards. He's come to see me on business, and Aunt Isabel suggested he should stay till over your birthday. He's had rather a hard life, though it's his own fault. I do hope he won't annoy you."

She was so garrulous, she almost followed me into the lavatory when I went to wash. She was looking very well, and showed a vitality which I hadn't remembered noticing in her for a long time.

I wondered if she really had taken it in when I told her, before going away, that I intended to make big changes after my birthday. Was she working herself up for a torrent of tears when I had to say, "Please have your things packed"?

She was the first woman I had talked to since Russia. The first female contrast. I suppose I may as well face the facts and admit that I can't allow Rose to mean anything to me now. I must marry, of course, but the daughter of an Oxfordshire farmer wouldn't do. I should have her mother, covered with imitation furs, sidling up to me and saying, "Can't you do something for my poor little Rosie? She's so unhappy. Do give her a new dress or a piece of jewellery. We didn't think she was marrying someone without a family and with all those fantastical ideas." And before I knew where I was, there'd be a scene, and I should have the fur-clad lady rolling about the floor. No, Rose mustn't do for me, though she'd make a splendid wife from the point of view of the family, if only they had the wit to realise it. Just as Dora was a splendid wife for my father—if only she'd had children. What should I have been like if I'd had half a dozen step-brothers and sisters?

Happily Rose's image has grown faint. The family don't know that they have only to get her over here to make me abjure all my virtuous resolutions. If they did, they'd send for her at once. At least, Aunt Isabel would. Whenever I say "the family" I really mean her. There's nobody else to mean.

After I'd got rid of Dora by washing my hands, I went to the library, and looked out of the window till I knew luncheon would be ready. "I'll meet Isabel at the table," I thought; "while she's at her food she won't be so occupied with me. It'll be a good place, too, in which to meet the uninvited guest, on whom I shall have to waste politeness for forty-eight hours." I have never been able to talk to middle-aged men. I'd rather have a crusted Colonel of eighty than someone who tries to understand you, and meet you halfway, and went through the war and thinks that that made him understand all about life.

While I was waiting, looking at my watch rather than at the view, Eames came in to say that the mistress wondered if I should like anything sent upstairs. I almost said that I should like all my meals sent upstairs for the next forty-eight hours, but told him to tell them I would join them in the dining-room in two minutes. I had meant to account for my lateness by saying I had been doing a little unpacking, but as Eames had caught me idling in the library that excuse was taken from me.

I came down slowly—the squire descending the *escalier d'honneur* —and went into the dining-room. Isabel was on her feet, helping herself to some salad on one of the side-tables. She came forward with a plate in one hand and offered me her other. "When and where," she asked, "did you have your last meal?"

I said, "I suppose you expect me to reply, 'In the Kremlin.'"

She answered, "I expect you to enjoy this very delicious oyster soup. Thomas Hill has sent down a barrel of oysters, and we thought they wouldn't all keep."

She rang as she talked to me, and Eames brought in my soup-plate. While he was putting it down in my place at the head of the table, she introduced Dora's brother, Stephen Payne. I had met him before, years ago. I think I had just left my first school, and in those days liked strangers who gave me half a crown. Stephen Payne had given me nothing. I remembered him as a sandy-haired little man with the look of a sentimental grocer. He hadn't changed much, except that the sandy hair was thinner. He made no attempt to remind me of our first meeting, but sat down as soon as he had shaken hands with me, and began to eat. I felt that he was sorry I had arrived. "This is a meal to be got over quickly," I thought.

I tackled Dora at once about her cruise. It had been a great success and she was very ready to talk about it. She had met such nice people, and the sea air had done her so much good. The ship she went on was going to cross the Equator at Christmas. Quite a number of her fellow-passengers had booked for the trip. She had been tempted to do so too.

This statement dried her up. It was too closely connected with the unknown future—the future which, on Tuesday, is to lie in my hands. "Well," I thought, "you'd better book, if you can afford it. You won't be here."

Aunt Isabel, meanwhile, was talking about rabbits to Stephen Payne. It seems that they are getting into the garden, and Payne shot one through the morning-room window, ten minutes after he arrived. He asked me if I shot.

I replied, "No, I have never learnt to shoot—unlike my father."

Those last three words showed how much I was on edge. I could almost feel Dora's shiver, and Isabel stiffening against me. It was a sign, in the eyes of both of them, that Russia hadn't done me any good.

Payne said, "I learnt to shoot during the war. But with a different kind of weapon." He didn't share in the tension I had created. No doubt he had forgotten about my father's death. Perhaps he had never heard about it.

Before serving coffee, Eames handed round the port. We all refused it, even Payne, who, I thought, was supposed to be something of a dipsomaniac. Perhaps he was on his best behaviour. We were all on our best behaviour.

When Eames had gone out, Aunt Isabel said, "About three, I'm going for a walk. I shall come back by Noakes' cottage, because I promised to drop in and see old Mrs. Noakes. Would anyone like to come with me?"

Dora said she had eaten too much and was sure she'd be sleepy. Payne said he would like to.

"We won't bother Ronnie," Isabel said. "I'm sure he'll be glad of two hours by himself—acclimatising himself to home again."

I answered, "Yes, I shall." It was the first thrust that they made at me.

3

It was a right instinct of mine not to bring any of my friends here for my birthday. However much we agreed politically, other *nuances* were bound to disturb us. Their energies would have been absorbed by the routine of the place—that routine to which I have been adapted from birth. They couldn't have helped me. I should have been more nervous than I am, seeing their discomfiture over trivialities, and more upset than I am, hearing them pay lip-service to the conventions. Or else there would have been a ghastly row, and I can't face that till I have my final row with Thomas Hill, who is coming here, it seems, for luncheon on my birthday. "If need be, he'll stay the night," said Isabel. I took it that this was her way of saying, "If you invite him, he'll stay the night," because on and after Tuesday invitations to stay at Carlice should come from me. In the past they have come theoretically from Dora, though Isabel's promptings have never been disregarded. Poor Dora! In the early days, when I was not aware of things, there must have been a lot of, "Don't you think, Dora, it would be a good thing to ask so-and-so?" And Dora would reply, "Of course, Isabel. I was thinking of that only last night." I played the same game later, though with more justification.

No, I'm glad I have no friends of mine here during these three days. They would only hamper me in the coming contest. Thomas Hill is coming to luncheon on Tuesday, and he shall stay just so long as it takes him to do his business. The bank manager is coming over after luncheon from Risely, bringing documents which he has been keeping in safe custody. I wonder if I shall find among the papers some sinister note from my father—some awful voice from the tomb disclosing a family scandal and telling me why he killed himself. I used to be afraid, five or six years ago, that my father killed himself because he had an hereditary disease, and had left a letter, somewhere, cautioning me to be on my guard against it. Well, I can look upon that sort of thing with more equanimity now. It was different when I thought that the attainment of my majority would open a gate for me to a life of cultivated egotism.

I had thought, that as soon as luncheon was over, I could slip up to the library and read, or even have a nap. Dora went to the drawing-room, and Stephen Payne followed her there with a furtive air. Isabel went to the morning-room—that has always been her room, just as the library has been mine, and the drawing-room Dora's—and left the door open. I loitered in the dining-room for a minute, pretending to look for the cigars, though they were always left in charge of Eames. When I thought the coast should have been clear, I crossed the hall to go upstairs. But Isabel was by her open door and called me.

"Ronnie, do spare me ten minutes."

I said, "Certainly," and sat down and lit a cigarette.

She got going at once.

"Ronnie, I do want to have rather a serious talk with you. I know it's a silly time to choose, when you've just come back from a tiring journey, but I want you to have as long a time as possible to make up your mind about what I'm going to say before—well, before Tuesday and Thomas Hill's visit."

She pushed an ash-tray towards me, giving me time to speak if I wanted to, but I didn't.

"I only know what your plans are from Dora," she went on. "She tells me that as soon as you come into Carlice you are going to hand it over to the Communist party as a kind of propaganda centre or school. Apparently you've met some girl near Oxford who attracts you, and you may be marrying her and living here as caretaker. A farmer's daughter, Dora told me. How far is all this true?"

"The second part is hardly true at all," I answered. "I did meet a farmer's daughter near Oxford, and she did attract me very much. I don't know if I attracted her, though I dare say she would have liked to make a good marriage like—you know whom I mean. But she wouldn't be able to help me in my work and I'm not going to be false to my principles for the sake of a love-affair. This may sound priggish, but I am priggish."

"My dear Ronnie," she said, "we should all far prefer you to marry a farmer's daughter rather than some intellectual tart from London who writes for the papers."

"I dare say you would. I happen to think that an intellectual tart from London—mind you, I don't know one yet—would be more likely to help the cause I want to help."

She looked at me without any show of affection.

"Well, we can leave that. You haven't yet met the woman you're going to marry. Now what about this handing over of Carlice to the 'party'?"

She pronounced the word "party" with a contemptuous inflexion.

"That is all perfectly correct. I shall make the place over as soon as I get it. On Wednesday, if it can be done so soon."

"You really are set upon this? You've thought it all out thoroughly?"

"Yes."

"Of course," she said, in a more reflective tone, "it upsets me and it will upset all our friends and all those who've been connected with us. You don't suppose that Noakes and Stephens and Jackson and Eames will take kindly to what you're doing? However, I won't waste your time by putting their case. They're only individuals and don't count for you. And I'm certainly not going to waste your time by asking you to give up your idea for my sake. Instead, I'm going to make you a suggestion, and I do ask you to take it very seriously. It seems very sensible to me, and I hope it'll seem sensible to you. It is this—that you should sell Carlice to me, lock, stock and barrel. I'll give you eighteen thousand pounds. That's as much as I can manage, if I'm to have anything left over to run the place with."

I thought to myself, "An offer of eighteen means that she'll go to twenty."

"My dear Aunt Isabel, that's more than the place is worth."

"Is it?"

"Yes, far more. I have been to one or two estate agents. They said that though a millionaire who fell in love with the place might give twenty-five, it would be foolish to reckon on more than twelve, or even ten. In a forced sale, we might only get five or six, or even find we couldn't get an offer at all. So you see, you're being unfair to yourself."

"Then you *have* thought that you might like to sell?"

"Yes. I thought the money might be more useful to the party than the house, but——"

"Well, I offered eighteen. I may be unbusinesslike, but you can have eighteen. Needless to say, I hope you won't pass the whole lot on."

"But I've decided not to sell."

Her face became so white, I thought she was going to faint.

"Not at any price?" she asked. "Suppose I go through my investments and find I could manage a bit more. After all, this isn't the only house of its kind. With my money you could have your pick of the market and make a profit on the deal."

I agreed with her that Carlice wasn't the only country house for sale. I agreed even that it wasn't the most convenient house we could get, either in its design or situation.

"Then," she said, "why not take the money and buy them something more convenient?"

"Because I've decided they shall have this house."

"Even if they don't want it?"

"They do want it."

"Yes, but have you told them what you could get for it in money?

You can't have done. You said yourself that you couldn't hope for more than ten or twelve thousand at an ordinary sale. Oh, Ronnie, why must they have *this* house of all houses?"

"Because it's my house, or will be on Tuesday."

"You mean you want a cheap advertisement. A headline in the papers. That's what it is, simply a silly personal vanity. You, who profess to think that personal feelings are contemptible. I always knew that you must be inconsistent."

"You're quite wrong. I don't think you'd understand my reasons if I told you them."

"Oh, I've no doubt you've bamboozled yourself with some frightfully subtle scientific theory. I don't suppose you've simply said to yourself, 'I shall get a lot of prestige by doing this dramatic thing.' It goes a bit further down than that with you. That's Dora's level, not ours. But underneath, it's just personal vanity—the same feeling exactly as Dora had when the Captain of her cruising liner asked her for a dance."

"I was afraid you'd see it in this light," I replied. "But in order to convince you that my feeling is not quite the same as Dora's—or yours—would be, I may tell you that, when the deal goes through, it will be announced publicly that I have *sold* this house to the party—not *given* it to them."

"Yes, but the party will know the truth."

"Only one or two officials. They won't care, and in any case they haven't much influence."

She put her hand behind her neck, and seemed to rest for a minute. And while she did so, I felt a minute's weakness. Was it, after all, mere vanity on my part? Or a silly desire to shock people without doing any good? Or even a mean revenge on my aunt, whose authority had weighed down my childhood more than she could understand? If she had said nothing, or even shed a tear or two, I might have given way. But she didn't. She sat bolt upright and burst into a long tirade.

"I suppose it's no use asking you, Ronnie, to be a little more lucid in your own mind. I've no doubt you think you've reached a stage of perfect and final lucidity, and it's almost impertinent of me to remind you that you're not yet twenty-one. But you aren't twenty-one yet, and things that seem so simple and obvious at that age seem less simple and obvious when you're thirty-three or forty-four, or even older. Surely you ought to realise that you may change. You *will* change. I can promise you that. It's only very dull people who remain the same all their lives, and I don't think you are dull. You're rather clever, and that means you'll change a lot. Do leave some little loop-hole for yourself. Don't throw everything away in an undergraduate's caprice. I'm sorry. I'd forgotten that you'd taken your degree and are not an undergraduate any longer, but I don't suppose that marks any great spiritual rebirth. Give yourself a chance. That's all I'm asking you. Keep Carlice going, as it is, for two or three years. Or let me buy it from you. I'll pay you as much as ever I can afford. I'll let you see my investment book. Drive as hard a bargain with me as you can, and give my money to the Communist party. Let me have Carlice. After all, if it's mine, it's in the family, and when I die there's nobody for me to leave it to but you."

She sat back and looked at me. I felt I couldn't go on talking to her any longer and said:

"That's exactly the reason, Auntie Isabel, why my mind is made up, and why I want the whole thing settled now. I don't want to make the best of both worlds. I don't want any secret expectations—if the present social order should last so long, which I doubt. I don't want to cater for myself, if I live, with any hope of a comfortable old age——"

"I suppose you know," she said quietly, "that even if you do make this gift to the Communists, you're doomed in advance. They've no use, really, for people like you. They may flatter you now, and think that 'Carlice Abbey becomes Communist Training Centre' will make a good headline in the gutter-press, but they don't care twopence about you. Apart from your money, you're no use to them. Even your theories don't count. They'll shoot you in the first purge after the revolution."

I said, "I know that."

"Then you're a fool, a fool, a damned fool, Ronnie!"

This, as the lawyers would say, precluded the possibility of all further negotiations between us.

"I'm very sorry," I said, as urbanely as I could, "that my decision hurts you so much, Aunt Isabel. Or rather, I don't want to be hypocritical even to you. I'm not very sorry. You've had everything life can give you—or almost everything—and you're still not satisfied. You ask for more. You want to interfere with the lives of other people—with my life. You'd sacrifice the population of China, if it would give you this house. I know you and your kind. Well, let me tell you that it gives me peculiar satisfaction to think that you're not going to live here, lording it over the tenants of the estate, and playing the Lady Bountiful when you've nothing else to do. This may be a personal vanity of mine, but, if it is, I'm going to yield to it. It will give me a very profound pleasure, when I sign the Deed of Conveyance of Carlice Abbey to the Communist party, to know that never, by any possibility, can the property come into the hands of Isabel Carlice."

I stood up, and she stood up and said, "Ronnie, I think you are a little over-excited. You had better go up to your room."

I went through the door without looking at her or speaking to her, and feeling very shaky about the knees.

My knees are still shaky.

Chapter XI: DORA CARLICE

I INTENDED to lie down after all that oyster soup, but Stephen followed me into the drawing-room. What a time to choose for a talk! Sunday afternoon after rather a heavy meal. Besides, he must have known there was nothing to talk about. I more or less said so to him, when I caught him alone for a few minutes on Saturday night. I said, "Look here, Stephen, I know perfectly well you've come here to try to persuade me to pull strings with Donald Rusper. Let me tell you this, I haven't any strings to pull. I've written him two or three times urging him not to be hard on you, and he replied that I must trust him to use his own judgment, as Daddy intended. So that's that. I think it's rather mean of you to have come here without giving me a chance to say we couldn't do with you. As it is, you're Miss Carlice's guest, not mine. She seems to have taken charge of you. Let her go on doing it, till Tuesday, when Ronnie is going to turn out the lot of us, with barely time to put our bits and pieces together."

That should have been plain enough, but he followed me into the drawing-room, even though I'd said at lunch that I was going to have a nap. I can quite understand that he didn't like to go into the morning-room where Isabel was, or up to Ronnie's library, but there was always the garden for him to walk about in. Heaven knows that's big enough. It isn't as if it were winter and one had to be indoors near a fire. It's early September, even if it isn't a very nice day.

He followed me into the drawing-room. I went straight to the sofa and he went to the easy chair by the fireplace and lit a cigarette.

The first thing he said was, "I don't like this room as much as the other rooms in the house. Why did you choose it?"

I said, "I don't agree with you. I like it better than the other rooms. It isn't so heavy, specially since I got new curtains and had the furniture done up."

He flicked his ash carelessly over the clean hearth, and asked me suddenly, "Where are you going on Tuesday?"

"Tuesday?"

"Yes, your nephew's birthday."

I said I hadn't settled anything.

"Haven't you asked your nephew if you're to go?" he said, as if I were a housemaid afraid of being given notice.

"No, I haven't. If I did, it would sound as if I was asking him to let me stay on."

"Do you want to stay on?"

"No. I don't want to be bustled out of the house, but I don't think I really want to stay. In fact I should only stay if he showed me that he really needed me here. And he won't."

"I see. So Tuesday brings no tragedy for you."

I spent a few minutes wondering what he meant by that. It was all leading up to *his* tragedy, I supposed. Well, there was no need for him to have any tragedy, if only he'd be sensible. He was waiting for me to speak, but I decided to say nothing. Besides, I had a good deal to think about. What was I going to do on Tuesday if Ronnie said, "Out you go!"? Dolly Headford had let her flat and had gone to some cousins near Whitby, so I couldn't ask her to put me up. Could I ask Isabel to give me a bed? No, I should be miserable there. The only thing to do was to go to a hotel—but where? In London and look round for a flatlet? It might be rather fun, setting up a little place on my own. Perhaps Ronnie would let me take some of the drawing-room furniture. After all, I'd spent my own money having it done up; and the curtains were certainly mine. (They'll find the old ones in one of the oak chests in the hall.) Not that I'm very satisfied with the way my new curtains have worn. Ever since Flora left the window open that wet day in April there have been stains on the curtains behind the writing-desk. If Ronnie knew how much I'd thought about that writing-desk, and how much that bottom drawer had meant to me, he'd give me it outright. The bottom drawer is still locked. Whoever opened it once can open it again, if he wants to put the box back. I shall look there after tea to-morrow. If the box is there, I shall give it to Ronnie and tell him I've been keeping it for him since Claude died. I shall say, "That's your father's writing on the label. I found the box hidden under his tennis clothes, when I went through his things after he died. I can't help what's inside the box, and, now, I don't really care."

I thought all this (just as I'm still thinking some of it now) while Stephen was silent after his remark about Tuesday bringing no tragedy to me. When, at last, I looked up at him, he seemed to be asleep.

"Stephen!"

"Yes, Dora?"

"You can't sleep here. You promised to go for a walk with Miss Carlice."

"Do you suppose she wants me?"

"*I* don't know."

"Dora."

"Yes?"

"Are you going to help me with Rusper?"

"I can't do anything."

"Yes, you can. Let me tell you."

And he started a long explanation of how I could give evidence in court that Don was acting against the wishes of the family in his capacity of trustee. He said there wouldn't even be any need to go to court, because Don would crumple up the moment he knew I was really against him. It all depended on me. If only I'd take a firm line, everything would be all right. Would I promise to take a firm line? I said I wouldn't promise.

"Then you really are with him against me," Stephen said. "Dora, what does that great brute mean to you?"

"Oh, nothing special," I said, feeling that I was blushing. "Only," I went on, "he did come closer to Daddy than you ever did, and I can't honestly say I think he isn't carrying out Daddy's wishes. I think he is carrying them out. You mayn't like his manner, but there it is. Daddy would have acted just the same if he'd been alive. In fact, if Daddy had been alive, you'd have still been a solicitor or a schoolmaster."

"No, I shouldn't," he said.

"Why not?"

"Because I still would have been expelled from the school."

"You wouldn't have dared to let yourself go like that. You only gave way because you knew you had four-fifty a year behind you."

Without even looking at me, he got up and went through the

French window into the garden—leaving the flap of the window open.

I got up from the sofa, shut the window, lay down and went to sleep.

Chapter XII: STEPHEN PAYNE

I'M done for now.

Utterly. Hopelessly. And through my own fault. They may have been right about me the whole time. I am unfit to be let loose. The third time, one can't hope to be given another chance. I got over that business at Barling House School because Duparc was a sensible fellow. Besides, I hadn't really antagonised Rusper then. He was only bullying me as he bullied everyone. He hadn't singled me out. I got over my second breakdown—though it was really a piece of bad luck, not a break-down at all—by running away from Rusper to Thurlow. By this time I'd made Rusper my enemy—and I made him still more an enemy when I paid him that idiotic visit on my way to Cornwall. (After all, I was only doing what Dora had urged me to do.) But this last exhibition I've made of myself is too much. I've put myself completely in Rusper's hands for good and all.

I suppose my attempt to have a talk with Dora after lunch was the beginning of it. I saw that she intended to give me no chance of talking to her, and I had to force the conversation on her. A bad move. But I couldn't wait for ever. She knew why I've come here, and she must have known, if she has troubled her head about me the least bit, that I should never have been able to screw myself up to invading her here unless I'd been desperate. Yet she allows me to loaf about the house and garden like an ordinary guest. She tells me, in fact, that I am an ordinary guest—"Miss Carlice's guest," till Tuesday. And on Tuesday, what then? Oh, she isn't even sure about her own arrangements. We'll see what happens on Tuesday when Tuesday comes.

There was really no need for her to drive me out of the drawing-room into the garden. I should have gone of my own free will. Otherwise I should have let myself go too far. I should have told her that she was as selfish as I am, without the same good cause.

I should have told her—but I'm making myself ill with these recriminations. It does no good to think of that now, it's all so very unimportant—and it wouldn't have done any good if I had stayed on in the drawing-room and spoken all that was in my mind. It was just as well I went out and ambled round the garden, till punctually at three o'clock Miss Carlice came out of the side door, and we began our walk together.

Beyond one or two preliminary words, we remained silent for a longer time than I should have thought possible. I can't remember ever having gone for so silent a walk with anyone. It was as if I were following her, not walking by her side, through the birch plantation, where a rabbit scuttled under my feet, out into the fields. When we had gone about a mile, she stopped suddenly and looked at the sky and then at me.

"It's going to rain," she said. "I ought to have told you to bring a mackintosh."

I said, "Oh, I don't mind getting wet. I've got another suit with me"; and we walked on in another long silence. I felt she was thinking as hard as I was—thinking about Tuesday, too, though for very different reasons. I hardly noticed the country we were passing—I, who, in my right mind, would have taken in the colours of every hedge and every tree-trunk, would have smelt the growing dampness of the breeze and the first trace of autumnal decay in the fluttering leaves. She too was looking at nothing, and all her thoughts were turned inwards. It seemed as if she were solving some problem with her feet, as she tramped like a man over the fields.

At length—we must have been walking for half an hour at least—I found myself saying:

"I can get no help from Dora."

She didn't reply for a minute, as though she were finishing up a private line of thought, and then she said, "Oh, Dora. It seems strange to think of anyone wanting her help. *I* haven't tackled her yet. I've had other things to think of. But I've another plan."

I interrupted, almost eagerly, "You mean, for me?"

"Yes, for you. It's on quite different lines. Something you don't know about. But don't let's talk about that now. I promise I won't forget when the proper time comes."

Can I build on that? Not now. Not after what has happened since then.

We came, silent as before, to the summit of a little hill. In the distance we could see the top of a line of beeches, and between them the side of the Abbey, melting into a background of grey sky. Miss Carlice stopped and looked at the view for some time, and then, making something of an effort, she began to talk, telling me about the boundaries of the estate, how her great-grandfather's land went so far, how her grandfather added this farm and her father sold that, how her brother had cut things down and made the place more compact, and how, for her own part, she wasn't wedded to the land outside the home boundary, except for a few special trees—"those beeches above all."

"We shall pass them when we go back by the road," she said. "You passed them when you were carrying your bag from Busley station. Good heavens, that was only yesterday afternoon. It seems more like a month."

I said, "That shows what a tedious guest I've been."

She didn't even pretend to laugh, but said, as the first drops of the rain-squall struck us, "You'll be wet through by the time we get to Noakes' cottage. You must go straight back from there and change, while I'm seeing Mrs. Noakes. I shall be all right in this."

I helped her on with a light mackintosh she had carried, and we changed our direction and got into a lane overhung by trees. It was raining so hard that the leaves were dripping already, and I soon felt my suit sticking to my body, while the water leaked in through my wretched shoes.

"This rain really marks the end of summer," she said. "This year, it's come too early. But we've been spoilt by the good summers of the last two or three years."

It took us about ten minutes to reach the cottage, where she dismissed me with the words, "You go straight on. You can't miss the way. When you get to the front door, ring, and Eames or Charles will deal with your wet clothes. Tell Dora that Mrs. Noakes will give me some tea. I'll be back later."

As she finished, a girl came hurrying out of the cottage. I said "Good-bye" and walked on up the road.

It was nearly a quarter to five when I got back. I told Charles, who took my wet suit away, what Miss Carlice had said about tea, and he told me that Dora had already had hers. Rather boldly I asked if he could bring me a cup of tea to my bedroom, and when he had done so, I sat there for a long time enjoying the spaciousness of the room and the sombre colours of the sky and garden. The rain was still falling heavily, and from time to time there was a flash of lightning to the west. I forgot my anxieties. I began "just living" again—fusing myself into the reality of that corner of Wiltshire as it reacted to the passing of that first autumnal storm. It was so dark, I might have turned on the light, but I didn't, and sat in a chair near the deep-set window, feeling in that unnaturally early darkness the coming darkness of winter, with its climax of mistletoe berries squashed in the carpet and sudden glimpses of a pale inactive sun seen in the intervals of cloud. Though it was only the first week in September, I had already begun to enjoy the winter—winter in the country, needless to say—days of damp mist followed by a sudden day of spring sunshine, wet soggy lawns, holly berries and ivy (lost in summer, but now coming into its own), the bare trees, most faithful of the friends that will outlive us, long meditative evenings by the fire, the exhilaration of white frosty mornings, the first snowdrop—the first faint sign of spring. The vividness of these delightful images was intensified by the desperateness of my own affairs. How would these thoughts flow behind the bars of Dr. Ebermann's asylum?

No, I would not submit myself to that. Damn Rusper and damn Dora. I would taste the joys of the sticky pavement oozing through my shoes, as I sold newspapers, or cadged at the street corner. Perhaps if I sold newspapers I should learn to be bored by the headlines. I could amuse myself with their posters, count the number of times they used the words "sensation" and "crisis" in a year. There is something in all life, provided you're not in overwhelming pain and are alive—by which I mean possessed of your own personality, which is your only means of contact with reality. But if Dr. Ebermann was to give me a personality of his choosing—well, as I've said before, we might as well kill Stephen Payne and let someone else be born in his place. And Stephen Payne has no wish to die just yet.

2

I sat in my bedroom till about half-past six. Then, as luck would have it, I thought I'd like a drink and was going downstairs, when I met Dora's stepson, Ronnie, on the landing.

He said, "Hello! Come and have a drink in the library, won't you?"

I said, "You're very kind. I don't want to bother you. Has Miss Carlice got back?"

He said, "I don't know," rather shortly and opened a door in the middle of the passage. It was a finely proportioned room, with a kind of arch in the middle and four windows looking on to the main lawn. I should say the walls must have been three feet thick. There were five or six bookcases against the walls, some shelves full of gramophone records and two corner cupboards containing china. I remember thinking, "I suppose this is all genuine antique stuff—bought by his ancestors at the proper time."

I asked him this, when he had settled me in a big carved wing-chair, and poured me out a very strong whisky-and-soda. His reply was so uninterested that I can't recall it. "He's doing his bit to entertain the unwanted guest," I thought, "but he might do it more gracefully than this." Then I recollected that in less than forty-eight hours he was going to turn Dora and Miss Carlice out of their home and give it to the Communist party. I supposed one couldn't feel quite normal before taking a step like that—it needed probably as much courage as I should need voluntarily to enter Dr. Ebermann's asylum—and I resolved to be indulgent to him.

Non-committally, I said to him, "How you must love having a room like this, where you can get away from people."

He answered, "What makes you think I want to get away from people? Privacy is a piece of anti-social luxury. In twenty years the word will have lost all meaning."

I said, "I hope not," realising that I had already taken sides against him, and he said, "I hope so."

After this unpromising beginning, we talked vaguely for a while. He asked me what I did. I told him that I had been in a solicitor's office and a master in a private school, but that if I had any gift at all—gift, that was to say, regarded from a public point of view—it was for novel-writing.

His reply to this was, "Then I'm sorry for you."

I asked him why, and he went on, "Because of all art-forms, the novel is the most bound up with the present very transitory form of society. Almost by definition, it is rooted in individualism, and it will perish when individualism perishes."

I said, "You might almost say, 'When life perishes'," but he said, "Oh, no, I mightn't. I amused myself three or four months ago at Oxford, by analysing three pages from a typical modern novel, and marking everything which in a few years will either be meaningless or censored. I don't mean obsolete details like the kitchen-range, that will be superseded by newer inventions, or even references to private property or class-distinctions. I mean passages which indicate a meaningless or criminal psychology—sentences like, *I picture myself sitting in that old garden on summer evenings.*"

I said, "What's wrong with that?"

"Well, can't you see?" he answered testily, "that it adopts altogether too egotistical an attitude towards life? We shall have lost the taste for so-called imaginative reveries. To indulge in them will be looked up as selfish, retrograde and vicious. I could elaborate the iniquities of that sentence for about half an hour. *Old* garden, too. As if there's any virtue in age. Of course, all novels aren't on those lines. It's quite true that attempts have been made to write the proletarian novel—praiseworthy attempts, too—but I should think, from the novelist's point of view, that the theme is even more restricted than the eternal triangle. You can't have a novel without characters, and the moment you begin to characterise you begin to individualise, which destroys your proletarian basis. I'm afraid the proletarian novel can never be really successful propaganda."

I replied, "Well, I'm afraid I'm not a proletarian novelist."

He said, "I gathered you weren't. I suppose you write for a few dyspeptic escapists who feel as you feel, and then you're surprised at not being a best-seller. There's no future for art which appeals only to a small and moribund class, you know."

"I certainly write for people who can read," I said. "And for people with personalities developed by some kind of traditional cultivation. I don't write for ants or illiterates. But one hopes that in due time everyone will be able to read and develop a personality."

"You write for people you think count," he said. "Well, I don't think they'll count much longer. That's hardly encouraging, is it?"

He gave me a forced little smile. I guessed he felt hypocritical even in forcing a smile.

"You said something just now about propaganda," I went on. "Do you think propagandist art can survive? Don't you think it becomes dead—as dead as an out-of-date scientific textbook—as soon as the cause for which it's written ceases to exist? We still read Milton's *Comus*, but who bothers about his Treatises against Salmasius and Morus? Personally, I think that of all art, propagandist art has the smallest chances of survival."

"I don't see why any art should survive," he answered. "When society changes, art must change or perish."

"But society changes in a circle," I suggested. "The literature of the French Revolution must have seemed very old-fashioned to Balzac, while he probably admired a good deal that was written further back."

"It's true," he said, "that till to-day we've never had a successful revolution. But we have one to-day in Russia, and we shall have one in England to-morrow. Besides, you've forgotten science—science practically applied. That's going to change things whether you like it or not. It *is* changing things. Every day it smashes some form of individualistic conceit, and paves the way for the mass-evolution of the social organism."

"I'm sick of science," I said. "Except for the invention of anæsthetics, which we aren't allowed to buy, I doubt if it has made life any pleasanter."

He laughed triumphantly.

"There you go! Because perhaps it hasn't made life any pleasanter for you, you say you're sick of science."

"Isn't that a good reason?"

"Do you really think the function of life is to make itself pleasant for you?"

"In one sense, yes. In another sense, I know life is quite indifferent to me."

"Oh, no, it isn't. It's watching you the whole time, waiting to see if you're going to make yourself pleasant to it—in other words an efficient link in the life-chain—an efficient member of the community."

"And if I don't?"

"Well, the community won't very much longer be able to put up with inefficient members. They're too much of a luxury nowadays."

"But it used to put up with them—if I *must* admit that I'm an inefficient member of the community."

"The community used to be unscientifically run. Now science has taken a hand things are going to be very different."

"I wish, instead of talking about the 'community,' or 'society,' you people would say, 'Mr. Jones, Mr. Brown and Mr. Robinson.' It would sound so much more human. After all, society exists for its members, doesn't it? It's only a public convenience—like a club, I mean."

"Oh, no, it isn't. The members of a society exist for society. Just as the cells in your body exist for your body. If they don't do their job properly, if they develop individualities and personalities of their own, they become cancer-cells, and have to be cut out. In the same way, members of society who develop personalities and individualities are cancer-cells in society, and will have to be cut out."

I said, "What book did you get that from?"

"I don't know. It's quite a commonplace metaphor in our propaganda. Let me get you another drink."

"Thank you. I see you maintain that man exists for society, and not, as I'd always thought, society for man. What does society exist for, then?"

He put the drink—another strong one—on a little table by my chair, and said, "Society exists for life."

"What do you mean?"

"I mean that society is the most efficient means for the carrying on of life, and as such is bound to survive and become intensified."

"Till the individual becomes nothing but an ant?"

"If necessary. If reducing him to that level is the most efficient basis of social organisation, I have no doubt whatsoever that he will become an ant."

"Do you think that desirable?"

"What does it matter whether it's desirable or not, provided it's biologically necessary?"

"I should have thought it mattered a good deal. Do you regard life—any kind of life—as an end in itself? Life, just in quantity, with no notion of quality? What value has life, considered by itself?"

"It has the only value—survival value."

I paused. There were so many things I could say. What did he mean by survival? Survival only in time? Is something that lasts a hundred years necessarily better than something that only lasts ten minutes? Is the life of a tortoise better than the life of a may-fly? To take this view was like taking mere size as a criterion of excellence—or mere numbers. I wondered how far he could possibly be sincere.

"And what," I asked, "when you've got life going to the uttermost—when you've peopled the earth till there's standing-room only—when you've peopled all the planets and all the stars? What then? What is the end? Why bother about it all? Unless the people who are going to live and die during those ages have a chance to develop personalities of their own and to stand outside the ghastly process and form their own reality and get contact with it in their own individual ways?"

He said, "They will be in contact with reality, if they're efficient members of society."

"Simply as ants, or cogs in a machine? I don't see that. Have you nothing more to offer me? Not even a distant vision of perfection?"

"Why should I have?"

"Because life is so meaningless without one."

"Well, if it is?"

"It becomes a nightmare."

"Well? Perhaps it is, to people like you. Personally, my own view is that one rubs along better by adapting oneself to life as it is than by going against it. However, life doesn't care whether I rub along well or badly, so long as I serve my purpose."

"Then why don't you adapt yourself to the capitalist system, which happens to be the prevailing mode of life in England today?"

"Ah, that's asking me to take too short a view altogether."

"Yet you won't let me take a very long one."

"I won't let you look forward to the Infinite. That's a very different matter."

"Tell me, are you a Communist on scientific or humanitarian grounds?"

"Both, though I realise that, ultimately, it's the scientific grounds which count. As the most efficient of possible biological developments, Communism is inevitable."

"If it is, why bother to help it forward?"

"Because I'm more comfortable if I adapt myself to the future than if I try to live in the past."

"Then personal comfort is a legitimate motive?"

"It's one of life's baits. Mind you, life doesn't want you to be comfortable, any more than society does. If it turns out that individual suffering makes for an efficient society, the individual will have to suffer. In fact, I'm afraid that endurance of a certain amount of bodily pain probably has a social survival-value. If it has, we shall all have to undergo, say, half an hour's torture every day, just as in time vivisection will almost certainly be practised on human beings. The fittest survive. The law of survival is the one law we know—and, ultimately, the only value worth recognising."

I felt I had borne enough, and finished my drink at one gulp.

"So you really think," I said, rather offensively perhaps, "that all our instincts, all our hopes and aspirations, all our private realities—and there is no reality which is not private—must be measured and valued by this one biological law. You think, because very feebly you're learning to recognise the glands without which we couldn't have emotions, that emotions can be ruled out as perceptions of reality. (You might as well say that the value of a rosebud is the manure round the rose's root.) You think that what survives, should survive. Science, to you, is the only means of knowledge. For the sake of science (mind you, the very rudimentary science of 1936, which contradicts the science of 1886 and will itself be contradicted in 2006) you're prepared to blot out in one blow the living influence of the past, all our traditions, all the sanctity of our age-long experience. Shall I tell you my vision of the future? You will find it very different from yours. In my future you will have a world not over-populated, so that the individual, in the course of his long life, will have all the privacy he requires for contemplation, and all the space he requires for the extension and development of his personality. There will be so much to browse upon—all the loveliness of the past, the vast treasury of the arts—not temporary propagandist arts, but those arts which are eternal bridges to reality. The individual will browse upon these arts, and upon his own direct personal realities also—which spring upon us from a host of intimate feelings and sudden convincing glimpses of nature. By nature I don't want you to think I'm indicating nature on a bold, picturesque or panoramic scale. Size doesn't count. A few matches littered in the dust on the floor of an inn-parlour, one leaf hanging from a twig in autumn, a muddy path leading to a farm gate—these and such other images are quite sufficient for my purpose. As I have said, there will be so much for us to browse upon that action will seem superfluous and impertinent—at best, an unpleasant necessity. As for this science which gives you people such a thrill, we shall very soon get bored with it. We shall take it for granted that every year we can fly ten times as quickly as we could fly the year before. We shan't really want to fly anywhere. We shall accept, perhaps, certain bodily conveniences which leave us freer for meditation, but we shall no more regard science as a fit object for our emotions than we now regard the sewage-farm."

"In Russia——" he said, and I said, "I dare say. I'm giving you *my* vision of the future—a future of contemplation rather than action, and of feeling rather than theorising, a future which lives on the past and doesn't bother itself about progress, a future in which life moves more and more slowly, like a clock running down, on whose face each hour is marked as longer and lovelier than the last—till finally, time stands still, and all our troubles are over."

I tried to take a drink, but my glass was empty. He got up quickly and refilled it for me.

"Well," he said, "if that's your vision of the future, I'm afraid you're going to spend the rest of your life having a series of disappointments, if nothing worse."

"I'm going to die," I said, "but at least I have a vision. I have something inside me that is an end in itself, and I shall have lived in contact with that something. It's more than you have, in your miserable biological world, with your pathetic belief that reality is a scientific subject, accessible by science. And by what science?

Yesterday's, to-day's or to-morrow's? They're not the same. What do you know, yet, of deeper causes and deeper effects? (If the law of cause and effect holds good at all. *I* hope it doesn't.) What entitles you to try to remould humanity for the sake of a scientific experiment, divesting men of every attribute which distinguishes them from animals? Wait till your science is as old as our traditions before you put it into practice. Why, you didn't even foresee the rise of Fascism! I'll tell you about your science. I'll give you a little scientific lecture, which may be new to you. You know that plants need water?"

"Yes."

"Do you know that in every so many parts of ordinary water there is a tiny drop of another substance called Heavy Water?"

"I seem to have heard of Heavy Water."

"Well, without this infinitesimal proportion of Heavy Water, ordinary water is less fitted for maintaining plant life. And inside this heavy water there is a still heavier water—I suppose you'd call it Tritium Oxide, Heavy Water being known as Deuterium Oxide. I don't think they pretend to know yet what the effects of Tritium Oxide are, but it may turn out to be a very important substance— even essential. And other discoveries may be made within Tritium Oxide. My point is that you, with your conception of society, with your imperfect rudimentary science, would have regarded Heavy Water as a dangerous antisocial abnormality. You would have said, had you been head-gardener to the community, 'We can't allow this wasteful monstrosity to exist. What we want is water, not Deuterium Oxide—that freakish piece of individualism.' And you would have trotted out your metaphor of the cancer-cell, and run the Heavy Water off into a concentration camp. You'd have done the same with the first proton that misbehaved with an electron— the first amœba that struck out for itself, the first monkey who tried to walk on two legs. Talk of the intolerance of the Old Testament or the Catholic Church! You're fifty times as intolerant, and fifty times as ignorant, because you would gaily sacrifice the known to a half-digested theory—the freedom of the individual soul to the discipline of an ant-hill."

He heard my last few sentences impatiently, and asked, "What book did you get that Heavy Water business from?"

"A botanical magazine I found on a table in the morning-room here."

"Oh, yes. My aunt has them sent here, and reads them when she comes to stay. Is that the end of your lecture—or should I call it parable?"

"Yes. Though I could elaborate it a good deal."

"Rather a case of the Devil quoting Scripture, isn't it?"

"Well—if it is?"

"I'm afraid it doesn't convince me. I still know that the only possible values are biological values. The fittest survive. A fit nation will beat an unfit nation. An organised nation will beat an unorganised nation. And the best organisation is quite obviously Communism."

"Regarded purely as an economic theory, or as a spiritual theory as well—forgive the word 'spiritual'?"

"From both and all points of view—the spiritual theory being, ultimately, irrelevant, since the desire for spiritual values arises either from faulty upbringing or faultily functioning glands."

"If you had argued purely from the economic standpoint," I said, "and only attacked economic individualism, I might have been prepared to concede a good deal. But when you say that there is no other level, when you deny that individuals are ends in themselves and assert that they are valuable only as links in the chain of life, then I cannot and will not give you an inch. It's death you are offering, not life—you with your talk of biological values. It's death to the soul, death to the spirit, death to *me as a person*. What do you offer in exchange?"

"I offer you the enjoyment of the rhythm of the mass-mind."

"The mass-mind! Usually manifested in lynchings and panics, I believe."

He turned savagely upon me. "At any rate, it's better than your miserable little warped ego. Why should people slave away and subsidise *you* so that you can go mooning about your inward reality and matches on a pub floor? What use are *you*? What right have *you* to ask for anything? You with your talk of the importance of property, and tradition and privacy, and quality being better than quantity and all the other mumbo-jumbo of your class! Why should I bother to listen to such stuff, any more than I bother to read your twopenny-ha'penny novelettes? Why should——"

I was so startled by his outburst I nearly dropped the empty glass I was holding in my hand. Then, almost deliberately, I threw it at his head. It missed and struck the glass in the china cupboard and smashed it. He jumped up, went straight to the door and slammed it behind him. I sat where I was for five minutes—ten minutes—half an hour—I don't know how long. I had begun to cry.

3

It was crying that saved me from fainting. I'm glad I didn't faint, or I'd have been carried to bed, or sent away in an ambulance—straight to Dr. Ebermann's clinic. I was wiping my eyes, when the door opened and Dora came in.

She said, "Stephen, Ronnie has told me."

I was irritated by a silly look of drama on her face.

"Has he told you we both lost our tempers?" I asked.

"You know that with you, Stephen, it was more than a loss of temper. It was a complete breakdown of self-control. It's exactly what you did at your school, when you threw the ink-pot at the window—or what you did at Boschurch, the night you threw the plant-pot at Catherine Rusper. I can't take the responsibility any more. It's too much for me. I ought never to have let you stay here."

I felt she was going to work herself up into hysterics, but instead she surprised me by saying with sudden calm, "I've just rung up Don Rusper. Luckily he was in. He's coming over here to-morrow about five. He can't manage to get here before, he's still so busy. He'll take you away, and this time you'll have to do as he says."

I jumped to my feet.

"You've done that," I shouted. "You, Dora! Well, you and your stepson are a pretty pair of sneaks. You don't want me in this house? All right. I'll go. I'll go now."

I went to the door and she shrank away as if I were going to hit her.

"Oh, Stephen," she said, "why can't you be like other people? You always were a worry, both to Daddy and to me. There *is* something wrong with you. Why won't you let yourself be cured?"

"There's nothing wrong with me," I answered. "If you suppose

I'm going to my bedroom so that you can lock the door on me, till——"

Then suddenly I felt it was quite futile to talk to her any more, and, in the middle of my sentence, I walked downstairs, took my cap from a peg in the cloakroom and went to the front door. At the top of the stairs, pale against the dark panelling, I saw Dora's horrified irresolute face. Before she could come down, or even speak, I opened the front door, went through it and slammed it behind me.

When I reached the end of the long drive, I realised that the rain had almost stopped. A good thing, I thought; for I shouldn't have to give the footman two suits to dry in one day—if I ever came back, that was. On reaching the road I hesitated, and then walked in a direction which I imagined to be northward—the opposite direction to that by which I had arrived from Busley station—full of hope, even then, though it was the hope of despair. Now I was hopeless. I had done for myself.

I *have* done for myself. I repeat the words with the rhythm of my stride. It has become dark, very quickly, and no stars can show through the clouds. Winter has begun already, as Miss Carlice said this afternoon—some twenty days too early. What will she think, I wonder, when Dora tells her? Will she say, "Oh, what a pair of fools, to quarrel over a theory?" (But it's more than a theory. It's a practical danger, that outlook of his.) Still, *she* must hate his theory. Her sympathies must be with me, even if she deplores my suburban lapse of manners. It's Board-School boys who throw ink-pots. I've thrown an ink-pot in my time. I threw one at the window in Barling House School.

This is a lovely night for a long walk, even though there are no stars or moon. The damp air carries the smell of the dying leaves to my nose. How I could wander through the Cornish lanes, finding a joy in every twist or sudden slope, every loose stone that trips me, every branch that brushes past my body, every sound of those uncommercial waterways. If twenty-eight and sixpence would take me there, I'd go—and die there, if I must, of starvation.

If there were no Don Rusper in the world—if he could be struck by lightning, or run over, or or poisoned, or shot by accident, I should be there in my own right—the honoured guest, perhaps, of the farmer who encouraged me to shoot at rats and

rabbits. I should be looking round for a little house, that I'd fill
with my own knick-knacks, forgetting the colourless creeds of
modern sociologists and preparing to embark on my own life—a
small thing, if one must reckon by the sum of things, but to me,
the central pathway through an universe. It's funny how clearly
I can think when slightly drunk. I even said *an* universe. (It was
his fault, giving me those three whiskies. He knew my failing.
Or had Dora kept my terrible secret from them? Why couldn't I
have had Miss Carlice for my sister?) So near and yet so far. The
more I have begun to discover happiness in myself, the more the
outside world threatens to smash me—with a new war, or a new
economic system, or an absurd caprice on the part of my trustee. I
have a feeling that if I weren't happy in myself, if I were ill or bored
or lonely and couldn't get through my days, the future would
seem absolutely secure. *I'm* all right. I've done my part. It's for the
rest of the world to do its part. It's for some motor-car to collide
with Rusper as he marches self-importantly with his stethoscope
through South Mersley Garden City. It's only an accident that I'm
in these straits. It's for an accident to put me right again. Perhaps
it's only an accident that I am what I am—an accident of badly
functioning glands, Ronald Carlice would say. Well, it may be. You
can explain away why I want what I want, but it is a fact, an objec-
tive, scientific fact, that I do want it very much indeed. And that,
being a person, I have an access to reality which the ant hasn't, and
won't have when the whole beastly brood are ants together. Oh, I
could have said so much more to him. (And, doubtless, he to me.)
Our talk was too short. We made our points too quickly, without
giving them an atmosphere. After all, he didn't disprove anything I
said. All he could answer was, "Well, you're going to have a nasty
time. The world isn't moving your way!"

And that was all a good deal truer than he knew.

4

It has begun to rain again—a drizzle this time. The stones on
which I am leaning are quite damp. What is it, the parapet of a
bridge over a river? No, a railway-bridge. A high one too. I can see
dimly the lines glistening far down there in the darkness. Across

the road, the ground rises steeply. It must be a bridge over the entrance to a tunnel. Perhaps it's the railway I came by—the line to Busley.

I'm getting wet—the second time to-day. I shall have to give the footman my suit to dry. I hope my other one will be ready. I'm talking as if I'm going back quite soon—as if this were a pleasant after-dinner stroll. I forget that I ran away, and that Dora is mopping her eyes with a silly little handkerchief, sniffing at smelling salts or ringing up the police. The police! Perhaps they're scouring the country for me. But they can't do that, till Rusper gives them the word.

There's a policeman over the road, talking to a man outside the pub, by the new red telephone kiosk. This must be a kind of village—or an important bus stop. Perhaps it's known as something or other bridge—marked on the map and all that—a real place. Perhaps some day I shall look it up on the map and say, "I walked there from Carlice Abbey, the night before I went to Ebermann's Asylum." Will map-reading be one of my accomplishments then? Will they leave me that? It is the one agreeable thing the war taught me.

I'd better not let that policeman see my face. I'll look down over the parapet on to the railway. If he went away, I could easily climb up and jump down. I wonder what it feels like to jump down. No one can tell us, I suppose. Probably it's no worse than turning on the gas or taking an overdose of something. But it sounds worse. It needs more courage. And if one didn't die? If one was left, all crumpled up, but living, till a train came along—as that one's coming along now. It's marvellous how far away you can hear trains on a still night. The wind has quite dropped. There it comes. I can see sparks shooting out of the funnel. Rumble, rumble. I have always loved the sound of distant trains. Perhaps one can make everything real, humanise everything, even modern science, by thinking about it and growing familiar with it. Nowadays, a train seems such a gentle creature, like a docile dog. And the railway line, flowing perpetually in a fixed course through the fields, is a romantic thing, like all old things which are wrapped round by the leisurely musings of mankind. If ever mankind stops musing, then there'll be trouble.

The man has gone into the pub, and the policeman's moving up the lane. No, he isn't. He's coming across the road to have a look at me. What shall I say if he speaks to me? Something fantastic, such as that I'm composing a sonnet or a sonata? No, simply "Good-night," and agree with what he says about the weather. He *is* coming here. He's coming to talk to me—to find out my business. I could get across to the telephone-box in time. Quickly. Now.

I'll look up Carlice Abbey in the Directory. They hang them so awkwardly by these bits of string. There we are. Mrs. Claude Carlice, Carlice Abbey. Maggerham 15. I must pretend to ring up somebody. He's watching me through the glass panel. Why must I have this bright electric light in here? I can't see him, but he can see me. I suppose I must spend twopence out of my poor twenty-eight and sixpence. I haven't any coppers. Only a sixpence. Shall I be really bold and ask him for change? Why not, after all?

"Good-evening, Constable. I wonder if by any chance you could change me a sixpence?"

"Sorry, Sir, I know I haven't any coppers on me. But they'll change it in there, right enough."

"Of course they will. Thank you so much. Good-night."

"Good-night."

An excellent idea this—a visit to the pub and a hair of the dog that bit me. Only one man drinking. He looks like a broken-down doctor—a down-at-heel Rusper. I won't speak to him.

"Good-evening, can I have a double Haig and splash?"

"You can, Sir, with pleasure. Nasty day it's been."

"Yes, very nasty. Thank you. Give me some coppers in the change, will you?"

What fun it is to part with your last pound note. I should like to die with a pocket full of silver. Which pocket shall I put it in, I wonder? Do the engine wheels grind all the coins together, or flatten them into silver strips on the rails? I should like to ask Dora that question. (How pale her face was against the panelling at the head of the stairs.) I could ring her up and ask her. Why not? Why not do anything now, however fantastic? Nine o'clock. They'll have finished dinner. Young Carlice will be sitting alone in his library, looking at the broken glass in the china cupboard door. Dora will be moping in the drawing-room, or else worrying Miss Carlice and yapping away about me. And Miss Carlice herself will be sitting very rigidly in a rather uncomfortable chair, flashing a ring in the light from time to time, not listening to Dora, but wondering about her own perplexities and searching for some master-card to play. I've had a feeling the whole time that she intended to use me—just as I came to Carlice intending to use her, if Dora failed me. Of course, not knowing how. Just hoping somehow that she could give me help, as she hopes vaguely for some help from me. A superstitious impulse, really. Or shall I give it one more desperate chance?

"Good-night."

"Good-night, Sir."

Insert two pennies. Yes. What a noise they make as they drop. No dial. I must wait for the operator.

"I want Maggerham 15."

"Maggerham 15?"

And now a pause. I suppose Eames will answer.

"Hello? Hello? Is that Carlice Abbey? . . . This is Mr. Payne. Has Miss Carlice finished dinner? . . . Will you ask her, please, if she would speak to me for a moment?"

She'll come. Never fear. She'll come. She won't be stopped by Dora.

"Yes? This is Stephen Payne. Miss Carlice, first I've got to beg your pardon. I had a frightful row with your nephew and threw a glass at him. Yes, I missed. . . . Oh, you've heard all about it? . . . And did Dora tell you that she rang up my trustee, Dr. Rusper, and that he's coming to-morrow at five to take me off to a——"

"*We can deal with him when he comes.*"

What is she saying? She'll speak to him herself. "Come home at once. Eames will let you in. Don't bother to say good-night to us, but go straight upstairs to bed, and come down to breakfast to-morrow as if nothing has happened. I think I shall have more influence than you imagine."

O great woman! (Lord, I nearly said that aloud.)

O great woman. She's rung off. Well, that's that. And so to bed.

But these things aren't so easy. There's more to come yet. And if she helps me, it won't be for the love of my blue eyes. The essence of a bargain is a *quid pro quo*. What *quid* have I to give her this lovely night of drizzle and no stars? The policeman has gone away, and the solitary drinker has just come out of the pub, lurching a little. Am I lurching a little too? Perhaps, poor devil, something was bothering him. Is he a city clerk turned farmer, and losing his little savings? It might be that. I ought to have talked to him. But he goes that way—over the railway-bridge—and I go this way. He stops, as I stopped, and looks over the parapet, as I looked over, on to the railway line.

Fifty feet? Sixty? The drop should be big enough. I don't like the way he's looking over the parapet. Perhaps he's wishing I'd go away, but I'll outstay him, if I have to stay here all night. Besides, I think that bridge is a lucky bridge. (Now don't get too elated, Stephen Payne. Troubles don't end so easily as all that. A few words from a great woman aren't enough. Still, she has spoken.) And now comes the last train; rumble, rumble through the rain; rumble, rumble through the night, showering tiny sparks of light. What immortal hand or eye Could frame thy fearful symmetry? His last chance. He might do it now. There's just time. And I, like a fool, couldn't stop him. I'm too far away—mouthing a mixture of poetry and doggerel. Rumble, rumble. I've got to see this out, then I can go to bed. Rumble-rumble-roar. He's missed his chance. He's too late. The train's in the tunnel. He moves on now and crosses the bridge. I shan't see him again. Lord, now lettest Thou Thy servant depart in peace. Depart in peace. In peace. . . .

Chapter XIII: ISABEL CARLICE

NOT one of our happiest breakfasts—in fact, I was thankful to have got it over. Yet, with the possible exception of Dora, we all behaved well. Especially Ronnie. I almost dared to hope that the row last night had produced a change of heart in him. It hasn't, but I think, despite himself, he feels we are entitled to a few hours' magnanimity from him, and he can't help giving us the benefit of it. He came down with his hair more carefully brushed than usual, and reminded me of a very young subaltern who has been given a kind but firm lecture by his Colonel—a young subaltern who very soon, perhaps, will be facing death at the front. There was an air about him, too, of a theological student who has strayed into a house-party, and, while keeping his spiritual values jealously intact, resolves that Mammon shall have no cause to reproach him for bad manners. Ronnie's manners were not only good. They were "obliging." He even said, "Do let me give you another piece of haddock." I hope he has the sense not to try to apologise to Stephen Payne, or take the blame for what happened. That would produce more emotional tension, and I can't do with any more.

Stephen Payne was filled with a suppressed radiance—the radiance of a fatalist. I can understand that. When you've been through an agony in anticipation, there's bound to be a period of frivolous relief, even though the real crisis comes nearer. I was able to mutter to him, "For God's sake, say nothing to Ronnie. It would embarrass him too much." He nodded at me like a conspirator. We were both standing by the hot-plate, while Dora was eating fastidiously by herself. Somehow Payne's complacency irritated me a little. I don't like such unstable people. Still, I shall have to do what I can for him.

Dora had not forgiven me for not backing her up last night. She still remembered how I had said to her, after dinner, "I think you've made a mountain out of a molehill. Can't you cancel your doctor friend's visit?" She tossed her head, as girls used to toss their heads when I was a girl, and said, "I know perfectly well I've done right. It's what father intended." And she went on to say that it was all for Stephen's good, and besides, she couldn't let Ronnie be insulted in his own house. It was only giving Ronnie a taste of his friends' methods, I suggested, but she wouldn't hear of it, and told me I was prejudiced.

So this morning, she's on her dignity, and, as none of us could gratify her taste for drama by pulling a tragic face, she feels herself slighted and unappreciated. What she intends to do about her own little worry, I don't know. Perhaps, like her brother, having lived through months of apprehension, she has found the peace of indifference. It will be a tame birthday, after all, with nothing to harass anyone but me.

In the stress of the last few days, I had forgotten about the case of *fritillaria imperialis* I had ordered in July. It *would* arrive this morning, of all mornings. Fine bulbs too. If Ronnie is, as I suppose, in his library, he can see me planting them here in the grass in front of the birches. Twice I've caught myself thinking, "I must give orders that this grass isn't to be mown next spring," then remembering with a shock that I'm planting flowers for Communist children to pick or trample on. And Ronnie, if he is watching, is saying to himself, "She's planting flowers for Communist children to pick. Let her go on."

I'm horribly afraid, though, that they won't be allowed to pick them. This part of the garden will be railed off as a rest-home for expectant mothers, and anybody who picks a flower will be sent to Siberia for five years. That's the difference between their practice and their theory. More and more do I believe that what belongs to everybody belongs to nobody. Material objects need private owners to make them live. When I've seen museums, I've always felt, "What a pity these things aren't in some private collection, littered carefully about a drawing-room or library. For students surely models would suffice." I am reminded of one of Gwen Rashdall's visits here last year, when Ronnie said, "In Russia there are eighteen thousand art galleries full of the great masters," and she answered, "And how many drawing-rooms are there, full of the great mistresses? A drawing-room is a much better proof of civilisation than an art gallery." Ronnie was furious. Like Claude, he has very little sense of humour.

I am planting bulbs whose flowers even the Communist children won't be allowed to pick. I really don't know why I go on. I ought to put them back in the brown paper bag and keep them till I get some earth of my own. Would Ronnie have a qualm if he saw them, as part of my luggage, to-morrow afternoon? Not he.

Here comes Stephen Payne, wanting to speak to me—or, rather, wanting me to speak to him. He says:

"In a few hours my horrible trustee will be here. He's confirmed his arrival by letter. Dora told me after breakfast. I can do nothing with her. . . . She's the last woman in the world I'd guess was my sister."

"Don't worry," I say. "I've got your trustee taped."

He watches me drive the bulb-planter into the earth. Fine big bulbs. One has to make three overlapping holes to plant each bulb properly.

"Can I help you?"

"No. I couldn't bear anyone else to have a hand in this."

He wanders away.

It ought to be thundery weather on this last day of mine at Carlice. Instead, it's just seasonable. Chilly at breakfast, then milder, with intermittent sun and threats of rain.

2

At luncheon, Ronnie could hardly conceal his boredom. The graciousness of breakfast had gone. I suspect he spent the morning looking at his watch—sometimes twice in the same minute—and saying, "O Lord, how long?"

Stephen Payne was still serene. While we were eating biscuits and cheese, two rabbits ran across the lawn. I said, "You must shoot those for me this afternoon. You shall go rabbiting among the silver birches." He said he would try, and looked dreamily out of the window, as if he saw the future outlined against the sky.

Ronnie struck in with, "They don't do any harm at this time of year. They never touch the vegetables till the winter."

I said, "They eat flowers, and I've always preferred flowers to

vegetables, just as Théophile Gautier said he would sell his bread
to buy jam. Do you read Théophile Gautier, Ronnie?"

"No," he answered. "The last generation wasted its time on that
sort of thing. We don't."

When the meal was over, Ronnie went inevitably upstairs to his
library, and Stephen Payne wandered into the garden. I went to the
desk in the morning-room, to write some letters, supposing that
Dora would go to her drawing-room to have her nap. However, I
had hardly been sitting in the writing-chair five minutes when she
appeared at the door and said, "Isabel."

"Yes, Dora?"

"I want to ask you when you think I ought to make my arrangements with Ronnie."

It was like one's cook suddenly saying, "I'm sorry, mum, but I
really must complain about the range."

"I should think this evening," I answered. "But what arrangements do you mean?"

"Oh, about the removal of my things. You know, some of
the things in the drawing-room were bought out of my private
money."

"I'm sure there won't be any difficulty about them," I said.
"Ronnie ought to let you have all the things in the drawing-room—
and in your bedroom too. I should ask him, after dinner, quite
openly. Young people don't understand our delicacy, you know.
I'll ask him for you, if you like, and will tell me what you want."

If she had been wearing an apron, she would have twirled the
corner.

"Oh, I can speak to him, if you think it's quite all right. Thank
you very much all the same, Isabel. I'll ask him if he can spare me
a few minutes after dinner. I thought it better that he should know
before he sees Sir Thomas Hill to-morrow. And I wanted you to
know what I was doing. And there's something else I ought to talk
to him about."

"What's that?"

"I'm afraid it's private."

I paused, wondering whether to tell her that I knew. But I
decided against it, and said, "All right. Only, don't harass him too
much. He's rather on edge with these big changes coming. And

you mustn't expect him to behave quite as you were brought up to behave. Oh, Dora——"

I called her back just as she was going to the door. "Yes?"

"Is this Dr. Rusper really coming at five o'clock?"

"Yes. I told you he was."

"Well, will you let me have a few words with him?"

"Why?"

"I have a reason. I've taken a liking to your brother, and I'm sure Dr. Rusper will view his case very differently when I've said what I have to say. You're quite willing to be guided by his view, aren't you?"

"Of course. But I don't see——"

"Never mind about that. When he arrives, let him be shown in here. I'll be waiting for him. You might be in the drawing-room, and I'll bring him in to you when I've finished. But let me talk first."

"But he's certain to ask for me."

"I dare say. But I'll intercept him. I really think it'll be wiser. We don't want another scene. By the way, have you arranged for him to stay the night?"

"No. He couldn't, I'm sure. He's frightfully busy. He's going to America with his wife at the beginning of next week. An international conference on pneumonia, he said. He'll catch the 7.50 back to London to-night. I suppose it doesn't matter sending him to the station in the car?"

"Of course not. And the idea is that your brother will go with him?"

"I expect that's what Dr. Rusper will suggest."

"Well, I shall tell him that I don't think it's at all a good suggestion."

She shrugged her shoulders unskilfully, pondered a moment and said:

"I do wonder what will become of Tan."

"I'm sure Ronnie would gladly give him to you."

"I think it's hardly fair to keep a dog in a flat, do you? He's been a great comfort to me while I've been here, though I think he prefers Eames to me."

"Perhaps Eames would like him. I wonder, by the way, what's

going to become of Eames—and the rest of them: I do hope they've been saving up. I don't suppose they have any idea, yet, of these changes. Ronnie hasn't said anything to them, and I haven't."

"And I haven't," she said defensively, and yawned.

"Well, I suppose in a few days we shall see everything more clearly and shall all know what we're going to do."

"I'm sure I hope so, Isabel."

She went into the drawing-room for her nap.

As I started writing again, I wondered if I could keep the members of the house-party separate during the afternoon. I felt unable to manage them collectively, and wished I could make it a rule that all their remarks must be addressed to me and no one else. Was I being proud, pathetic or idiotic in trying to play the mistress of Carlice till the very last minute? Or was I following a sound instinct? I have grown very superstitious these last few days, and am prepared to see omens in everything.

One of the letters I had to answer came from a spinster who organises our local flower-show. They are having a meeting to-night, at the village hall, and Jackson and Mildon—poor men, little knowing—are to attend. I ought to have answered before. I must send the answer round by hand. Charles can take it, after tea. Then we shan't have him here, if there's any unpleasantness on Rusper's arrival. And Eames is taking Simmonds to the carnival at Riseley . . .

DEAR MISS CARLICE,

Do you think we might beg the hospitality of the Abbey for our show next year? We have to settle these things well in advance. As perhaps you know, we can't count on Lady Ellerton as heretofore. I write to you because I am not sure whether I ought to approach Mrs. Carlice or your nephew, who I believe is very soon to celebrate his twenty-first birthday. We are holding a meeting in the Village Hall on Monday, Sept. 7th, at 8. . . .

What shall I say? "Dear Miss Eagre, in twenty-four hours Carlice Abbey is going to be given to the Communist party. I don't know their views on flower-shows, but I suspect they are unfavourable."

No, I must say, "Wait and see. I'll write again as soon as I can." She'll read the letter aloud at the meeting. I must take care . . .

Ronnie said he went to some house-agents about the value of this place. We had always imagined it to be priceless, because it seemed inconceivable we should ever sell. The agent said we couldn't hope for more than twelve thousand and should probably only get five or six. Or we might have difficulty in selling at any price. I think Ronnie enjoyed telling me this. (And yet people are clamouring to pay fifteen hundred pounds for shoddy little bunga-lows on the outskirts of Riseley.) If I became owner of Carlice, would it lessen my enjoyment to know that I owned an unsaleable property? This is a question to be put and answered very secretly. Honestly, I think I can answer "No." But it depends very much upon one's mood. The real me says "No." It must say "No." If I were the owner of Carlice, if I could live here and become rooted in the stones and soil and felt the root of every tree, the forma-tion of every border and piece of lawn depended upon me, and I on them—— But it is useless to work myself up like this again. All I have to do is to answer these letters, perform one little act of charity—that shouldn't be difficult, with a suburban doctor to deal with—and then go round the house collecting one or two little odds and ends which are legally mine, and say good-bye. Oh, why did Claude beget a lunatic for his son? There was no weakness on his mother's side. The weakness must be in us. Claude should have been the girl who married and went away, and I should have lived here for ever. A fairy story . . .

3

Charles brings in the tea.

"Charles, when we've finished and you've cleared away, would you walk round with this note for Miss Eagre? I want her to get it before six. You know where she lives? The house up the hill beyond Major Inchley's."

"Yes, 'm."

He's getting too fat here. The walk will do him good.

"And you might tell Flora that we're expecting a visitor about five

—a Dr. Rusper. He will probably ask for Mrs. Carlice, but I should like him shown in here, where I shall be."

"Yes, Miss. Mr. Ronald said he's going for a walk and won't want any tea."

"All right. But we are three, you know. We shall need a third cup and saucer. Mr. Payne will be here."

The lad can't even count. And here is Mr. Payne, coming in by the garden-door.

"You were quite right about those rabbits, Miss Carlice. I counted six as I walked through the birch wood. And I rather think one of them got into the garden."

"You must shoot them all after tea."

"Hadn't I better try now? My trustee's coming after tea."

"I think there won't be any harm in letting him see you can handle a gun. Let him see you with a gun in your hands."

"Oh, I've tried impressing him like that before."

"Well, my persuasion will be added this time. I'm not advising you to shoot *him*, mind! In any case, here's tea. We have it early, because Dora likes to be roused from her nap by it. Charles, you might go and knock at the drawing-room door."

"Yes, Miss."

"Dora likes me to pour out. Very weak, and no sugar?"

This takes me back to the tennis tournament days, and the first tea here after their marriage, when she asked me to pour out. To-morrow, if I pour out tea, I shall feel that I'm pouring it down the throats of expectant Communist mothers, though I think they would like it stronger than we make it here. And, of course, not China.

Now Dora comes in, still yawning.

"Do you know, I've had the most extraordinary dream?"

"What was it, Dora?"

"Oh, I'm so sleepy, I feel as if I were talking in my sleep. Perhaps it's this changeable weather. I dreamt we had all been dreaming we'd ever lived here—Ronnie, you and I. I'm not quite sure about you. But Ronnie said if he'd been here it was in a previous incarnation. And I said I'd never been here at all and that I belonged to South Mersley and would vote for South Mersley through thick and thin. How silly it sounds!"

"And did I say anything?"

"You said, 'I haven't been here yet, but I shall be in my next incarnation.'"

"Oh, Mr. Payne, do leave that heavy scone and have a sandwich. Mrs. Sowerby makes them so badly. Yes, Dora, what happened then?"

"Nothing. Charles knocked on the door and woke me up. But it was a frightfully vivid dream. I still feel I'm standing at the top of the little hill that leads to Elmcroft—you remember it, Stephen?— outside a polling-booth, draped with election colours, and saying, 'I vote for South Mersley for ever, through thick and thin!'"

Chapter XIV: RONALD CARLICE

"RONNIE!"

Damn! She sits like a spider at the centre of its web. Doors open, window open. She sees and hears everything. I'd have stayed out till dinner, only after luncheon she begged me to be back about five, just in case there was a scene between Payne and his trustee. I hoped I could slip safely upstairs to the library. But it was not to be, as they say in obituary notices.

"Ronnie!"

"Yes, Aunt Isabel?"

"Ronnie, Dr. Rusper has arrived. You know—Stephen Payne's guardian whom Dora stupidly sent for after that bother last night——"

"Well, it wasn't my fault."

"No, of course it wasn't. Now, Ronnie, you're not going to be bothered with any of us much longer—oh, I know exactly what you feel—but to-day you've got to be a little gentleman. You can be a little Communist to-morrow if you like. Dr. Rusper seemed very much upset to hear that Stephen Payne was shooting rabbits. I asked him to shoot them, and, till to-morrow, if the rabbits belong to anybody, they belong to Dora. Dr. Rusper broke away from me in rather an ill-mannered way as soon as he heard a shot outside——"

"How did he know it was Payne shooting?"

"I told him. I said, 'Your ward is shooting some rabbits for me, in the garden.' He said, 'Payne shooting?' I said, 'Yes, why not?' and he told me that I was under a very grave misapprehension and stalked out on to the lawn. I'm afraid there's going to be a most frightful row. Yes, there is. There they are, coming towards the house, Stephen carrying the gun. What a fool the doctor is to touch it like that. I'd shoot him if I were Stephen. But that's what you've got to prevent, Ronnie."

"Why should I?"

The two men, one big and black, and the other flimsy and fair, are crossing the lawn. The flimsy one carries the gun.

"What do you want me to do, Aunt Isabel?"

"Just to be ready. That's all. Wait a moment. I suppose you haven't been thinking things over, Ronnie?"

"I've thought a good deal, but not your way, I'm afraid."

"Dr. Rusper!"

Good heavens, what a voice the woman has!

"Dr. Rusper!" she shouts again.

They're coming this way. Payne leads. Poor flimsy little man. I was an idiot to tell Dora about my row with him last night. It was my fault for making him drunk. If only she hadn't caught me on the landing, as Isabel caught me in the hall just now.

"Dr. Rusper, this is my nephew, Mr. Ronald Carlice."

Rusper gives me a quick bow, and says, "In one moment, Madam." He follows Payne closely to the gunroom door. Can't Payne do anything but walk like a sleep-walker? Yes, he does. He turns round and makes a stand.

"If you'll kindly remember your manners, Rusper, I'll put the gun away at my convenience."

"You'll do nothing of the sort. You'll hand it over to me here and now."

Payne goes inside, and the doctor follows him. Has Payne been drinking? The whisky is out on the side-table. Yes, and a glass not quite emptied. It's *she* who gave him that.

"Now, Ronnie, you see . . . You've got to stop this quarrel."

"In there?"

Shall I remind her of what happened in there? But she remembers all right. Trust her for that.

"Ronnie, please go in and take the gun from Mr. Payne. He'll give it to you. And send Dr. Rusper over here to me."

"Do you know, Aunt Isabel . . ."

"Ronnie, go quickly. I order you to go."

Oh, Lord, the fool in the gunroom is shouting now! "Weapon in the hands of an irresponsible . . ." He ought to have said "lethal weapon." That's the usual phrase.

Ronnie, you must go.

Did she say that, or did I? All right, I'll go.

"Let me past, Dr. Rusper, please. Now, Payne, don't be a fool, there's a good chap. We can straighten all this out afterwards. Just give me that gun. It isn't done, you know, for two people to hold a gun at once. It isn't, really."

I'll give it you as soon as Rusper clears out of here.

Now the other one's talking.

Mr. Carlice, I wish you'd leave this matter to me. I know how to handle these cases.

"Well, you don't know how to handle guns, either of you. The safety-catch doesn't turn that way, you fool. Oh, Dr. Rusper, I wish you'd get out, for God's sake . . ."

I know my duty, Mr. Carlice. Now, Payne——

Get out, you damnable interfering fool. Didn't you hear Mr. Carlice tell you to get out?

Oh, Lord! Oh, Lord! Never let them spell your name with an "s" my boy. My father said that. And it's all quite irrelevant.

"Rusper, my good fellow . . ."

Take your bloody hands off.

And there's Aunt Isabel's face peeping round the door.

"Aunt Isabel, can't you call this maniac off?"

I'm not a maniac, Carlice. I'm only——

"I didn't mean you, Payne. I meant the other fool."

Carlice, leave this to me——

"That's the trigger you're touching. Aunt Isabel, you're——

Don't point the muzzle here——"

Now they're all shouting at once.

Payne, I command you——

Command yourself, you——

Please, Dr. Rusper, you're making a fool of yourself——

"You're fools, all three of you—Oh—Oh——"

Chapter XV: DORA CARLICE

I

WHEN I heard the shot, I was in the drawing-room, looking in the bottom drawer of my bureau. I'd decided it should be the last time I would look there. If the box was still missing, I should simply say to Ronnie: "After your father died I found a tin cash-box in one of his bedroom drawers. It was labelled, in his writing, 'For my son Ronald Carlice, to be given to him on his twenty-first birthday.' I kept it for nearly ten years in the bottom drawer of my bureau. I looked for it last June, soon after your sister was killed, and it wasn't there. I looked for it yesterday, and it still wasn't there. I'm very sorry. I can't do anything about it." And it was as I'd expected. My half-finished embroidery with the pink rose was there and the boxes of old photographs—but Claude's box hadn't been put back.

I knelt for a long time with the drawer wide open. The shot had sounded as if it came from the house, but I supposed it must have come from the garden—one of the men after a rabbit, perhaps. Just one shot, and then a very long silence. Then, suddenly, Isabel came in and shut the door behind her. She was very pale, and I knew that something must have happened. She said, "Dora, there's been an accident. Ronnie has been killed."

She came over to me, walking like a man through the room, and caught me by the arm. "I know this is a great shock to you," she said, "but you mustn't let yourself give way yet. I want you to come with me into the morning-room. Your brother and Dr. Rusper are there."

"It wasn't Stephen who shot him?"

"Oh, no, no. I tell you it was an accident. Now will you please come? We have some very important things to settle quickly."

I had to go with her. When we were both through the morning-room door, she locked it and took the key.

"That will keep unauthorised people out of the gunroom," she said.

(*Unauthorised*. What a funny word for her to have used.)

"Why, was it in the gunroom?" I asked.

"Yes, it was."

Don and Stephen were both sitting in armchairs when we came in. I felt they hadn't said a single word to one another since the accident. They were both of them as white as could be. Don's face seemed even whiter than his stiff white collar.

Isabel sat down and told me to sit down too. Then Don got up, just a bit shakily, I thought, and said: "With your permission, Miss Carlice, I will now telephone to the police-station."

"When the time comes," Isabel said in her most icy voice, "*I* will telephone to the police-station. This is *my* house now." For one moment she looked as though she were startled at having said this. Stephen was so still, he might have been dead. I was frightened that he might come to life at any moment and do something awful.

Then Don said, "We shall be asked why there was all this delay, Miss Carlice."

"We shall be asked a good many questions, Dr. Rusper," she said, still in the same voice, "and you'll have to answer them."

"I? My position, at least, is perfectly clear."

"I think not."

"What do you mean?"

"Well—you were the direct and also the indirect cause of my nephew's death. If responsibility has to be taken for this accident, it will be taken entirely by you."

"It will not!"

"I think it will."

"How dare you say that, Miss Carlice? I saw you push the gun towards your nephew's face."

"I am prepared to swear in the witness-box that it was you. Your hands were flapping with terror. You were beside yourself with terror—and wounded dignity."

She laughed thinly, making little notes like somebody practising a flute.

Don turned towards me and said, "Dora, I want you to bear witness that I wish to ring up the police at once. I don't understand Miss Carlice's attitude."

"Stephen," I said, "are you quite all right, Stephen?"

He frightened me, sitting there with glazed eyes and saying nothing. While I spoke, Isabel got up and mixed two glasses of whisky-and-soda. She gave one to Stephen and one to Don, who took it, to my surprise. I was surprised, too, at seeing the whisky decanter out on the round table—the "gallery-table" they had taught me to call it, because it has a little railing running round the top. Had Stephen being drinking before the "accident"? As I wondered this, he took a sip and smiled at me. I felt we were all in a kind of dream.

Then Isabel sat down again and said, "Sit down, Dr. Rusper. I've a good deal to say yet. When I ring up the police, I shall give them to understand that the explanation of this tragedy rests entirely with you. I don't think you'll want to appear as having acted like an idiot—and an incompetent idiot at that—will you? I mean, you will be at some pains to safeguard your reputation, when you tell your story. And of course *our* reputations, which, though not quite so vulnerable as yours, are quite important. You see what I mean? You need a little time to think things over."

Again Don turned towards me.

"You've heard Miss Carlice," he said; "you'll bear witness, won't you, that I am asked to defeat the ends of justice and join a conspiracy to——"

Isabel interrupted him.

"One moment, Dr. Rusper. What story are you thinking of telling the police?"

"What story? The truth. You had given a lethal weapon to a man who, to my personal knowledge, was utterly unfitted to handle it. When I was attempting to disarm him, you urged your nephew to interfere. He did interfere. There was a struggle for the gun, and at the critical moment you came to the gunroom door and gave the gun the fatal push which set the weapon off in your nephew's face."

"That is untrue. Mr. Payne was shooting rabbits at my request, and you tried, tactlessly and without any authority in the world, to take the gun from him. Mr. Payne will bear out this statement. Unfortunately, through your obstinacy, there was a struggle for the weapon and I had to ask my nephew to intervene. He didn't seem very successful and I came up myself—too late to prevent you from pointing the gun at my nephew and jostling Mr. Payne so that it went off. We shall never know, believe me, whose hand touched the trigger. . . ."

Don, for the third and last time, looked at me, and then looked back as Isabel went on:

"We should none of us come out of that very well—and you least well of all, I think, Dr. Rusper."

His reply was a kind of sniff, as if something very big and important were being sucked up those hairy nostrils of his.

But Isabel was still talking. She seemed quite sure of herself now.

"Before we say any more about all this, I want to read you two letters—here they are in my bag—written ten years ago in South Mersley. That is to say, in 1926, the year of the General Strike, and the year in which my brother Claude committed suicide in the gunroom here. So listen, my little suburban apothecary. Listen to this——"

She opened her bag and pulled out two envelopes—greyish purple envelopes. I felt they were probably scented. She compared the dates on the postmarks and then took the notepaper out of one of the envelopes. "The heading is Elmcroft, Diana Road, South Mersley," she said, "and the date is July 19th, 1926. The letters are both addressed to my brother."

And she began to read:

DEAR SIR,

I had better explain at once that I am housekeeper to Dr. Payne, your wife's father. You may not know, but I am very attached to the doctor, and now that he is so ill and cannot manage his affairs, it upsets me very much to think that things aren't going on in his house as they should. I regret to have to tell you that there is trouble between your wife and Dr. Rusper, the master's partner. I feel I owe it both to the master and to you, Sir, as his son-in-law, to let you know that things aren't by any means what they ought to be. I trust I have spoken plainly enough and that you will be grateful to me for the warning I have given you. Should you desire further particulars both myself and Lily Jones, housemaid, will be able to supply the same.

Yours faithfully,

Eudoxia Greeg (Mrs.).

As Isabel paused for a moment before taking out the second letter, I felt as if something extraordinary was happening to me. I didn't know what. I looked at Don, but he didn't look at me, and sat staring straight in front of him, as if he were diagnosing something in the panelling on the wall. I noticed in that moment how thin his hair was on the top of his head, and how his stomach stuck out when he let himself go. "It wasn't with *him*," I thought. "It wasn't with *him*. It was somebody else who's been dead all these ten years."

Then Isabel started to read the second letter:

"Elmcroft,"

Diana Road,

South Mersley.

September 28th, 1926.

Dear Sir,

I confess I was very surprised at having no answer to my first letter. I almost feel you never got it, or doubted that it was *bona fide*, though it wasn't as if it was an anonymous one. So let me tell you straight out here and now, that I'm not out to get anything for myself, and it isn't a case of blackmail, as I told Dr. Rusper himself——

"Dr. Rusper, did Mrs. Greeg speak to you on this matter?"

"The cook-housekeeper at Elmcroft tried to blackmail me. I told her that if she had anything to say, she had better say it to my solicitor. That stopped her little game. She didn't say anything more."

"Yes," said Isabel, "she said this." And she went on reading:

Dr. Rusper seems to think he can take advantage of my poor master being so near to death, and then, I suppose, come into the practice as bold as brass and marry some poor young woman. But I don't intend to let the honour of the family I serve be tarnished so easily as all that. No, Sir, and in case you don't think the written word of Mrs. Greeg is good enough, I'm giving you the names of others who know what I know and will be prepared to swear to it in a court of law, if necessary. First, there's Lily Jones, housemaid at this address. She doesn't want to make trouble, but she's a good girl at heart and knows the truth from a lie. Then there's Tom Eynstop, who delivers milk for Messrs. Bradewell, dairymen, of 103, High Street, South Mersley. He was going across the common only yesterday afternoon and saw Mrs. Carlice and Dr. Rusper cuddling there. Cuddling—well *he* can tell you himself what he told Lily this morning. I prefer not to put his words in any letter of mine. But mind you, he's a truthful young fellow even though he's a bit of a lad. And then there's Nurse Grader of St. Paul's Hospital. She won't speak straight out to me, but I know what she thinks. And she's a good woman. And Mrs. Trempley too, who comes to oblige: 150a, London Road, North Mersley, is her address. As long ago as June, she was doing the hall, when she heard a noise in the drawing-room which made her think a thing or two. And shortly after, she said, out comes Dr. Rusper fingering his tie, and ten minutes later, Miss Dora, I mean Mrs. Carlice, looking red and sheepish. That's what she swore to me——

Isabel stopped suddenly, and said, "I don't like reading this out. Besides, we haven't much time."

"How did you get those letters?" Don growled.

"They were in a tin cash-box, addressed to Ronnie when he should be twenty-one, in my brother's handwriting. You see, my brother must have known. . . ."

"Within three weeks of Dr. Payne's funeral," Don said, "this Mrs. Greeg was taken to an Inebriates' Home. She died there a few weeks later of alcoholic softening of the brain."

Then Isabel looked at me quite suddenly and said:

"Dora, I suppose all this is quite true, isn't it?"

"Quite true," I said, and heard Isabel saying, "So you see, for the honour of my family, I ought to have the inquest on my brother's death reopened."

She was adding something about the British Medical Council, when the ceiling seemed to come down with a rush on my face, and buried me, and I died.

2

I think I was lucky to have got out of it all like that. When I came to, I was in my own bed, with a watery sunset beating feebly on the window. At least, that was when I really came to. I seemed to remember dreaming that I had woken up before and been given something to drink and told to go to sleep again.

As things began to come home to me, I wished I could have slept for a whole year. How much easier life would be if, when anything awful happened, you could simply fall asleep and wake up when it was all stale news and somebody else had done anything that had to be done at the time. So that you could say, "How about that murder?" and they would say to you, "Which murder? Oh, that one. We've nearly forgotten that now."

But I knew it was still the same day. It seemed impossible that days could ever be so long. I listened for sounds below, but this isn't a house like Elmcroft. It's full of sounds, but you don't hear them distinctly from one room to another. The walls are so thick. In Elmcroft I could have heard anybody coming to the front door. No doubt Mrs. Greeg heard things too, that we didn't reckon for. I tried, though my head wasn't very clear, to remember what we had done that Mrs. Greeg and Lily could have found out. It was hard, because I had to think myself back into being quite a different person—somebody who gloried in what was happening and didn't care and set no store by the future—a little fool, I suppose some would call me, carried away by her first real love affair. But it was worth it. Even though that fat, pompous, middle-aged man downstairs was the man I'd fallen in love with. He wasn't the same person then, just as I wasn't the same.

The clock on my mantelpiece had stopped at twenty minutes past five. "It must have been exactly then," I thought, "that Ronnie was killed in the gunroom." Oh, my God! wasn't it enough that Claude had chosen to kill himself there—after getting that second letter from Mrs. Greeg. How he must have been thinking over it, poor man. My father wasn't even dead when she wrote it. A whole month and more. That was why Claude was like that at the funeral—like a churchyard ghost already. He didn't seem angry with me, but very sad—sadder than I could be about anything. Oh, Claude—oh, darling Claude, I *did* love you in quite a different way—a better way—a way that lasts longer. . . .

I looked at the clock again, because it frightened me to look at it. Twenty past five. Yes, it was just then that the gun went off. I heard the shot in the drawing-room when I was looking for those letters that *she* stole. Why didn't I think of her as being the thief before? It seems so obvious now. But it had never occurred to me that Joan would talk to *her*. And I was in such a state that I could have believed anything—anything except the obvious. What shall I say to Isabel when she comes in to see me? For she's bound to come in. I've something against her now. If I'm an—adulteress, she would say straight out at me—she's a thief. A common thief. Looking in my private locked drawer. Is that the tradition of these old families? Give me South Mersley every time, if it is.

When would she come? I couldn't help looking at the clock on my mantelpiece. Twenty past five. Then suddenly I remembered that it had stopped this morning. It had stopped before I awoke, and I hadn't thought of asking Flora to see to it. She ought to have seen to it without being asked. But she never was one of our brightest.

For one moment I wondered whether Ronnie would keep her on, after I left. Then I remembered, and pictured him lying huddled up on the gunroom floor, like Claude, with a face one couldn't look at. "You pushed the gun towards your nephew's face," Don said to Isabel. Oh, God, that couldn't be true. I'll not believe that. After all, she's a living woman. We mustn't think that about her. And even Don gave way. It was the first time, the very first time, that I've ever seen him fight a losing battle. I suppose he carried me here—and undressed me, perhaps. Oh, that's too much. Isabel couldn't have allowed him to do that. She and Flora must have done it. I won't ask her.

If this were Elmcroft, I could hear the police arriving. I suppose they *have* telephoned. Oh, why couldn't I sleep longer?

She comes. I knew she would come.

"Come in."

She walks, almost on tip-toe, and sits down in the tub-chair.

"Well, Dora, are you better? I do hope so."

Though she only says that, she is sweet—I can tell it at once—very sweet, like something you saw when you were a child behind the plate-glass of an expensive confectioner, and couldn't afford to buy—and have never bought.

"Dora, you must forgive me about those letters."

I turned over on my side and said, "Oh, I thought I should have to ask *you* that, and you've known since June. Was it June?"

"Yes, Joan told me about your secret. She was worried on Ronnie's account. I thought I had better know what the truth really was. I ought to have told you—that's where I went wrong. I thought, when you missed the box, you'd think Joan had taken it. And that would have meant no harm, because you had confidence in her, as we all had. I should have said and done nothing—as you know—but with Dr. Rusper there I had to use the letters. You understand this, don't you?"

"You mean, for Stephen's sake?"

"For his sake and mine and, in a way, Dr. Rusper's sake, too. We were all in it——"

"Like a lynching," I thought suddenly. But I didn't say that.

"And Ronnie?" I asked. "What's happened to him now?"

"That's all right, Dora. You mustn't think of that. The police have been here and Dr. Rusper has seen them. He says Ronnie took the gun and turned it on himself. He'll tell you to-morrow what he said to them."

"He's staying here, then?"

"Yes, for to-night."

"Isabel, I don't want to see him to-morrow. I can't see him. You know why."

She went to the window and pulled the curtains together. It was now quite dark, and she switched on a little lamp by the dressing-table. It made funny shadows. It was the first time I had ever seen that lamp on without the others. When she spoke, she was almost soapy.

"My dear child, do believe this. I think no worse of you for anything that may have happened ten years ago. Good heavens, it was none of my business. You did no harm."

"Except to Claude, you mean."

She sat down again near my bed.

"Those letters grieved him, of course, but I do know this, he would never be one to bear malice against you. If you had known him as well as I did, you would never have worried about that box."

"How do you account for it, then?"

"In the first place, we don't know when he put the two letters in it."

"Yes, we do," something forced me to answer. "When I found the box, there was a date on the corner of the label. I tore it off, because I guessed what was inside. I was going to destroy the whole box—only somehow I didn't. I couldn't."

"What was the date, Dora? Can you remember?"

"November 7th, 1926."

She put her hand to her head. I felt she was trying not to say, "That was two days before he killed himself." But I didn't care if she did. I was too far gone to care, and it was only a kind of vague curiosity which made me remind her—if she needed reminding— so as to hear what she would say next.

"That would be after we'd left for Leamington," she said. "You know, Dora, the more I think of it all, the more certain I am that it was influenza and nothing else which killed Claude. After all, he'd known—about that matter—for some time. Mrs. Greeg's first letter was written as far back as July and even her second letter was written in September—five or six weeks before. If he hadn't had that horrible influenza, he would never have had such a morbid impulse to put those letters in that little box. You know he'd been ill for a few days before we went to Leamington."

"Yes, but he seemed better. We shouldn't have gone if he'd been really ill."

"It's the after-effects that do the mischief. Any doctor will tell you that. Well, he put the letters in the box on the Friday. I don't suppose even then he had decided to do anything. Otherwise he would have seen that the box got into someone's hands, and not left it to be found by you, or one of the servants."

"I always thought he did that to punish me."

"No, no. That wasn't like Claude. He put the box away, vaguely, because he hadn't settled what he was going to do with it. He probably would have done nothing, if he'd recovered. But he didn't recover, poor boy, and on the Sunday, as we know, he had that fit of depression—unconnected, very probably, with the box. It's reasonable and best to think like this. One thing at least I can promise you—on his behalf—he would never have left that box lying about—wherever you happened to find it—if his mind had been made up. It wasn't intended for you, or to torment you. He only thought—and even so, he wasn't himself—'This is part of the family history. I suppose Ronnie had better know about it when he comes of age. It's just possible it may make some slight difference to what he does.' You must remember, Dora, Claude was ill, and we shall never get right into his mind, as it worked during those sad days. We still know as little why he did it as at the time—in spite of everything."

"Isabel," I asked, "were there only those two letters in the box?"

"Only those two letters. Nothing more."

"No letter from Claude about me?"

"No. Nothing more. . . . Now, I'm tiring you?"

I turned on my other side, away from her, and said nothing. If I had spoken, it would have been to ask her if she had loved Claude very much. But perhaps even she didn't know the answer to that.

She went round the bed, on tip-toe, to the door, and said, "I'll come in later, to see how you're getting on."

3

Flora came in soon afterwards to ask if I would like anything to eat. I said "No," and she tidied up the room and lit the fire. I told her I didn't need it, but she went on:

"Miss Carlice said I was to light it, 'm. Besides, it's winter now. There's a real chill in the air these last two hours."

I thought if she cried I should cry, but she seemed quite grim and cheerful. When she went out I did cry gently to myself.

I felt I had been let off, almost too lightly, and I knew, dimly, that when I had got over this feeling, I should be very happy. What had I done to deserve such happiness? Perhaps, as poor Ronnie was fond of saying at one time, people don't *deserve* things. But that isn't really very comforting, because, if that is true, you can't say, when you're suffering, "I don't deserve this pain." When I was frantic with worry over that box, and the day, coming nearer and nearer, when I should have to give it to Ronnie, I used to say, "It's too unfair on me. I don't deserve what they will say about me. I'm not like that. Besides, it was all so very long ago."

If it were true—as Isabel said—oh, she was all sweetness and light to me—and Claude had no thought ever of punishing me—if that were true, and all along he meant me to be let off, as I have been let off—somehow I felt very small and very happy, like a little thief to whom the judge might say, "I've got nine murders to try. I can't bother with you. You can go." Very happy—and very small. If any one wants to despise me, he can do so. All I ask now is to slink away and have a bit of fun from time to time—for what's life without fun?—and be myself, not a heroine or a great lady or someone whom they'll talk of in the newspapers. Some people will say it's all very contemptible. I don't see that it is. Is a cat contemptible because it sits a whole afternoon purring by the fire? I never asked to be born a human being—especially nowadays, when human beings are supposed to do such terrible things.

It's half past eight by my wrist-watch. I wish that clock on the mantelpiece hadn't stopped at twenty past five. (But twenty past five *this morning*—not this afternoon in the gunroom.) Half past eight. They must be having dinner. Can they eat? Yes, she can eat, and so can Don. About Stephen I don't know. I've hardly thought of him yet. Was it he who killed Ronnie? And what will they do to him now? If he's made friends with Isabel, he's all right. She's got Don well under her thumb. It's extraordinary Isabel and Stephen being so friendly! I can't imagine two people more different. I think I've been very unsympathetic to Stephen. But he was always so strange. One of those people who do odd things for the sake of doing them, and let you down at the very first chance. But I've been very unsympathetic towards him. I must ask Isabel about him when she comes to say good-night. Never fear, she'll come. I don't mind that very much. The ice is broken between us. I don't want to see the others—even Stephen. I should like never to see either of them again. If only I could fall asleep and wake up in a nice little flat in South Kensington. I ought to be able to get something for a hundred and fifty a year. With gas fires and constant hot water. What a lot they seem to mean to one, these silly little details. But I'm a cat, and I want to purr by the fire—the gas-fire. I'm not someone who'll be noticed or remembered two centuries from now. Why should I be, anyway?

4

"Come in."

"Were you asleep, Dora?"

"Oh, half and half. I suppose you've all had dinner? You know, I feel almost lazy, lying here."

"I'll only stay for five minutes."

She sat down in the tub-chair again. I suppose—to her—it was like visiting an invalid.

"Have you had dinner, Isabel?"

"Oh, yes. It passed off fairly well. Dr. Rusper talked most of the time about pneumonia. Apparently modern pneumonia is quite different from the old disease. You don't just have one crisis and either die or recover—you go on with it for quite a long time, like a war of attrition. Your brother was most interested."

"Did he eat anything?"

"Moderately."

"Isabel, I do hope he's all right. I feel I've been unsympathetic towards Stephen."

"Oh, don't you bother your head about him, my dear. He'll be all right. I'll see to that."

"How long is he staying here?"

"Till the inquest's over."

"The inquest?"

"Of course. But he knows what he ought to say. He'll simply back up Dr. Rusper."

"What did Don say?"

"He told the Police Inspector that Ronnie seized the gun from your brother and killed himself. We hadn't time, really, to prepare the story fully. Perhaps it was just as well. Dr. Rusper is a very clever man. I think I should call him in if I were ill—provided he had an interest in keeping me alive."

"Shall I have to give evidence at the inquest?"

"Why, no. You were in the drawing-room when it happened. The most they could do would be to ask you about Ronnie's state of mind."

"And what do I know about that?"

"Nothing, I should think. Except that he'd just been to Russia. If we mention Russia, that'll explain everything to the jury."

"And that row with Stephen, last night?"

"It would only be misleading to mention that."

"But, Isabel—the servants?"

"You know that Eames was out for the afternoon with Simmonds. I had sent Charles out with a note for Miss Eagre. I don't know where Flora was, but she can't have seen or heard anything. Mrs. Sowerby and Liza would be in the kitchen. The servants don't come into this at all."

"They must have known that the glass of the china cupboard in the library was broken last night. They know how Stephen rushed out of the house, and how poor Ronnie—oh, Isabel, I don't see the end of this coming so easily."

"My darling Dora, I promise you Stephen didn't shoot Ronnie."

"But Stephen was holding the gun."

"We were all four of us holding the gun, my dear."

"Then, who——?"

"Don't you see, we have got to a stage when that doesn't matter? Suppose it was Dr. Rusper, pushing the barrel desperately away from his face. Isn't it better to call it the accident it was?"

She went to the dressing-table and straightened something. Then she passed the fireplace, put on a little more coal, and straightened herself, saw my clock on the mantelpiece which had stopped at twenty past five—this morning. She wound it up, and, looking at her wrist-watch, set the hands to five minutes past ten.

"Isabel."

"Yes?"

"I suppose this house is now yours."

"Yes, I suppose so. Do you—want anything? You said something to me this morning, or was it the other day? You must take just what you want. There's plenty for both of us here. Oh dear!"

She yawned.

"You're more tired than I am," I said.

"I think I am. Sleep well."

She gave me a quick look, as though wondering whether she ought to kiss me.

"Shall I turn out this light?" she asked.

"No, I'll turn it out."

"And there's nothing you want?"

"No, thank you."

"Good-night."

"Good-night, Isabel."

5

Our Father which art in Heaven——

Grant, I pray, that my sins may be forgiven. Thou knowest my weakness and what I have suffered through my foolishness and my forgetfulness of Thy Will. If thou hast been pleased to spare me the punishment I was afraid of, I give Thee my most humble and grateful thanks. And grant, O Father, that I may go from here not too broken up with what I may still have to endure, and grant that in due time I may settle down and be allowed to grow old like my friends without being too unhappy. And if it may be, I will try to do some good as I pass through this life, after my fashion, trusting in Thy Infinite Wisdom and mercy to guide me to the happiness of the world to come.

And bless, I pray Thee, my sister-in-law, Isabel Carlice, and my brother Stephen and also Donald Rusper, and give them Thy peace.

And have mercy on the soul of my poor stepson Ronald Carlice, and grant that he may now be at peace with Thee in Thy most holy kingdom.

Amen.

Chapter XVI: STEPHEN PAYNE

*I*T *was an accident.*
   It was an accident.

(To the tune of *La Donna e mobile*.) I think it was Aldous Huxley in one of his earlier books who said you could teach the wheels of a train to say anything. But when once they've learnt their text, they can't help repeating it. These wheels will go on telling me that it was an accident till we reach Cornwall—though I suppose we're bound to stop at Exeter, or even before.

It was an accident. It's funny how accidents are supposed to be inartistic. If Macbeth had died through being accidentally bitten by a poisonous owl on the battlements, the play wouldn't have been a tragedy, even though he might have suffered more than he did when he was killed in his duel with Macduff. We were taught that at school. You must have retribution to make a tragedy— something, proceeding from the characters of the tragedians, so that the victim, in a sense, destroys himself through some fatal weakness of his own, like Othello's jealousy.

To think it wasn't an accident is simply a morbid craving for the artistic. And it's still more morbid to think of retribution. You don't have retribution for accidents even in literature. And in real life you don't have retribution at all—or very often you don't. I must keep sane on this point. I mustn't go imagining a last act, with the last curtain covering a heap of guilty corpses. That's a morbid literary impulse, and will break me up if I indulge in it. That's what I'm afraid of—being broken up by a morbid literary impulse. An utterly fantastic fear. . . .

And yet, on thinking all this business over, as I've done far too often during these last few days, I think I could make a tragedy or at least a tragicomedy out of it. One could start by going back to Dora and her little folly of ten years ago. Strange how I never guessed that—how confidently I used to say, "Rusper never seduces," thinking the worse of him on that account. And all the time . . . It needed Dora's lapse to explain why she couldn't help me in my trouble. If she had helped me, I should never have come to Carlice Abbey and Isabel would have had to find someone else to shoot the rabbits on the lawn. And there's a second line of thought. If Dora's husband had never killed himself with a rabbit gun in the gunroom, then Isabel would never—but it isn't fair or right even to think of that.

It was an accident.

I'm wasting time, when I ought to be looking out of the window. I suppose some day my fantastic fear will leave me. I shall get over it. I must still be suffering from a good deal of shock. Before the inquest I was numb, and didn't worry. Rusper and Isabel pumped strength into me, and I became their creature. I could feel their wills forcing me to keep going. The alliance began when Isabel was putting Dora to bed. Rusper and I were left alone in the morning-room, each with our two arms trembling on the arms of our chairs. A long silence, then Rusper suddenly looked me right in the face and said, "Payne, she's too much for us. You and I are in the same boat now, and it's up to me to pilot us both ashore." I nodded, and rather self-consciously he got up and shook hands with me. I wanted to laugh, but thought I might break down if I did. He did laugh—at least he made a couple of noises in his throat symbolical of laughter. Then he sat down and told me what he was going to say—the simple story that I have learnt by heart, of how he was examining the gun with me in the gunroom when Ronnie burst in, said, "Give me that gun," snatched it from us— we were both holding it—went to the far corner and shot himself dead.

The Police Inspector and the family doctor swallowed it whole. Why shouldn't they? So did the Coroner and his jury at the inquest. Before the inquest my chief fear was that I should be asked if I had a licence to carry a gun. Apparently the licence for that particular gun was in Dora's name. Did they cover the household and guests in the house? During the evening we hunted up books of reference, and even then we weren't quite sure. The answer seemed to depend on the meaning of the word *vermin* as used in the *Gun Licence Act* of 1870. Are rabbits *vermin* or are they *game*? They are not treated as game by the *Game Act* of 1831, but they are by the *Ground Game Act* of 1880. As a former solicitor I ought to have

known all about it. The next day, when the family solicitor, Sir
Thomas Hill—a man I didn't take to—arrived, we asked him, and
of course he didn't know. He said, however, that the point was
most unlikely to be raised. Nor was it. Indeed the whole inquest
passed more easily than I could have believed possible. I told
my story, and was only asked one question afterwards. "During
your acquaintanceship with the deceased, did he say anything or
give you an impression which might lead you to suppose that he
contemplated taking his life?" I answered "No." It was the magic
word *Russia* which did the trick. Both Dora and Isabel testified
that Ronnie had just returned from a holiday in Russia and had
declared his intention of making over Carlice Abbey—"which," as
the Coroner put it, "this unfortunate young man was to inherit the
very next day"—to the Communist party. Then the Coroner asked
Miss Carlice, "Would this have been a matter of great distress to
you?" She answered, "Yes, a matter of very great distress." In her
voice there was just the faintest suspicion of a break. I couldn't
say whether it was natural or artificial, but it told. "I think we may
conclude," the Coroner said, "that this problem, this question of
giving up an ancestral property to the Communist party, was also a
cause of very great distress to the deceased. We must picture him,
I think, as torn between two loyalties, the old and the new. Young
people of to-day are apt to take their politics—particularly when
those politics are of a certain type—with an enthusiasm which
persons of greater maturity and balance can only regard as hysterical. We have had evidence to the effect that the deceased was, in
fact, highly strung and unstable in temperament. No doubt—and
it is sad to have to say this—despite the wise attempt made by his
relatives to conceal the details of his father's death—I refer to the
death of the late Claude Carlice in similar circumstances some ten
years ago—he must sooner or later have become acquainted with
that tragic story, and the ever-present memory of it, at a critical
moment in his own affairs, was too much for his sensitive and ill-
balanced nature. Gentlemen——"

There was no doubt about the verdict. Suicide while the balance of his mind was disturbed. And a rider of sympathy to the
surviving relatives.

That night, as I lay in bed in my big bedroom at Carlice Abbey —a room I had grown to love for its air of unforced comfort and effortless dignity—I thought the inquest over, not only as it had actually gone that afternoon but as it might have gone, if we had told the true story. And I imagined, when it came to my turn in the witness-box, these questions being put to me, and myself being compelled to make these answers:

Q. Why didn't you unload the gun before bringing it into the house?

A. Because Rusper accosted me when I had just loaded, and I was too flustered to think of unloading.

Q. During your struggle with Rusper by the gunroom door, Ronald Carlice came up and tried to separate you?

A. Yes.

Q. Did he approach you of his own free will?

A. No. His aunt urged him to intervene.

Q. Did you hear her speaking to him?

A. Confusedly—yes.

Q. What did you hear her say?

A. Something like this: "Ronnie, you must go and stop them. I order you to go."

Q. When Ronald Carlice joined you, who was holding the gun?

A. Rusper was holding the barrel. I also held the barrel lower down with my left hand, and my right hand was near the trigger.

Q. Was the safety-catch on or off?

A. It was on at first. It was Rusper who pulled it off, with his left hand.

Q. Do you think he knew what he was doing?

A. No. I think he thought he was putting it on.

Q. Did Ronald Carlice know that it was off?

A. Yes. He told Rusper to push it the other way.

Q. When the gun went off, who was holding it?

A. We were all four of us holding it.

Q. All *four* of you? Who was the fourth?

A. Isabel Carlice. She came up and put her hand round the barrel quite near the end.

Q. Who pulled the trigger?

A. I don't know.

Q. You don't know? Think again. You must know.

A. I suppose my finger must have touched the trigger.

Q. Did you actually pull the trigger? Did you exert any muscular pressure against it?

A. I don't know.

Q. How do you mean, you don't know?

A. The moment Isabel Carlice put her hand on the barrel I was fascinated by the glitter of a large diamond ring on her finger. As the poet Dowson said,

> *I was always a lover of ladies' hands.*

(Sensation.)

Q. You state on oath that the moment Miss Carlice touched the barrel you don't really know what happened?

A. I state that on oath.

★   ★   ★   ★   ★

Q. Who, in your view, was morally guilty?

A. I can't answer that unless I know what your code of morals is.

Q. What about your code?

A. It isn't clear. Perhaps we were all morally guilty.

Q. Though there was nothing in the nature of a conspiracy between you?

A. No, nothing at all. At least——

Q. At least what?

A. I was relying on Miss Carlice to help me out of a difficulty. No doubt I felt, half-consciously, that I ought to help her in return.

Q. Let us deal with Miss Carlice first. She stood to benefit materially by her nephew's death?

A. Yes.

Q. Do you think she conceived the staging of this "accident"?

A. Who am I to judge her?

Q. You must try.

A. I do not think she conceived it very consciously—at least, till things developed as she may secretly have hoped they would develop.

Q. That is involved.

A. I can't make myself clearer.

Q. That first afternoon, when she asked you to shoot that

rabbit on the lawn, do you think it possible that she thought—very secretly, as you would say, and perhaps only semi-consciously—"What a pity that clumsy dipsomaniac Stephen Payne can't shoot Ronnie by accident!"?

A. Yes, that is possible.

Q. And later, when she heard of Dr. Rusper's impending visit, might she not have thought, "If Dr. Rusper catches Stephen with a gun, we shall have a jolly old row. Is there any way I can turn that row to my advantage?"

A. It is possible that she thought this too.

Q. And when her nephew came into the room so opportunely—is it possible, by the way, that she asked him to be at hand?—don't you think her thoughts may have become a little clearer and more conscious?

A. Yes.

Q. And, finally, was it Miss Carlice who pushed the muzzle of the gun towards her nephew's face?

A. I don't know. I was fascinated by the glitter of her ring.

(Renewed sensation.)

Q. Now let us turn to you. Did you at any time wish to shoot Dr. Rusper?

A. For one mad instant, yes.

Q. Was that when you pressed the trigger?

A. I'm not sure if I did press the trigger.

Q. At all events, for one mad instant it did occur to you that you might press the trigger and shoot Dr. Rusper?

A. Yes.

Q. Miss Carlice had offered you a whisky-and-soda before Dr. Rusper arrived, and you accepted it?

A. Yes.

Q. Are you aware that drink is apt to have an unfortunate effect on you?

A. It has sometimes, but by no means always.

Q. Did you ever have an impulse to shoot Ronald Carlice?

A. I don't think so.

Q. You're not quite sure?

A. I felt—after a quarrel I had had with him—that he was one of my enemies, standing, as he did, for everything I stood against, but he was not my chief enemy. My chief enemy, of course, was Rusper.

Q. Might you have felt, "If I can't get one, I'll get the other"?

A. I don't know.

Q. Did you consciously wish to kill Ronald Carlice?

A. No.

Q. Was he unbalanced or of suicidal tendency?

A. No. He was over-sensitive and highly strung and filled with a monomania, but he was perfectly sane.

Q. Assuming that we can acquit you of intentional complicity in this affair, are you in any way indirectly guilty?

A. Yes. If I hadn't allowed my weakness—as you will call it—to master me years ago, or if I had been a stronger character, I should never have been victimised by Rusper or come to Carlice Abbey in such circumstances. But then, you might also say that if my step-sister——

Q. We will leave that lady out of it, if you please. Now, take Dr. Rusper. What moral guilt can you attach to him?

A. The fact that he was a bully and a fool. The fact that he was eaten up with his own dignity which he thought I had offended. The fact that he was over-bearing, stupid, pig-headed and vain, meddlesome and incompetent——

Q. Thank you very much, Mr. Payne. We were not asking for invective. You may stand down.

★   ★   ★   ★   ★

It was an accident. It was an accident. The carriage wheels still sing the same words to the tune of *La Donna e mobile.* I have taught them to sing those words, and I won't teach them to sing any others, for the sake of all the artistry in the world. Especially now that they're beginning to put up little tables for luncheon. Every minute the smell of food grows stronger. The old lady at the end of the carriage puts a grey rug round her knees and asks the attendant why the heating isn't on. "But, Madam," he says, "it's only mid-September." She makes a long reply. We pass through endless fields, leaving the Great Wen further and further behind us.

I am going to Cornwall—let me remind myself—where I intend

to live. My annuity has been paid, and will continue to be paid, as long as such things are payable. Rusper is resigning from the trusteeship. "Really, my dear fellow," he said, "there are now so many calls on my time that I am not justified in performing functions of this kind." What a changed Rusper! When I said good-bye to Dora, she said, with a tear in her eye, "So you see, everything's come all right in the end, Stephen." And after a moment's pause, she added irrelevantly and untruthfully, "You remember, I told you to be patient!" Poor Dora. Are the next ten years going to be happier for her than the last ten? I wonder how much she worried about that box. Up to a point, her guilty conscience made her guess quite rightly that the contents of the box had something to do with her. But as Isabel Carlice said to me, it is utterly fantastic to think that Claude Carlice left the box about in order to take a post-mortem revenge on Dora. He wasn't that kind of man. If he meant anything, he meant the box to be kept by his trustees and handed by them to Ronnie—who would have tossed the contents straight into the fire. A mountain out of a molehill. But who can blame Dora for that? Don't we all invent mountains? Am I not inventing one, travelling, a free man, to Cornwall with a big cheque in my pocket. I know exactly what's gnawing at me. I might almost say it out loud and get it over. I'm afraid that some day I shall imagine I'm a murderer, and go about confessing publicly like a character in an old-style Russian novel. I know I'm not a murderer now, but imagination and one's nerves can play such nasty tricks. Well, if I think I'm a murderer I must go to Rusper and ask him. He'll very quickly disabuse me of the idea. Or I could ask Miss Carlice. She'd put me straight. People like me always have a worry when they ought to be full of joy. I remember the time I won a scholarship. Even my father seemed pleased with me, and for two or three days the congratulations poured in. For about the first time in my life I was thoroughly pleased with myself. I really had achieved something. When I heard the result of the examination, I thought, "Life is too wonderful." Then I developed a slight pain on the right side of the abdomen, and thought I'd got appendicitis. I daren't ask my father about it, for fear he should want to have me operated on at once, and I went about convinced I was going to die. The pain lasted till, five or six evenings later, my father said to me, "Well, my boy, you may have won a scholarship, but I'm afraid by itself that's not sufficient to make you a career." Then ordinary life seemed to begin again—the life of friction, competition and restraint—and the pain left me.

I'm "escaping" from ordinary life now, as this train with its musical wheels hurtles me towards Cornwall. Isabel Carlice, herself serene as the ice-maiden, said to me, as she saw me off this morning: "I'm glad you're getting away at last to your dream-world." She was making conversation while my luggage was being brought down to the car. I answered: "I am afraid you may think the worse of me for that—for trying to 'escape realities.'" And she said, "No, I admire you for creating them. There's nothing real in a realist's view of life. In a few days you will be very happy." Then Charles came up with my luggage, and I hadn't the proper tip ready.

It was an accident.

Yes, my good wheels, every time you say that, we're twenty yards nearer to Cornwall. Already there's something different in the air. The old lady loosens the grey rug about her knees, and orders stout. The two young girls put down their magazines and yawn, then smile at something they've whispered together, and the man with the conical head pulls out his flask.

"Yes, waiter. I'll take a *single* gin and a small tonic-water, please."

THE END

ALSO AVAILABLE FROM VALANCOURT BOOKS